Dark
Edge

To Alan,

My fellow Hollybush,
philosophers

Roger.
April 2009

By the same author

Crystal Spirit
Out of Nowhere

Dark
Edge

ROGER GRANELLI

seren

seren is the book imprint of
Poetry Wales Press Ltd
2 Wyndham Street, Bridgend
CF31 1EF, Wales

A Cataloguing in Publication record for this title
is available from the British Library CIP Office

ISBN 1-85411-204-X

Cover images by Martin Shakeshaft

*Published with the financial support of the
Arts Council of Wales*

Printed in Plantin by CPD Wales Ltd, Ebbw Vale

The clack of a woman's heels came to Elliott out of the night. Approaching the house insistently. Matching the throbbing in his head. Clack-pain, clack-pain, clack-pain. The heavier tread of a man accompanied it, and low, murmured voices could be heard. Not happy. Not sad. Just drunk. The footsteps faded away but his headache was going nowhere. It hadn't for weeks.

He finished packing his bag, taking enough clothes for the week the sergeant said they would be away. They were arranged meticulously, with a paperback on top of the neat folds. Its violent cover had attracted him weeks ago. Muscle-bound mercenaries cleaning up some banana republic. Beefcake making life simple. Like Elliott, the book was a veteran of two previous trips, thumbed but unread.

He changed into his uniform and attached his truncheon. Letting the twirled handle protrude from the right hand pocket. He always felt sheepish when he did this, like a schoolboy going off to camp. The weapon was hopelessly inadequate for modern policing and made him yearn for the guns police carried all over the world.

Checking his appearance in the mirror, Elliott came to attention instinctively. He probed the bruise to the right of his eye. It had faded, but the imprint of a ring was still visible. He could still make out his father's first initial, the *L* of Lyndon Byron Bowles. It was a ring he had always wanted, but it had passed to his elder brother, Edwin.

His appearance pleased him. He saw a tall man, a broad, erect frame tapering to a fit waist and athletic legs. Black hair was swept back over his crown and held in place with a touch of gel, and dark brown eyes were enhanced by the moustache bunched thickly over his upper lip. The eyes could be considered black in some light.

He zipped up the canvas holdall and looked in on his two daughters, Sarah and Sally. Nine and seven, they slept soundly in the back bedroom. He did not like leaving them anonymously in the night but it couldn't be helped. He had a job to do. And the girls lacked for nothing. Their bedroom was the size of the whole top floor of the terrace he had grown up in. Had endured. Where he had shared a rickety, undersized bed with Edwin.

He stroked the hair of his daughters, lightly, but enough to make Sally murmur in her sleep. They were pretty girls and he was proud of their looks. He went downstairs, where his wife Susan dozed in front of the television. It was in his mind to slip out without waking her but Sam the labrador got up and shook himself on Elliott's entry, rousing his wife. Susan had named the dog as she had the children and Elliott was glad his name did not complete the family alliteration. Neatness appealed to Susan. She was a practical, caring, seemingly faultless woman to the outside eye. A perfect copper's wife.

'You're off then,' Susan said.

'Aye. I've got to be down the station at ten. We'll be in Mansfield at first light.'

'And you don't know how long?'

'I'll phone, I've told you. Depends on how things go.'

'You know how they'll go, that's why they are sending you to the other side of the country.'

'Don't start,' Elliott said. 'I've been on double time, just about since the strike started and you like the money as much as I do.'

'You'll be telling me next we never had it so good, as you go off practically risking your life. And what comes after, Elliott? This is a village and we are – you are – on the wrong side of it. Most of the village is connected with the Top Pit in some way or other. Look what –'

'You *are* starting. It's my job, how many times do I have to tell you? My job and our living.'

'The strike has been going on two months and look what is happening around here. And you fighting with Edwin. What will it be like when it finishes, if it ever does?'

'It will finish all right, and with only one outcome. Times have changed in Wales.'

'They certainly have with us.'

There was a moment's silence as he brushed the top of her head with his lips. Her grey strands were getting noticeable but Susan made no attempt to colour them out, as Elliott would have liked. She was forty, five years older than him.

'Right, see you some time next week,' Elliott said.

Susan did not turn towards him, but she managed not to steel herself when he touched her.

As he drove to the station Elliott felt excitement stir within him. This was his third Yorkshire tour and was the nearest he would get to going to war. He liked it, meeting aggression with aggression but having the safety net of his profession to fall back on. For ten years the arrogance of the miners had grated on him. It ran parallel to his estrangement in the village. Not that he lived there any more.

He had bought a house on the new estate overlooking his birth-place, built on the woods of his childhood. Many local people had campaigned against its development, but had lost the fight, as they invariably did. Elliott put the resistence down to jealousy. A few of the oaks he had climbed were left scattered about the estate, like intruders.

He liked his house, it at least gave an illusion of space, and did not cling to another. He had worked hard to imprint his personal-ity on it, hanging horse brasses and a brace of reproduction flint-locks over the fireplace which did not have a fire. It was made of blue and puce stone, with a television and video housed in the grate recess. He had been the first person on the estate to have a video. Outside, the garden was a miniature version of a country estate he had once been called upon to police. An ornamental pond held oversized, ornamental fish and was bordered by carefully layered rocks. A mix of infant trees lined the garden wall.

When his Chief Inspector once called Elliott had been proud of his property. He had escaped the terraces, where people were going nowhere, yet thought they had a God-given right to mind everyone else's business. Moving to the estate was his way of con-firming a different route. When he joined the force his mother's surprise was tinged with pride but Edwin resented it. Elliott's social contacts now were with other policemen, though he did not call any of them friend.

The strike would give him a chance to reinforce his new iden-tity, and repay the blow from Edwin many times over. Promotion might come quickly afterwards, and he could move away, to a bigger house on a bigger hill. Elliott knew he was being monitored by his superiors, all officers from mining communities were, in case conflicts of interest arose. He found there was no conflict at all for him.

* * *

As Elliott took his place in the police Transit, to be sped north to the Yorkshire coalfield, his brother Edwin was also busy, chairing a late meeting of his local action committee, a group set up to

7

support the striking miners. He sat at the head of a long pub table, letting others talk, a head shorter than his brother, and lighter in complexion. He favoured his mother's Irish ancestry. Slate grey eyes edged with blue, an open-pored skin and a gap in his top teeth. A thin line of a scar, like a faint trace of blue crayon, highlighted his paleness. A legacy of his days underground.

The action committee was a disparate bunch. Five union members, 'Scuttle' Davies, a retired miner; the two Jenkins sisters, in charge of family aid; and Ceri Griffiths, a union official from regional headquarters. Scuttle had volunteered his presence as a representative of tradition, always available to tell how it was in the old days.

Griffiths had the floor. He was a man Edwin did not much trust. An opportunist, using the strike to give himself maximum publicity whilst offering the strikers nothing more than words. He was talked of as a future Labour member of parliament. The sisters were indomitable and well-organised, which disconcerted some of their male colleagues. Women's aid groups were gathering momentum in the valleys.

Griffiths gave his standard pep talk, which they had all heard before. Edwin worked his hands through his shortcropped hair and tried to look supportive. Unlike Griffiths he had no skill with clothes. Whatever he wore covered him and he thought no further than this. He was a bachelor and some might have said his appearance reflected this.

The members jockeyed for position, grinding individual axes under his loose control. As a senior lodge official it was Edwin's task to mould them into an effective force. Hence his clasped hands. This strike was so different, Edwin had felt it from the first. The rules were different, the opposition fitter and very much meaner. He had been turning thirty in '74, at the peak of his powers and beliefs, and the miners had been inexorable then, carrying other unions in their wake, crippling the government until it bent its knee, and with the vital element of public support throughout. It had been the coming together of thirty years of progress in the coalfields and the culmination of a century of effort. Unlike the older men, Edwin had always thought they might have to do it all over again. He did not share their almost childlike belief that their status was now assured, that they had won for good. Now, each time he took his place in the line he remembered the words of one old collier, a man who had played

Jonah even in the midst of their greatest triumph. They had been in the Labour Club, drunk on emotion before they started the ale.

'We've gone and done it now, boys,' the old man had said, 'brought down a bloody Tory government we have. It will shake the buggers to the core and that lot are good at revenge, believe me. Don't forget, it was like this when we tossed Churchill out. Thought we had swept away the rubbish for good and all. Five years later it was back again. It taught our boys what bloody wine to drink and it was back to bloody normal.'

The old man was drunk and he had tipped beer over Edwin before departing but his words stayed with him. There was a knowing hopelessness about them that rang true. Edwin kept these doubts to himself now. In his quiet way he was good at rallying people, his tenor voice rising to strength as he made his points. When people came to him with their own doubts he reassured them, called up the ghosts of past victories, talked about the spirit in their community and put the coal stockpiled by the Board to the back of his mind. He had done so tonight, as he visited the lads picketing the Top Pit. On his way back he saw Elliott driving through the village, on his way to the doll's house he lived in.

★ ★ ★

It had been a wet start to May and a persistent drizzle accompanied Elliott to Mansfield. They had passed through mining districts like his own, suburbs of ribboned terracing leading to drab town centres crying out for attention. But there was more space here, mining did not have to follow the tortuous contours of his native valleys. Different conditions had nurtured different attitudes in much of the Nottinghamshire coalfield. With modern productivity deals miners here earned more than their colleagues elsewhere. Elliott remembered his grandfather talking about Notts miners with a mixture of envy and contempt. Most of the miners in this region had ignored Scargill's call to strike and Elliott loved this. It proved that workers' solidarity was bunkum.

Some officers were dropped off at Mansfield, but Elliott and the rest were taken on into Yorkshire, to the Orgreave coking plant, south of Rotherham. The landscape grew bleaker, and the rain heavier. Large council estates dominated the towns they passed, sprawling grey presences that pointed the way to the pits they surrounded. There were more than thirty of them in this area.

The Transit parked behind the local police station, joining many from other regions. Police from every force had been moved in. Their intelligence was good and hotspots of picket action could be anticipated. Elliott hoped he was here for a major one.

It was certain that Scargill himself would be on the picket line at Orgreave in the next few days. Elliott had seen the miners' leader on his first visit to Yorkshire. A short, stocky man, like Edwin, with firebrand hair that was easy to pick out in a crowd. He always reminded Elliott of Punch, red-faced, exasperated and ineffectual. A fanatic inflamed by outmoded rubbish, eager to take on everyone as it became clear he was losing. That man could not accept change and talked about the great British working class, but Elliot knew this was a delusion. There was only an underclass, with just a lack of money cutting it off. And most of them deserved to be there anyway. He had gotten out of this, pulled himself up, and in a more honest way than the educated crowd who talked about the glorious traditions of their beloved valleys from afar.

The rain began to ease and traces of blue penetrated the edge of the sky. Elliott fingered his bruise lightly and felt his head start up again as he took his place with the others.

He marched with pride to the coking plant. He was part of a force that had identity and purpose and which knew it had a future. For years, in canteens and staffrooms, he had found his views echoed by his fellows. They had been nurtured by men who thought like him and were right like him.

Elliott was in the first rank of men behind the police horsemen, one of a thousand officers. Alongside the police trailed the media, sharing the excitement and imagining they were part of things. White lines had been drawn around the perimeter of the Orgreave plant to mark out its boundary and any miner stepping onto Coal Board land would be arrested. Orgreave was a major focal point of the strike. It supplied the Scunthorpe steelworks with fuel and was a vital target for the miners to nullify, especially as it was so close to NUM headquarters.

The day was long and uneventful, although the air crackled with tension and the cacophony of chants, insults and taunts coming from the massed pickets. Many of them wore the black work jackets of their employer, with orange plastic on their shoulders. Even in times of rebellion the coal industry marked its own.

Elliott was bored and disappointed by the hours spent facing his enemy without incident, but night brought what he wanted. They heard that trucks were coming to take coal to Scunthorpe, and to the miners trucks meant betrayal. The police formed lines to make a corridor leading to the Orgreave gates and the miners made this a gauntlet to be run. Lights were set up overhead, shining into the faces of three thousand angry strikers. Bricks flew. Missiles were thrown from behind the first line of pickets, mostly clattering onto police shields. One carried over to hit its mark and a sergeant collapsed near Elliott, his face mauled by a piece of house brick. Elliott knew this would allow them full rein.

The first truck appeared, anonymous, untaxed and bald-tyred. The owner's name had been obliterated with black paint, another secret treachery the miners noted. The trucks came on far too fast, daring any pickets to try and stop them. One man tried to jump up to a driver's cab but was struck a glancing blow. He bounced back into the crowd. Flash point.

Pickets rushed at the police, a swirling coming together as inevitable as it was violent, given the long hours of intense proximity. The battle that followed echoed the past. There were no guns here, just boots, fists and hand held weapons. They were back in a darker age and Elliott revelled in it.

A young man with a shock of blond hair tried to jump over the wall of police shields but crashed back to the ground. Elliott put a boot on his neck, yanked back his hair, and dug at him with a baton. Other officers joined him and the man was soon inert, and his blond hair red.

Meanwhile the miners almost succeeded in breaching police defences. Waves of men crashed against the shielded ranks, probing desperately for an opening. Police responded by pulling men from the mass and pummelling them with their sticks. The blond man's friends came to his aid and tried to take him back to the main body of the pickets. A policeman went down and Elliott saw he was in anger of being cut off. He flailed about him and charged back to the police lines, adept at this tactic. The quick rush to someone vulnerable then a retreat back to strength. There was an excited glaze to his face and his breath came in short, exhilarated bursts. He had not been hurt at all.

Police horsemen tipped the balance. They managed to create a wedge between the two sides, and pushed the pickets back. Elliott watched with satisfaction as the pickets' force dissipated. He wished the cameras could show how well he had performed but he knew it would be edited out. Most of the media operated behind police lines, under their umbrella. It was the pickets' actions that were caught on film, their violence that was seen: lenses always pointed from one side. Men like Elliott operated with impunity under these conditions.

The pickets dispersed into the night, herded away by the now dominant police. A collective murmur of disappointment hung over them as their anger turned to tiredness. Out of the darkness a lone voice shouted defiance.

'We'll be back, you bastards.'

Elliott smiled. The voice set the final seal to his personal victory. He picked his way over the battlefield, his uniform splashed with blood. Fifty miners and a dozen policemen were hospitalised. The picket who had tangled with the truck had a set of broken ribs and a fractured skull. There was talk that he might be the second picket line fatality, adding to the man killed at Ollerton. Someone noticed the blood on Elliott and asked if he was all right. He said he was fine.

Elliott and the other policemen from the valley had been billeted in a small hotel. It was a three star place, much better accommodation than most of the drafted-in men had. They checked in quietly at six in the morning, men anxious to sink into sleep before the next night's work. Elliott did not join them. He phoned for a taxi from the hotel desk and quickly changed as he waited for it to take him into Rotherham.

The town was typical enough of a northern industrial centre to be a caricature. Elliott knew it a little now, though it had not taken long. It was a larger but equally depressing version of his own community, a town hanging on to the rump of humanity with deprivation etched across its face. What it relied on was coal and heavy industries, and they were dying. This was a place for losers – for Edwins – and Elliott felt the privilege that came from being an outsider.

The taxi dropped him at the better end of town. What wealth there was was gathered here. Rows of pre-war detached houses, four and five bedroomed, with spacious, obediently green gardens. This was the next stage of living for Elliott, when he made Inspector. He rang the bell of the second house in the row and the door was opened by a woman in a dressing gown.

'Good God, Elliott. It's only seven o'clock. Why didn't you ring?'

He stepped inside and grabbed her.

'No time for that.'

For Elliott this was the perfect distillation of the night's fever.

★ ★ ★

Edwin saw Susan walking down the street towards him. He wondered if she would cross over to the other side but she came on steadily.

'Hello, Ed,' Susan said, 'I thought it was you, though it's hard to see much of you under that coat.'

He was in a black duffel coat that swept below his knees, ridiculous for a May morning.

'I put the thing on out of habit,' Edwin said. 'I suppose it is a bit too warm for it.'

He shuffled with some embarrassment, and hid the hand that had struck Elliott behind his back.

'Elliott has told you about our little fracas, no doubt,' he said.

'Not at first, but he couldn't hide his eye, could he?'

'I shouldn't have hit him, I know but –'

'Don't try to explain, Edwin. It's been coming for years, ever since he joined the force. Does your mother know?'

'Not from me.'

'Well she doesn't, then. That's something.'

'I'm surprised Elliott hasn't been down there.'

'He's up north all the time, he was one of the first to volunteer.'

The younger Jenkins sister walked past, acknowledging Edwin with a nod of her head but looking through Susan.

'Sorry about that,' Edwin said.

'I went all through school with Marge Jenkins,' Susan said, 'people are so bitter this time.'

'Aye, seems that way.'

'Are you confident you'll win?' Susan asked.

Edwin shrugged.

'Too nice a day to talk about that,' he said.

He took off his coat, revealing a faded blue shirt.

'How are you managing?' Susan asked. 'I hear the single men are getting nothing.'

'I'm all right. I've got some savings, and not much to pay out on.'

They walked along the street, Edwin matching the stride of a

13

woman he had known all his life. They were the same age and had shared the same school classrooms, but he noticed Susan used the word 'you' when she talked of winning. After fifteen years he still could not believe she had married his brother.

They parted at a corner and Edwin walked on through the main street of the village. The central area was a collection of shabby shops, built into the fronts of the larger terraces, or utilising two houses knocked into one. They sold goods that city centres would have laughed at but were not yet threatened by new ways. Here 'out of town' meant the hillsides, the preserves of sheep, youths on makeshift motor bikes, cranky solitary walkers and now miners like Edwin, experiencing fresh air in greedy doses.

Even with the pit in production Edwin knew his village had run down. There still remained some of the qualities which had been so strong in his youth but they had been thinned by changing times. For years there had been an undercurrent of unrest, a sense of dissatisfaction that they were cut off from the mainstream of development. Youngsters still talked of 'going down to Cardiff' as if it was the Mecca of a land far away, not the de-nationalised provincial city it was. He loved and hated his community. A complex sense of inferiority balanced with aggressive pride. He was aware of this dichotomy and thought it might be the one unique quality of the Welsh.

Edwin had seen many villagers leave, usually the ones at either end of the financial scale. The young poor drifted out in search of work and the few that money came to rarely stayed. They flew away quickly with a denial of their roots on their lips. The ones starting to thrust upwards, like Elliott, retreated to the new, fenced-in settlements. But Edwin still believed in his birthplace and its old ideals, no matter how beleaguered it had become. His socialism was a fundamental part of him, as vital as his heart and lungs, and was not for turning.

Edwin was on his way to his mother's but thought better of it. He let himself into her backyard and stashed his coat in the shed. Here there was a collection of walking sticks from which he chose his favourite, the thick ash with a carved badger's head for a handle. Sticks were a habit gleaned from his father. He strode out down the back lane for the hillside, his head still full of the clash with his brother.

At fourteen Elliott had breached the five years between them by matching Edwin in size. At this age he began to take on his elder brother by behaving as aggressively as possible, more so when their father died. He liked to manufacture anger, stoking it up until he was able to rush at Edwin, fists flailing, yet with one eye on the expected intervention of his mother. After two years at the coalface Edwin was easily the stronger but he found it increasingly hard to fend off Elliott without hurting him. One day, after a gruelling shift, his brother performed after being dropped from the school rugby team. He threw half a lamb chop from his dinner plate at Edwin when their mother was in the kitchen. Edwin lost patience and swiped him across the head, knocking Elliott out of his chair. Rowena Bowles arrived on cue to castigate Edwin's bullying. She invariably took her youngest son's side. It was never the same between the brothers after this. What brotherly unity they had disintegrated, the last fragments blown away with their first fight two weeks ago.

Elliott's job as a policeman was a permanent affront to Edwin. Although he had never been in trouble, not even in the last strike, he harboured a keen mistrust of the police, put in place by his instinct and the traditions of his family. He was well versed in mining folklore and the great struggles of the past, and his early childhood was marked by his grandfather's bitter memories of the Tonypandy riots and the 1926 strike.

'They got English bastards in,' the old man told him, 'police, scabs, troops, you name it, as if we didn't have enough Welsh bastards of our own. Police, don't ever talk to me about them. They were hand in glove with money then and they are now. For ever and always.'

His grandfather was proud of his lack of forgiveness despite his meticulous attendance at chapel, and his view was shared by many. The few scabs who remained in the area from those days had never been reintegrated into the community. They were on the outside, outside life itself, Old Man Bowles was wont to say, with relish.

Edwin crossed the river that split the valley and walked up the slope behind the terraces. This near hillside was a mixture of rough mountain turf, untidy, sectioned off fields where a few horses grazed, and pit waste. Debris had been dumped on the land for generations. Older tips were covered by a thin crust of green scrub, the only growth that could take hold on them. Fresher deposits from Edwin's pit gleamed dull black, and were just as lifeless. A derelict landscape some said, so expected that it

15

had become a cliché. Yet Edwin liked what he saw. His land had been scarred and changed by man but not destroyed. It retained a wildness which laughed at the pits below. He preferred to think that if contours had been changed they had also been added to, each tear at nature a testimony to the personal histories of thousands of men and women. He knew every fold of the high slopes, the best points to sit, the finest slabs of stone, the unexpected copses. His single state had given him time to develop this knowledge, and the sense of belonging that came with it. Most men let it fade with their childhoods, and even children were a rare sight on the hills now. Boys playing were an endangered species, having been snared by television and the smallness of its world.

Edwin knew that he was out of date. His world was being sliced up by new ways. It seemed to him that personal greed fed by empty promises was the dominant philosophy now. Striking for him was about more than the fate of the pits. It was an attempt to maintain a fingerhold on respect, to fight against unemployment, the old spectre that was stalking the village once again. If the strike failed they would be back to the deadly twins of no work or wage slavery, this time yoked to the new barons from the Far East. It seemed that there was always an outside power eager to use Wales. In the last ten years miners' wages had increased to a level that was reasonable, a minimal platform to achieve independence. To lose it all now was hard to countenance.

Edwin's village was four streets of terraced housing twisting into each other like a sculpture of slate and stone. They were flanked by a river on one side and a banked railway on the other. At one end of the village was the colliery, still called the Top Pit, though the others had long since gone. Its winding gear was the village's one landmark, sitting black and round and solid on the skyline, a liar in its image of permanence.

Fronting the village was the new housing of Elliott's world, built on the landscaped and greened slope alongside the road out, the road taken by so many in the last fifty years. A cluster of red and yellow bricked houses, detached, but still within touching distance of each other. Imported turf made up their gardens and a tall wooden fence, emphasizing its determination to be apart. Edwin was able to pick out his brother's house by its garden shed, where all his electrical gardening gadgets were housed. These days Susan tended the garden. Elliott had no time.

Edwin sat back in one of his favourite spots and glanced up. The sky was cloudy-bright and he imagined he knew every configuration of cloud formation it might offer, so many times he had watched them scud over. It was a small sky, hemmed in by hills and matching the communities below, but it was his sky. He drifted into sleep, as he sometimes did on the hillside. It was a way of catching up from night picket duty and the endless meetings.

He was on the railway line with his brother, strictly forbidden by parents but always done. The 'line' was one of the mainstays for village children, its holed defences easily breached. It was 1958 and Wales had just lost to Brazil in the World Cup. They had listened to it on the wireless and Edwin had been jealous of the one family who had the new television and had not asked anyone to share it. Elliott did not take much interest in football, his new passion was flattening pennies on the railway line. Children would place the coins on the track minutes before a train fat with coal thundered down the valley. The result would be pennies transformed into copper pancakes. Some were crushed out of all recognition, the ones that still had a distorted Britannia were shown off and traded. For boys on the fringe of work, like Edwin, it was necessary to place the coins just before the train came, to gain credibility with their fellows. To dash onto the track, place the penny, dash back to the bushes with the engine hooting and its steam clouding your face was the ultimate. He was never bettered at this and was proud of the praise he gained and the hero worship of his brother.

The younger boys, not yet allowed pennies, would run ahead and climb the wooden foot-bridge, to stand feet spread on its slats as the train passed under them. They were enveloped in smoke and feared they might be sucked into the engine's fiery maw. This was an initiation ceremony, to be endured many times until they were allowed to graduate to the pennies.

The brothers were good together then. Edwin did not mind looking after his little brother, for his authority was never challenged, but playing with trains stopped abruptly that day in 1958. The Tucker boy from Williams Terrace got stuck on the line, no-one knew how. Edwin heard him scream, a piercing chill sound that carried over the screech of brakes. They all ran, unable to bear what might remain of Billy. For a heart stopping moment he could not find Elliott and thought it might be him under the wheels, but his brother appeared from the undergrowth to be dragged away from the scene. Parents and the railway authority cracked down after this and then the diesels came and the attraction was gone.

Edwin woke up as the sun struck his face. He sat up and instinctively looked for Elliott's house. Susan was in the garden, prodding at the flower beds with a hoe. It seemed such a short time ago that they sat close to each other in school and he was hastening away a bawling Elliott from the death scene of Billy Tucker.

* * *

Elliott read the banner headline of the morning newspaper. It said that miners were striking at the heart of democracy in a statement by Margaret Thatcher. Elliott agreed with it, he supported all the prime minister's utterances. This was one woman he could really admire. She was what the country needed, someone who had shown more balls than the men around her and led by example. She had also showered the police with money. Elliott had always kept an eye on the advance of Edwin's wages but now his own surged ahead. Another victory. Thatcher had shown him the way forward. Opportunities were there to be grasped, if one had the bottle. Like him, she had no time for losers.

'Where's my breakfast, then?' Elliott shouted from the bedroom.

He emphasised his Welsh accent, knowing that Lisa liked it. He had met her on his first Yorkshire tour, serving beer at the local police club. It was an instantaneous affair, the type he liked to specialise in. For five years he had dallied sporadically with other women. They were usually met in the course of his work and he had grown adept at picking the ones least likely to cause trouble. Those safely tucked away in moribund marriages they did not want to end, or the recently divorced and eager. They were good for a few months, until he could manage another faithful spell with Susan.

Lisa was perfect. Besides fulfilling Elliott's usual criteria she lived two hundred miles away from his family. She was a tall, well proportioned girl, with hair dyed light blonde and lips painted into a vivid pout, someone who liked to work out in gymnasia and play squash. Lisa had a certain reputation at the club which Elliott sniffed out very quickly.

'Look at the arse on that,' his sergeant said when they first

18

drank there, 'and it's got a skirt right up to its nostrils.'

With his looks and Lisa's availability it was easy. She became the release for the energy he stored up for picket control, another plaything to help perpetuate his myth about himself.

Lisa came into the bedroom with a tray of cooked food, the full English breakfast that Elliott always demanded. She had never made one for her former husband.

'Thanks, love,' he said, 'home from home, this is.'

He sat up in bed with the tray on his legs.

'This is right,' he said, shaking a fork at the newspaper, 'I like that woman. And we showed them last night, got those trucks in and out no trouble.'

'I heard there was a lot of fighting,' Lisa said. 'I don't know why people get so worked up about it. This politics stuff is over my head anyway, just a lot of old men talking.'

'They got to be shown, see,' Elliott said. 'They're trying to take us on, and communists are behind it all. You know what it is like in Russia, don't you?'

Lisa looked at him blankly.

'My grandad was a miner,' she said. 'His black face used to frighten me when I was a kid, and he was always knackered. Anyway, eat your breakfast, you need it, a big man like you.'

Elliott grinned and tucked in, as Lisa undulated her way to the bathroom.

* * *

Edwin joined five other men at the entrance to the Top Pit. There had been no trouble in the village and this was deemed enough token force. Despite the season they still had a brazier going, filled with glowing coal and topped up with assorted pieces of wood. Most of the men sat around it, smoking, watched by a solitary policeman stationed at the pit's gates. It was a far cry from Orgreave and Yorkshire but Edwin was not sorry. For once South Wales was not at the heart of the disturbance, which meant there had not yet been any real violence. Their war with the police was more banter than battle.

Edwin stood away from the fire, leaning on railings. The men clustered around the heat could have been a scene from another century. Working men pitted against all elements. He half listened to the chat whilst he looked down the curve of the valley. The

19

hills loomed black against a lighter sky and lines of orange lights marked the roads below. Edwin knew all the men with him, had known them all his life. This pooled knowledge gave his community its identity and strength. But its way of life had become one of platitudes. He heard them coming from the men now, about sticking together, fighting the Tories, and the evils of capitalism. Edwin knew them all like a catechism and believed them, but knew they were proving ineffective for modern times.

Scargill had called the strike at the end of winter. A traditional ally had not been utilised, coal stocks were high around the country, the union could not afford strike pay, and support from other unions came in trickles.

'Ed, that's right, isn't it?' a voice called from the brazier.

'What's that?' he replied.

'That more will come to our side the longer we stick it out.'

Edwin assumed his delegate role.

'Aye, like in '74. The public will see what this government is trying to do.'

'See,' the man said, turning back to the others, 'you got to have faith, like Edwin here.'

'That don't go far with my missis,' another said, 'they're not all on action committees, you know. Mine just sees the bloody suite going back, perhaps even the telly next month.'

'No, not the telly,' someone mimicked.

They laughed and the mood lightened. No-one wanted to think of failing.

Hearing the laughter, the policeman walked over to them. He was a contemporary of Elliott's. Edwin remembered him from the railway line days.

'John Reynolds, isn't it?' Edwin asked.

'Aye, that's right. Cold today boys, for this time of year.'

No-one answered.

'Look,' Reynolds said, 'no hard feelings, right. I'm just doing my job, and it's not Yorkshire down here, is it.'

'Only obeying orders are you?' Edwin said.

'Aye,' Reynolds answered eagerly.

The policeman stood by the men, waiting for conversation. After a few minutes of silence, enhanced by the sucking on cigarettes and the odd spit on the floor, he walked back to his station.

'Bastard,' someone muttered, 'they all are.'

He was dug in the ribs by his mate.

'Remember Edwin's brother, mun,' the man whispered, but loud enough for everyone to hear.

Edwin fingered his right hand with the left, working over the contours of the fist that had struck Elliott. That action had been more of a shock to him than his brother.

The fight, if one blow could be called that, had taken place in their mother's kitchen. Elliott had returned from Yorkshire during one of the early weeks of the strike, flushed with overtime pay and excitement. For his mother's sake Edwin had kept quiet as long as he could, holding his tea-cup so tightly he feared it might crack in his hands. Not that his mother showed any concern. She did not cease knitting as Elliott described how 'they' controlled 'them'. It did not seem to register with her that she had a son in either camp. As usual she was on another plane, such was her detachment.

Rowena Bowles was a small woman, with her hair and eyes a matching silver grey and a shapeless body that seemed forever hunched over a piece of work. She looked older than her sixty-four years. Rowena was known for her endless patience, and she never passed an opinion on anything. In the village this was perceived as a strength but it frustrated Edwin, as it had his father before him, and neither son had received much maternal guidance since their father had died. With hindsight Edwin realised it was their mother's approach which had encouraged him in his solitary ways. Her distance had nurtured his inability to overcome his shyness, which had not diminished with the passing of years, whereas Elliott's selfish egotism had blossomed after the early loss of his father, and it had gone unchecked ever since.

Despite this placid, non-committal backdrop, Rowena did have occasional outbursts of temper, which always took Edwin by surprise. He sensed frustration within her, as if she had blocked off great parts of her being from him, without apparent reason. For years he had tried to break down this barrier, but to no avail. She would subside with a 'that's how things are', or her other well-worn saying, 'you can't change anything.'

Edwin tried to maintain a filial duty but his brother was now a rare visitor to the house. When he did come it was to gloat about his lifestyle. He was gloating when Edwin hit him, going on about 'picket control' as if he had been sent out to herd errant sheep.

Edwin had gone into the kitchen and had thought about going out the back way before he gave in to his seething temper. The strike had brought his feelings about Elliott's job to the fore. He had watched the riot scenes on television. Every charging policeman was Elliott, every baton raised was raised by Elliott, every boot that sank into a miner was swung by Elliott. Sibling rivalry had changed to direct challenge, and although understated, Edwin had an ego of his own. Elliott followed him into the kitchen.

'What's the matter, Ed, don't like my stories? Mam doesn't seem to mind.'

He sidled very close to Edwin.

'Are you going up to the Top Pit tonight? Don't worry, you'll be all right. You boys down here are no trouble, well-trained and docile you are, like poodles.'

Edwin could not resist the goad. He turned and swung his fist up into Elliott's face, knocking him backwards across the kitchen table. Elliott fell to the floor with much clattering of utensils. He jumped up quickly with his fists raised and for a moment the brothers faced each other as still as stone carvings, only face muscles twitching with hostility. Edwin knew that if they continued they would hurt each other badly and fought down the desire. A last echo of his childhood, the knowledge that Elliott was of the same flesh and blood stopped him. Elliott had no such consideration.

'You'd like me to fight, wouldn't you, you bastard,' Elliott shouted, 'like to fuck up my career, but I'm not that stupid. I'll fix you another way, later.'

Elliott's face was fire-red and he breathed hard, with his right eye already closed and puffed up.

'You lot are finished,' he said, 'and you most of all, butt.'

He pushed past him and went out the back lane door. Edwin went back into the parlour, where his mother still sat knitting.

'Elliott's gone,' Edwin said. 'He left the back way, had a call on his radio.'

'He's got such a busy job, hasn't he,' his mother said, 'always rushing somewhere.'

She did not notice the way he held his fist. He burned inside, at his lack of control, and, if he was truthful, his jealousy. He had known that Elliott was prone to violence for years, but it was he, Edwin, who had struck the first blow. But if he felt shame he also felt elation that he had shut Elliott up with his fists. Perhaps they were more alike than they thought.

★ ★ ★

Elliott returned home for a few days' leave. He helped his younger daughter Sally dress. Usually clumsy with domesticity he was more so when he was having an affair. He assuaged what little guilt he felt by increased parental care. This lasted for a short time until he slipped back into the role of absent father, a man who lived for his job under the pretext of providing for his family.

The outward appearance of his brood was very important to Elliott. His daughters would grow up to be very attractive, they had the best features of their parents and were already tall and clean limbed, miniature Lisas. His girls would not marry at eighteen and look forty ten years later. Their friends were the other children on the estate, and their grandmother was their sole contact with the old terraces. It was easy to instill snobbery in such young minds, when it came so naturally to Elliott. Sally especially aped his materialism. She knew the price and prestige of each new toy and was adept at receiving information from the television screen. When Elliott came back from Yorkshire he brought gifts for his daughters, ones he had sent Lisa out to buy.

'You spoil them too much,' Susan said, on his latest return.

'You can never give kids enough,' Elliott replied. 'And we've got the money now, you don't even have to keep that job up.'

'That job' as Elliott usually called it, was as a teacher's aide in the local primary school. Susan loved the modest post and the money it brought in had proved useful in the early days. But Elliott had never liked her working, a trait he shared with the miners in the village, the rigid clinging to old ways which meant men worked and women stayed at home. It had taken years for Susan to wear down Elliott's resistance to her job but she used the money as a bribe. She let him usurp her first year's wages and buy the new car they did not need.

It was the job that began to change Susan. At the school she worked with other women, from the Head down. She saw her own sex in another light, saw that women were just as capable as men, more so in many areas. Within six months, Elliott's chauvinism, which she had always taken for granted and let flow over her, started to chafe.

The village was too small for strangers so Susan had always known Elliott, becoming aware of him through his brother. She had been in the same year as Edwin in school and they walked home together with a bunch of children with the infant Elliott tagging along behind, five years younger and a nuisance.

When Susan was sixteen her mother had been immobilised by a stroke and her father made it very clear it was her duty to look after his wife. There was no-one else available. This put paid to any thoughts of further education. Susan left school and became a permanent, unpaid nurse. Her clutch of six 'O' Levels were put in a drawer and forgotten.

Nursing her mother, never an easy tempered woman, was hard for an inexperienced girl. Susan had to learn to interpret her mother's mouthings, shakes and slavering demands. At first she did this willingly enough, accepting the duty thrust upon her. But she soon became aware that other girls were rushing on and away from her. Her mother was a trap that held her for ten years. A prison sentence.

When Susan was twenty-six her mother died, three days before Christmas. A merciful release for them both. It was then that a twenty-one year old Elliott came back into her life. He stopped her in the street, reintroduced himself and offered condolences. Although she had met Edwin Bowles occasionally whilst briefly out shopping and maintained a fragile link of past days with him, Susan had completely lost track of Elliott. He was now a tall, young policeman, going places. Very attractive and going places. He was full of talk of life outside the village, seductive talk for a woman who had not yet done anything other than lie on the shelf her family had provided for her. She could not believe Elliott was interested in her but things moved quickly with them. They were married within a year, before the aura of Elliott's flattery waned. She did not understand how his mind worked until much later, when she got to know him, and his mother Rowena. And then it was too late.

Although her job had broadened her horizons Susan was still isolated, unable to escape the confinement that had dominated her early years. She did not have any real friends, despite Elliott's attempts to integrate her into other police families. The strike had taken this a step further, proved by the snub by Marge Jenkins. She feared that might herald a more tangible hostility and her children were now affected. Susan worked at their school but did not see them much throughout the day. She dealt with the younger children of the infants' school. Sarah came to her one dinner time with Sally in tow. They were in tears and it was some time before Susan could understand their problem.

'Why is daddy a pig?' Sally asked, through her sobs.

The girls had been surrounded in the playground and subjected to a chanted taunt they did not understand any more than the children who chanted. The mood of parents was filtering down, and two-thirds of the school's children were from mining stock. Susan had struggled to fight off Elliott's desire to send the girls out of the valley to a small private school.

'What's wrong with that?' he had demanded. 'It'll get them away from this dump, open their eyes to what they can achieve.'

But Susan did not want the girls uprooted at a price they could ill afford. Fortunately the costs involved proved a potent argument. Elliott simmered over his lack of money but had to let the matter drop. Ironically, Susan saw her community being fragmented anyway, with families like hers very much in the minority.

The headmistress, though concerned, made light of the incident as a game, part of the ritual of growing up, but neither woman believed it. There was little to be done, other than admonish the chanters.

'It's a one-off occurrence,' the Head said, 'your girls will soon forget about it, and I'll make sure it doesn't happen again.'

When Sally asked again about pigs on the way home Susan told her the other children were jealous of them. She made the girls promise not to tell Elliott and she dared not mention it to him herself. He would rage and then blame her. That was his way, to turn anger into frustration, and then recrimination. In the last year Elliott had struck her twice and the second time sealed the realisation that she did not love him, and never had.

Elliott had swept her away and she doubted if there had been real love on his part either. She was a mirror for his vanity, attractive but dependent. Susan had long known about his affairs. They had started very early on, in the first year of their marriage. She knew the signs well. The even greater attention he paid to his appearance, the illusion of caring he spilled around the house and his shallow spoiling of the girls. For him these were necessary payments for his deception. The last time he came back from Yorkshire Susan knew he was at it again. There was the small remnant of a love bite on his shoulder he had tried to pass off as a bruise and another woman's fragrance on his dirty shirts. Elliott was becoming lax as he got more involved with the strike.

As time passed Susan came to know the real Elliott, a series of revelations which moved her from the pain of initial disappointment to the despair of betrayal. Their relationship was a sham, any true feeling fading into the conventional setting Elliott seemed to think necessary for the advancement of his career.

Elliott developed into a vain bully but Susan knew there had once been something else in him. The brash young man who had charmed her fifteen years ago had a desire, even a need, to do good. Susan was sure of this, but it had got lost somewhere, turned sour and withered. Perhaps a different kind of woman might have nurtured this quality, but she refused to take the blame for the way her husband had turned out. She was not even sure of Elliott's role as a father any more. Outwardly he showed the expected paternal qualities but she thought Sarah and Sally were images of his own self-esteem. She doubted that Elliott himself knew what he was doing these days. Like all skilled liars he had the ability to deceive himself. This was the man she was tied to, whose perfumed shirts she washed.

* * *

Edwin sat in the lead car of a convoy of vehicles taking the mountain road into the next valley. Here there was a pit where two men were attempting to work. They had gone back in the early weeks of the strike, shaming and infuriating their fellows. Although many Welsh miners had not wanted the strike when it was called they had shown their traditional solidarity. The active lead given by Kent and Yorkshire miners took hold in South Wales and chances of violent confrontation increased as specific sites were targeted. Young miners were fired up, eager to translate into action the exhortation of Scargill's words.

Edwin led a group of thirty men to help picket a neighbouring pit. He had a list of potential strike breakers in his area and brief outlines of their work histories. Ceri Griffiths had told him to study it to see what conclusions could be drawn. The men could not easily be linked, they ranged through many years of mining experience, from the once popular to the feckless workshy who had lived on 'the sick'. Now they were united as outcasts.

It was Edwin's job to keep the pickets under control though he knew the feelings of his grandfather coursed through their hearts as they did through his own. Those with him tonight were amongst the most committed, and many Welsh pickets were active throughout British mining areas. But as the talk grew hot in the car Edwin felt more despair than anger for the miners turned scab.

The mood was vibrant in the car. Edwin had made sure the men had received the latest copy of *The Miner*, the organ of the NUM. It told of a crumbling Conservative government and had a sketch of a stone Margaret Thatcher falling to bits on its front page. Banner headlines displaying a dazzling optimism. It was good propaganda for those who wanted to believe it and perfect fare for the night time picket.

The cars wound down the other side of the valley, a line of ageing vehicles well marked with union stickers. They had not yet learnt to seek anonymity on their incursions. It was a light summer's evening and Edwin clearly saw the winding gear of their target in silhouette. There would be hundreds of pickets out this night, eager to show how they felt to anyone who was interested. No doubt there would be equal numbers of police, Griffiths had warned Edwin of this.

As they descended the steep hillside in low gear their way was barred by two police Landrovers. It was all they could do to stop in time. Edwin's leading car was surrounded by policemen, who came from either side of the road. He wound his window down to be asked where they were going, by an Inspector with a London accent.

'What's it got to do with you?' Edwin countered.

'We are here to discourage people like yourselves. We don't want you travelling all over the country, causing trouble.'

'We can go where we want,' Edwin said.

The Inspector seemed resigned, his coolness contrasting with the rising anger of the convoy. Edwin and the others in the car were ordered out and a policeman stood by each of them. Two other officers stepped forward and smashed the windscreen of the car with their batons.

'You can't do that, you bastards,' one of the men shouted, walking towards the Inspector. Edwin dug his hand into the man's shoulder, feeling the heat of his body surge into his own.

'Leave it,' Edwin hissed in the man's ear, 'leave it now.'

'Very wise, Mr Bowles,' the Inspector said.

Edwin hid his surprise at the knowledge of his name.

'Driving without a windscreen is an offence,' the Inspector said, 'but if you turn around now we'll overlook it. If you don't other screens will go the same way and you'll all be charged with having unroadworthy vehicles. I dare say there's a lot of things we could find wrong with them.'

Edwin was very close to the Inspector. He smelt the man's bad breath and saw that he wore a moustache identical to Elliott's.

'So this is how it is to be,' Edwin said.

'I've got a job to do,' the Inspector answered. 'Nothing personal.'

'Then why don't you fuck off back where you come from,' a voice shouted from the rear.

It was an awkward moment but Edwin kept a firm hand on the man's shoulder.

'Come on boys,' he said, 'we'd best get back.'

Each car turned in the lay-by picked out by the police and went back over the mountain. They drove back to The Merlin, a village pub they tended to use more than the Miners' Institute, which was now a decaying building in semi-disuse, a monument to grander times.

Men crowded around Edwin in the pub's car park and he let them vent their disappointment with questions and garbled threats. They had suffered a major humiliation which Edwin felt keenly. The fact that his own brother was a policeman made the strike that much harder for him. It was like a knife at his back that he could not see or move away from, yet no-one mentioned Elliott as they settled in the bar and drank their meagre picketing allowance. Edwin advised them to go home and take their change to their wives, then he too joined the wake. Two quick pints helped him back into the role expected of him, an exhorter of flagging spirits. Ceri Griffiths joined them and Edwin told him what had happened.

'We wondered what happened when you didn't show,' Griffiths said. 'So they've started that down here. It's been going on in Yorkshire for weeks.'

'They were London police,' Edwin said, 'wouldn't know coal if they fell over it.'

'How expertly history repeats itself,' Griffiths said, 'it's just like the twenties when they –'

'I know, Mr Griffiths, I was brought up on it too,' Edwin said.

He did not want a college monologue from Griffiths, or a session in mutual zealotry. Griffiths would come out of the strike all right whatever happened, and Edwin did not like having the man around. He was one for the remodelled times, for cameras and television.

★ ★ ★

Elliott Bowles had his first weekend off since the strike had started. Susan had insisted on it, for the children's sake. It was an attempt to bring some normality back into her married life but she regretted it as they sat in the front of the car, sharing a hostile silence. Elliott drove the large estate, which held the family, dog and toys with room to spare. It was a heavy July morning, without a freshening breeze, and the sun punished whenever it broke through the dirty clouds. In the back of the car the girls bickered with each other as they grew sticky, and teased the panting Sam. The dog tried to distance himself from the proceedings, prodding his slavering tongue against the back window. He knew it would be a long day. The girls were edgy in the company of their father since the school incident and took it out on each other. This was an enforced trip with none of the naturalness that made for successful outings.

Elliott drove to a seaside resort, a once vibrant town whose fortunes were largely tied to Welsh miners. It had lost much of its bustle but could still boast a full teeming beach on days like this. Susan had never liked the place, not even as a child, but it was where Elliott wanted to go. He sat hunched over the wheel, driving too quickly and barking orders at the girls. He had returned from Yorkshire late on Friday but he no longer talked about his business there. This time there had been bloodstains spattered over his trousers.

The Bowles family added five more dots to the beach, a large expanse of sand cleaner than Susan remembered, perhaps in recompense for the putrid sea that broke against it. This was a mixture of human and industrial waste mixed to a gun-metal grey that Susan would not let the girls paddle in.

'Come on, Dad, come and play with us,' Sally said, brandishing a beach ball.

'I will in a minute,' Elliott answered, sinking back onto the rented deckchair. Susan appraised his long body, what her mother would have called a 'fine figure of a man' but she looked on him coolly. It had been years since Elliott's masculinity had aroused her. Looking away she turned another page of her book.

'Edwin had a shock the other night,' Elliott murmured. He looked up at the sky with hands folded behind his head.

'What's that?' Susan asked.

'The bastard had his come-uppance. Got stopped going over the mountain, got turned back with his tail between his legs.

We've learnt that up in Yorkshire, stopping the buggers getting about.'

Elliott fingered his eye but it had lost all trace of Edwin's blow. Susan tried to concentrate on her book but prepared for one of his fraternal diatribes.

'Sometimes I think it would be better for me to work on my own patch. Pickets down here have had it too easy, just a bit of pushing and shoving at the steelworks.'

'We are alienated enough as it is,' Susan said.

'We don't mix with rubbish. I don't call that alienated. Look, I'm doing well in work, getting noticed again. Now I've passed my sergeants' exams it's only a matter of time. I could join the Met, there's opportunities up there and they think right.'

The girls moved away from them in pursuit of their ball and a half-hearted Sam lumbered after them, sucking in air in great gulps.

Susan wanted to ignore Elliott but found it impossible.

'For Christ's sake will you stop going on about your bloody job,' she said. 'It means more to you than me or the kids – Elliott's glorious career, I've had enough of being a fucking slave to it.'

Elliott's rising temper was briefly checked by Susan's language, he thought swearing a privilege of his own. Looking around to check where the girls were he grabbed Susan by the shoulder, twisting her skin in his hands.

'Listen, you cow,' he whispered, 'I'm not in the mood for your whinging. I've brought you all down here, haven't I, and it's my first day off in months. You've got the whole summer off with that poxy job of yours.'

'God, you play at being a father for one day and you expect praise for it.'

Elliott's hand clenched into a fist and Susan was glad of their public display.

Sarah called out and Elliot tensed. His headache started back. Would he ever get rid of it? Talking of Edwin brought a rare flash of memory into his mind. His father standing with his back to the fire, cleaning out his pipe. A scratching sound which was the only noise Elliott associated with him. But there had been comfort then. Playing with Edwin on the line, enjoying rugby at school. No terrors echoing in his head. A sliver of warm feeling started to creep into Elliott but he squashed it instantly, treating it like an invader. A silent sod, the old man had been, passing through life like a ghost. He was proud he was nothing like him, and nothing like his brother.

'I'm going to get a drink,' he muttered to Susan.

He stood up and shook sand over her. As he strode over the beach he joined in his daughters' game, kicking the ball high over their heads. Sam thought of following him but returned to his water bowl. Susan's nerves were so taut she was grateful for the dog's presence.

The girls tired, and rejoined their mother. There were a few minutes of silence until thoughts of food and fairgrounds entered their minds, and Susan savoured the lull. She let her head sink back against the coarse warm sand and closed her eyes against a hard blue sky. Elliott would not return until it was time to leave the beach. The stink of beer would be on his breath and he would doze on the way home.

'Dad said we could go on anything,' Sarah said, 'anything we want.'

'And he gave us five pounds,' Sally added. 'I think he's the best dad in all the world.'

A brief time with the children and Elliott was god again. A god who left her to dole out discipline with the food.

* * *

Rita Jenkins drank the tea Edwin had made for her. She slurped it and left a moist ring around a mouth which had puckered with emptiness as it awaited its false teeth. Her toothless state, combined with a careworn face, made her look ten years older than her forty-nine years. Rita looked after her father Jack, a contemporary of Edwin's father and a notable union man in his time. Jack was now a senile fixture in Rita's kitchen, in front of the fire in all weathers, fighting class battles in his head and stroking the dog that had been dead and buried ten years ago.

'We are used to him,' Rita said, 'but it takes an effort, mind. The language my father comes out with now, well, it's a good thing Mam's gone.'

'I'll have to get over to see him,' Edwin said.

'Not much point. He wouldn't know you from Adam now, and a strange face sets him off. It'll be fuck this and fuck that, and him a lifelong chapel goer. Makes you wonder what's locked up in the mind.'

31

'I've heard about The Merlin,' Edwin said, 'that's a stroke of luck.'

Ken Davidson, the owner of The Merlin Hotel, had given it over as a base for the women's support group. Besides being a miners' watering hole and occasional stopping place for wayward travellers it was now a soup kitchen and centre for the group's activities. Davidson's beer trade had slowed to a trickle but he was free from any brewery restraint. He was also an ex-miner.

Rita Jenkins led a team of fifteen women in her group, an organisation which had sprung up quite suddenly when it became obvious that the strike would be a long one. Edwin watched Rita mould an effective force in a short time without any prior experience. He was proud of her, but also amazed. Without the traditional route of early marriage he'd managed to cast off much of the male chauvinism of his fellows but its roots trailed deep and it was strange for him to see village women so actively involved in their men's world. Married women working full time were still a rarity in the village. Most followed the role laid out by tradition. Taking charge of children and household and getting their men to work. In this they had always been the ally of the pits, ensuring that a steady supply of labour took the cage down. Their hatred for the dirty toll paid by their men was balanced by regular pay packets.

Initially Rita faced an incredulous, even mocking response from her own side but it had not shaken her resolve.

'I think we've got it worked out now, Ed.' Rita said. 'We are going to help all the families in the three valleys.'

'That's all four pits,' Edwin said.

'You can't leave anyone out, can you? They'll only get a basic food parcel, mind, it's a gesture more than real aid.'

'Don't sell yourself short, Rita.'

'That's not the way my Ronnie sees it. I think he's a bit proud of me in his way but he can't adjust to it. He said I'll want to go down the pit next, like women did in the old days. I told him his own mother worked two heavy machines in the war making tank tracks and he shut up.'

'It will make some of the lads uneasy,' Edwin said, 'times are changing so quickly.'

'Ceri Griffiths was down The Merlin this morning,' Rita said. 'I can't work him out. He seemed genuinely cufuddled that we have got it together and he kept saying what an example we all were, but I felt his nose was out of joint, somehow.'

'Of course it was, he wished he'd thought of it first, that's all. There's a lot of jockeying for position in this strike.'

'Aye, I'm learning that. Politics, Christ it's worse than being back in school – girls in the corner bitching like banshees.'

As she grew animated Rita spluttered.

'I'll be glad when I get these teeth,' she said. 'You don't think I look too gross, do you, Ed?'

He was touched by the question. Rita was the wrong side of twelve stone, with a roughly hewn face which looked as if it would reject any female embellishment.

'I wouldn't like to meet you down a dark alley,' Edwin said.

'You cheeky bugger.'

She flicked the last of her tea at him and Edwin was careful not to dodge it. They laughed.

'That's the first chuckle I've had since this lot started,' Rita said.

'Nothing will stop you doing that for long.'

'Maybe. I'm an "indomitable spirit". Ceri Griffiths said so.'

'That and twenty pence will get you a cup of tea.'

'You're a hard bastard, Edwin Bowles. Don't forget I remember you in your nappy.'

Rita drank another half cup of tea and left. She was unable to close a door quietly, it was in her to slam them shut and this time she left a reverberation in Edwin's front passage. The sound echoed off the stone floor, making the house seem larger than it was. Since the strike began Edwin had felt its emptiness. It was something he had managed to banish from his mind in the last ten years, as he immersed himself in the welfare of miners, but now, without work, loneliness stalked him once again.

Crippled by adolescent shyness, his fumbled attempts at early girlfriends had been disastrous. The sensitivity he hid so well from men but dared show these girls was badly singed, to the point where he had not been able to build on any experience. When Elliott developed into such a ladies' man his lack of success became glaringly obvious. Becoming involved in the union gave him an identity and fellow miners stopped ribbing him about his lack of women as he gained their respect as a delegate.

When called upon to speak in the early days he had felt panic well up inside but his commitment conquered it. He developed a quiet fluency that gained attention. By then he was in his early thirties and the girls of his youth were married mothers. It did not occur to him to look further afield for a partner any more than it occurred to him to learn to drive. He could walk to the pit and the places he frequented, and there was an adequate public transport system if he needed it. If he could have foreseen the decimation of public services he might have joined the drivers but this, like marriage, was a lost opportunity.

Edwin had not strayed far from the parental home. Two streets and less than a hundred yards away he bought a two-bedroom terrace. The smaller bedroom became his union office, a desk and a few chairs he had salvaged from a demolished chapel, a typewriter that functioned despite its age and the box-filed paraphernalia of union business. One could enter the house and ascend the stairs to this room without seeing much of Edwin's world, which suited him. Innate shyness had nurtured his sense of privacy until it was central to his character and the badge of distinctiveness in the village that gained him respect. Yet Edwin knew it had stunted his personal development. Privacy was too handy a refuge, too easy to portray as a strength when it was a weakness, a familiar, comfortable weakness.

The rest of Edwin's house was strewn with books. His main furnishings were home-made bookcases and shelves which he quickly filled. Books unable to gain a neat place were heaped around. Before the strike began Edwin had thought of moving again. To have space for his books was the reason he had left his mother in the first place. It was an addiction, another mark of difference in his community, another facet of his aloneness. Reading had taken hold of him in his early teens, partly in defiance of his secondary education. His grammar school entrance examination had been botched in much the same way as his experiences with girls; too much nervousness, too little time. His grandfather had a ready collection of classics and Left ideology and more importantly, the old man lit the fuse of Edwin's imagination by introducing him to libraries. Edwin found he was able to understand and enjoy material other working-class kids did not touch.

When his first wages came Edwin's book acquisition ranged ahead of his reading. On trips to Cardiff he picked up bagfuls of second hand hardbacks, which he added to the growing piles on the floor of his bedroom, which was filled by his mid-twenties. Here the black dust of the coal face turned to the detritus of ageing paper but he liked the atmosphere of his miniature library.

The strike halted Edwin's book acquisition but this did not

bother him as much as he had expected. He felt the need to turn pages weakening. He began to realise that his life had been too carefully mapped out, vacillating between the sedentary life of the reader, the hard graft of the pit and union business. The strike had broken a routine he had thought permanent. Now he was beginning to think that every minute spent in a book was a lost one, compensation for the void in his life. Heresy, Bowles, he told himself, with a wry laugh. Unthinkable just a few months ago. He was changing. Pent-up frustrations were causing him to question his whole way of life, but he disguised his unease, still presenting to the world the solid reliability of Edwin Bowles.

The telephone rang, it was Griffiths wanting to see him that evening. They met in the back room of The Merlin.

'We are worried about the escalating violence,' Griffiths said, 'it's getting out of hand up north. Ten thousand were at Orgreave and Scargill himself was hurt there. We are playing into this government's hands.'

'Perhaps,' Edwin said, 'but what do you expect? It seems to me that it is a case of lay down and lose or fight and lose. At least the latter is easier to stomach for many of the lads.'

'Yes, but the majority in our area didn't want to strike in the first place, remember.' Griffiths lowered his voice. 'Are you still hopeful, Edwin?'

'I have some hope left. This will go on much longer, if we can get more outside support. Christ, our own women are doing more than other unions.'

'Exactly,' Griffiths said, 'that's our best chance, to get other working people on our side, and that's why these violent scenes are doing us no good.'

Edwin agreed with the man but did not think Griffiths could tap into the hearts of the rank and file. He thought in terms of moderate negotiation and his education irrevocably distanced him from the men he represented. The strategy of men like Griffiths was pre-doomed. Decent and cosy ideas of social democracy could not stand against the new breed of this Conservative government. The woman who now led Edwin's traditional enemy was a throwback to the older times she lauded. She had a black tunnel vision lit by bias and motivated by the need for revenge against the miners. That Margaret Thatcher was a woman Edwin thought a bitter twist of irony. He knew many women had voted for her because of this fact and in doing so had helped unleash a chauvinism more rampant than that shown by most of their men. In Thatcher the government had its own Scargill. Each had the same unshakeable belief in their own righteousness, but only one had the power to back it up. Edwin had not forgotten this woman quoting St Francis of Assisi when she came to power. And had loathed her ever since.

Edwin realised he had not heard the last minute of Griffiths's talk but he was able to pick up the thread easily enough. Griffiths was one of the new speechmakers who talked a lot, but about nothing, when one dismantled the words. Edwin understood the riotous scenes at the collieries and Griffiths did not.

'What's to be done about our smashed windscreen?' Edwin asked.

'We have lodged an official complaint,' Griffiths said.

'Ah. There's been no mention of it in the media.'

'You can't really expect it. Everyone is looking over their shoulder at the moment.'

'I've noticed when we are on that thing,' Edwin nodded to the wall-mounted television, 'that the cameras are always pointing from the police side. We don't get the same coverage as '74.'

'No, that's why we need more restraint,' Griffiths said.

'You are always telling me what we need, Ceri, but it's not what we've got, is it?'

'We haven't recovered from that mess in 1979,' Griffiths said. 'The winter of discontent.'

'Don't use their slogans, for Christ's sake. That was working people on peppercorn wages trying to better themselves, as far as I'm concerned, and being let down by a bloody Labour government.'

Edwin knew this was one way to get rid of Griffiths, show anger and talk about need.

'Look Ed, just try to keep the men in hand. I'll see you next week, when I get back from London.'

Edwin finished his pint and wondered who would calm his own fever. Ronnie Jenkins came over to him. Rita had given him a rare night off and he was already well into a celebration.

'Evening, Edwin. Haven't seen you since the strike started, not since the old woman got into the action. She's made me look after her father.'

'I know, and you are making a good job of it.'

'Don't bullshit me, Ed, I'm not that pissed. What do you think of it, though, this support group? Jesus, she's a different bloody woman. Always had more chops than a lamb, but about the usual things. You know, my drinking or time on the sick. Now she's around the place like Nye bloody Bevan.'

'Don't knock it, we need all the help we can get.'

'I know, but everything seems arse backwards. I feel useless, if you want to know the truth.'

'You shouldn't, Ron. You've been a miner for more than thirty years. Until this lot started, the changes you've seen have been good ones, haven't they? And this is another one. Whatever the outcome of the strike we have gained the other half of the village.'

'Aye, well, if you put it like that – but you're not married, are you. You don't have to live with them.'

Ronnie lurched back to his table. Although Edwin had been quick to damp down any talk of uselessness he recognised the mood. A growing undercurrent had begun to flow, making men capable of the violence Griffiths feared. Edwin offered the men in the bar another confident slogan as a way of saying good night and left. Now the strike had clearly defined his role he felt the weight of the responsibility. It would have been good to go home to a Rita, to have someone else to tap into the feelings he kept locked inside.

* * *

Elliott took his place in the Transit, his usual seat in the corner. He travelled north in the wake of another row with Susan, his own anger still ringing in his ears. This time he had pushed her too hard, causing her to fall heavily in their front porch. He'd left quickly before the neighbours noticed anything. At the station he phoned to see if she was all right and Susan affirmed this, in a voice emptied of any emotion. Elliott would have preferred recrimination but did not think about it overlong. He knew his marriage had disintegrated into a limbo of distance and bile with the children the only common ground. Lisa was on his mind more now. He could not wait to see her, for she excited him more than any of the others. She lived for each day and did not get bogged down in all the crap that entwines people. Elliott wished he could show her off publicly.

Elliott glanced around at the faces of his colleagues. They were calm and serious and one man snoozed. For them the strike was a job that had to be done but for him it was a war and he was on the side that could not lose. He looked forward to getting back into the fray and mixing with the boys from the Met again. After three tours they had accepted him and did not treat him like a woollyback.

As he dozed to the drone of the van's engine Elliott dreamed of taking Lisa to London. He was perfectly in tune with big cities and as his ambition grew he knew he could cope with being an absent father as long as he had access to the girls. It was career and money that concerned him now. The thought of having to share everything with Susan churned his stomach and darkened his mood. He saw her as a millstone around his neck, slowly asphyxiating him. His wooing and chasing of her was forgotten, filmed over by his spite until he saw himself as a man trapped. A man who wanted to lose himself in the action of picket control and in Lisa's bed.

Now that the government was using criminal law against the miners the hand of the police was strengthened further. Striking miners had also had over eight million pounds of tax refunds withheld. The more they were being squeezed the more he liked it. Each blow the authorities dealt out incited the hotheads into more reckless action and each mass picket was an opportunity for men to drink. This fired them up nicely and made them careless. Elliott wanted their collective pulse to match the frenetically racing beat of his own.

This time he was going to a colliery west of Doncaster. It was early August in a dry summer and the state of the Yorkshire coalfields had been one of fever pitch. As a few miners drifted back to work trouble escalated. At Elliott's pit, miners had already broken into its control room and attempted to burn the manager's office. He learned of these incidents and welcomed them. This area was becoming more like Northern Ireland every day, the miners more crazed and the country more indifferent to them. Elsewhere, people went about their business, intent on ignoring the strike. There were the usual holiday delays at airports, his fellow policemen talked about another English cricketing collapse. The miners' struggle had been marginalised, portrayed as the death throes of a spent force. Even Elliott was surprised at how quickly and effectively this had been done. He thought of his own valley, its skyline once punctuated with many pitheads, and coal permeating every strata of life there. Now he was part of a force that was sweeping it away, which made him feel special. It would be something to look back on when he grew old.

Nothing much happened on the first two nights of duty. He was able to get over to Rotherham on the third day. As usual he turned up at Lisa's house without warning but this time she was not at home. He phoned the police club but Lisa was not there. This brought immediate anger, then a long sulk into suspicion. Elliott had checked Lisa out carefully when they got together and there were no other men around then, but that was a month ago and for this woman that was a long time. He paced the large living room and remembered how Lisa had obtained such a house. She had married a man more than twice her age, given him a few years exhilaration then cast him off in a manoeuvred divorce. She took the house as a settlement. His 'leaving present', she called it. Lisa had not wanted to give Elliott a key but he had insisted on it, and felt in charge when she had assented.

He poured himself a large whisky from Lisa's drinks cabinet and took it with him to the bathroom. Here he took a leisurely soak in the corner bath, which was peach-coloured and not quite big enough for him. Lisa did not come back. He waited as long he could, flicking through the daytime television channels and taking a few more drinks. She had spoilt his day, and ruined his preparation for a night with the pickets. He focused his mind on this work now. Lisa would have to explain her whereabouts later and he tempered his annoyance with the knowledge that he would have an excuse to play rough with her. She liked this as much as he did. He left a note for her on the kitchen table, brushed his hair into place, checked himself in the mirror and went back to his war.

On this tour Elliott was part of a force protecting miners who wanted to work. He knew that for the pickets this was an even more emotive issue than the coal trucks. A trickle of men were attempting to return to the pits. If the police protected them others would join them and the strike would be broken. Elliott was told this by his superiors but he had no desire for it to end. He was hooked on its excitement and the extra money it brought him. Whenever his police van passed pickets he always made a point of waving a ten pound note at them. He liked to think he had started this trend, now copied by police and truck drivers alike.

Elliott liked to see miners breaking ranks. They were a cancer to militant miners. Pickets vented their frustration with incoherent shouting, some dissolving into tears of anger as they shouted themselves out. At this colliery ten men were to be bussed in, with thousands of police and pickets to witness it.

Nothing happened that night. There were too many police and inadequate numbers of pickets. The early advantage in numbers had been taken from the miners. Elliott was tired of standing in line, one of two thousand officers flanking the approaches to the colliery. The fine rain in his face kept him from sleeping on his feet and he had plenty of time to think about Lisa. He crushed any doubts that she could be with someone else. That would never happen to him.

The next day brought a cloudless sky and strong early sun-shine. The summer was a good one. On grass verges opposite the police pickets sat in groups, soaking up the sun in T-shirts and trainers. Elliott had no such freedom of clothing. From the box covering his genitals to the thick padding under his jacket, his full face helmet, riot shield and steel capped boots, he was protected. By the time he left his station to queue in front of one of the breakfast vans he was saturated by sweat. It gathered under his clothing to keep him angry. He ate a bacon sandwich and drank coffee as he watched the miners' ranks increase.

'Where are they all coming from?' Elliott asked his sergeant.

'Change of tactic, boy,' the sergeant answered. 'We've eased up on the road-blocks for this one – practically waving them on today, we are. We want them all here.'

'Why?'

'Come on, Bowles, use your head. This is going to be a big one. The government has been putting millions, billions some say, into breaking this strike. They want results and today we are going to give them one. It's what we have been training for.'

Elliott licked the grease from around his lips.

'Aye, you like that, don't you, Bowles? I've been watching you. You love all of this, you're always amongst the first to get stuck in.'

'Just doing my duty sarge.'

'Oh aye, we're all doing that all right.'

Elliott went back to his place in the police line. He noticed that numbers of women were present. They were there at Arthur Scargill's exhortation, to try to lessen the violence meted out to their men. The miners' ranks had increased by several thousand by the time the working miners arrived. Taut hours had been stretched by the knowledge of what would inevitably happen and the sun burned in celebration. There was a strange intermingling of history here, the mounted police communicating by crackling radios astride man's oldest form of transport. The police had adopted another tactic from the past, beating on their shields as they advanced, a primeval response of men reduced to their most primitive essentials.

As vans carrying the workers approached a roar went up from the pickets. The air was filled with a dissonance of shouting. The names of those in the vans were spat out and chanted and projectiles began to rain on the van roofs. The pickets had already been isolated on one patch of ground to the left of the gates, now mounted police pushed them into a tightly knotted group, like one great caterwauling animal being herded to slaughter. Elliott was in the front rank of advancing police and his fellows were now as fired up as he was, intent on striking at something they did not want to understand.

'Get the mouthy ones out,' an officer bellowed.

Whoever was heard shouting above the general volume was hauled from the massed pickets and beaten, before being taken off to waiting police vans. Miners rushed forward in an attempt to protect these men and the struggle divided up into many small skirmishes. Policemen suffered as the miners fought back and their control was threatened for a short time but the conflict was unequal. The imbalance between the two forces was glaring and many pickets were unprepared for the violence offered them. They were also handicapped by the awareness of what arrest might mean.

The police had no such compunction and Elliott played his full part. Whilst others struck out at bodies he went for heads. Several men sank down at his feet as he ploughed his way through them, his baton flailing swordlike. He felt a sharp pain at his side. A woman dug at him with something and screamed for him to stop pummelling her man. Elliott did not hear her clearly, her screams were coming from somewhere else, so lost was he in his actions. He swiped the woman away with a blow to her face and dragged the inert man to a van. The fighting moved away from the colliery gates and the strike-breaking miners entered. Men who sat heads down, some covered in blankets but known and marked forever by their communities.

The main wedge of pickets began to break up. In groups of fifty, men started to flee, pursued at first by mounted police. These looked for individual targets, lashing them with their sticks as they rode past. One woman was narrowly saved by looking up at the policeman's face. He preferred escaping backs. Elliott ran behind the horses. He saw acres of unprotected flesh and wanted more of it. In his cocoon of defence he felt so powerful, and this time the battle did not end on the pit site.

There was a mutual awareness that whichever side lost the fight this day would lose the war. Pickets were chased into the neighbouring council estate. With others Elliott entered one house in pursuit. He rampaged through the house, scattering furnishings and ornaments in his wake. He crunched the glass out of a television with his foot and worked his baton into anything that would break. A woman screamed. Later he had a collection of sounds and images but no clear recall of what he had been involved in. An exhilaration he had not felt since a young boy had taken hold of him, and he was running amok in a way he had never been allowed to as a child.

It was the most violent day of the strike. There would be others but it was the apex of the struggle which confirmed the superiority of the police and began the disintegration of union resolve. Hearts had been crushed as much as heads.

★ ★ ★

Elliott let himself into Lisa's house at dawn the next morning. He was elated by the action at the colliery and felt victorious as he enjoyed the beginnings of another sunny day. The dew on her lawn was drying on his boots and he carried the milk the roundsman had given him. He thought to go straight upstairs to Lisa but found her waiting for him.

'I heard you talking to the milkman,' she said, 'that means everyone here will know about you.'

'As if they didn't already,' Elliott said. 'People always notice the uniform.'

He was wild-eyed, unwilling to come down from his high as he drew her towards him and tried to fumble his way under her dressing gown. Elliott hardly noticed her avoidance of his lips and had forgotten her previous absence in his eagerness.

'Don't you ever get enough?' Lisa said.

She smelt Elliott's work on him. Layers of sweat had dried under his clothes in the last day, his face was lined with dirt and his breath betrayed his hasty eating of junk food. It would make it easier for her.

Elliott began to feel her failure to respond to him. Lisa tensed in his arms as if willing herself to be elsewhere.

'What's the matter with you?' he asked, as again his mouth sought hers.

'You just turn up here and start pawing me like an animal.'

'You like it, it turns you on.'

'Turns you on, you mean, and at seven o'clock in the bloody morning.'

She broke away from his grasp and looked for her cigarettes.

'Where were you yesterday?' Elliott asked, as memory came back to him. 'I left you a note.'

'I saw it.'

'Well?'

If you don't tell me you are coming you can't expect me to be here. I went to see my mother, if you must know. She hasn't been too well lately.'

'Let's go to bed,' Elliott said, pulling her towards the stairs.

Lisa broke away from him and pulled hard on her cigarette.

'Look,' she said, 'I'll run you a nice bath, you can unwind first, and clean yourself up.'

He acquiesced, to their mutual surprise. The realisation that Lisa meant something to him curtailed his anger.

Lisa had expected Elliott, despite her feigned surprise. She knew he would have been part of the violence her television had highlighted the previous night, and he always came to her afterwards, to include her in his games. The violence had shocked her. Since she had married there had been few thoughts in her mind about the mining community she came from. That was a place she wanted to forget about, if not deny had ever existed. But seeing what had amounted to a battle fought out in front of a pit she remembered, and the sight of women present, had discomfited her. She found it hard to understand commitment to anything, and to fight over the closure of lousy pits seemed crazy to her, yet the mistreatment of people who had been her own made her uneasy. It occurred to her that she might use this to finish with Elliott, if he proved difficult.

Lisa had decided to break with him weeks ago, before she met Ken, the new man in her life. Elliott had been exciting for a while, he was more her age and had the looks, but his boorishness had soon outgrown his appeal. They were all children but Elliott was a real man-child, full of dreams, lust and selfishness. Lisa could match him in the latter quality and now she wanted him gone. When Elliott began to talk of a future together, of going to London, of him leaving his wife and kids, alarm bells had rung loud and clear. It was ridiculous, Elliott earned peanuts whilst Ken had even more money than her former husband. She had taken Elliott at his word when he said he wanted just a short period of fun. Watching him splash about in the bath, with his legs sticking over the end she kicked herself for not knowing better.

Elliott took his time over the large whisky Lisa gave him. He sipped it carefully, letting the clouded ice cool his teeth before allowing the liquid to sting his stomach with warmth. Drinking at this time of the day, in a ponced up bathroom big enough to play squash in, he had a glimpse of another life. A rich life. Wealth always fascinated him, and the jealousy he felt when he read about people's luck was tangible. Each time someone won a fortune was a direct blow. Money mocked his lifestyle, laughed at his hopes of advancement in the police force and he knew that even the highest ranks only earned wages. He could not escape this system by drinking early morning whisky in peach-coloured baths. Elliott knew he could not throw off his dreams, it was the only weakness he recognised in himself. They had soured his marriage and made reality all the harder to bear.

Elliott shouted down for another drink and Lisa brought it up for him. As she walked away from the bath her back had never seemed so finely tapered. It led to the flare of her hips, the swell of her buttocks and then the long legs. He loved tall women, those able to come up to his shoulders. Five foot three was good going for the girls he grew up with, women as small as their horizons. Lisa was not like those at all, she was a self-made woman, with her future already provided for. Elliott had probed her finances, discreetly at first, but more openly when he was sure he had her hooked. She had told him there was just the house, big and valuable but not capital. Why else would she work in a club? Elliott did not believe her but let her have her way for the present.

He sank back and let the water come up to his ears. The whisky was talking to him. If Lisa sold up they would have a good start in London. He could get out of the force early, build something up. Security was the coming thing. There were fat contracts to be won if you had the money and the men on the ground worked for peanuts. He thought of employing ex-miners, there would be many of them about soon. It would be a final screwing of the bastards.

The second whisky was three fingers tall and Elliott was quite drunk when he had finished it. He was not sure how long Lisa had been standing there.

'Careful you don't drown,' she said.

He stretched out a wet hand but she evaded it.

'I feel good,' Elliott said, 'never better.'

Lisa struggled to help Elliott get out of the bath. They lumbered around and fell over on Elliott's journey to bed. He giggled as he promised her a good time, filling the air about her face with whisky breath. As Lisa hoped Elliott fell asleep as soon as she got the covers over him. He really did look like a boy now, with a stick-on toy moustache. Childish contentment was in his face as he began to snore, a nasal, rattling intake of air then a wheezing pucker of lips as he exhaled. She felt nothing for him at all.

She went downstairs and phoned Ken, catching him before he left for work. He knew about Elliott but was unconcerned, as long as she got rid of him quickly.

'Tell the bugger today,' Ken said. 'We're going to Paris this weekend, don't forget. Might get you something fancy there.'

Ken ran a chain of bookmakers. Lisa's father had made them his second home and now she wanted some of the money her old man had helped generate. It was not remotely possible that she would ever love Ken, but he would provide for her for the rest of her life, if she played it right. There would always be plenty of Elliotts if she needed them.

Elliott slept and snored his way to three in the afternoon. Lisa had made plans but was still nervous. This man was immature to a dangerous degree and more than a little punchy. There was a thread lose in him somewhere. He liked to play games when he went from very dominant to helpless.

Elliott murmured as she shook him by the shoulder.

'What time is it?' he asked.

'Past three. Don't you have to be back with the boys in blue?'

'Christ, why didn't you wake me?'

'I just did.'

'My head is splitting.'

He drank the tea she had brought him and perked up.

'I've got to be back on duty at six,' Elliott said, 'but we've got time for a quickie. It'll cure my hangover.'

His arm groped for her once again. It would be Lisa's one lasting memory, that hand reaching for her as if she was a plate of food.

Lisa stepped away from the bed and Elliott sat up, blinking the sleep from his eyes.

'What's up with you?' he asked.

'I've got my period.'

'So what? That hasn't stopped us before.'

'I don't feel well, and I'm worried about my mother, she's got to see a specialist.'

She wanted to tell him to fuck off and that her mother had never had a day's illness in her life. Elliott had an amazingly inflated idea of his powers but because he'd once excited her Lisa was close to hating him. She wanted to deny his small part in her life.

Lisa's plan was a cautious one. In Elliott's jacket pocket was a letter she had taken a long time to compose. It had all the usual rubbish in it about him being a married man, it not being right, that she would let him go for the sake of his marriage. It would be touch and go whether he accepted it, though she had tried to massage his ego as much as she could. Whatever happened she would be in France with Ken and the locks on the house changed before Elliot had the chance to react.

Lisa lit another cigarette.

'Christ, do you have to do that,' Elliott said, 'especially in the bedroom.'

'It's my bedroom. It's my house for that matter.'

'What is that supposed to mean?'

'Nothing. Look, love, you can't expect to have everything your own way all the time. That's not real.'

She saw his face redden and expected Elliott to bound out of bed at her but he stayed put. Lisa felt a rare moment of guilt as she thought of him going back to his wife and taking it all out on her. She knew Elliott would do this, after the initial shock of the letter had worn off. He was the type who found it impossible to keep a secret for long and he would want Susan to share his pain.

'I'm fixing you some food,' Lisa said. 'You'll just have time to eat it if you stop messing around.'

'You shouldn't have given me that last drink,' Elliott said. 'Jesus, it was more like half a pint than a short.'

'You needed to unwind. I saw some of the action on the telly last night.'

'Didn't video it, did you? We stuffed them, didn't we, no doubt about it.'

She knew that one way to lessen Elliott's sexual appetite was to get him talking about his job. When he did this he reminded her of her uncle, the one who came home from the war and used stories gleaned from it to impress the family, though only the kids listened after a time. Elliott talked his way through the meal, encouraged by Lisa's silence. At five thirty she helped him into his jacket as a taxi waited outside.

'This feels like my real home now,' Elliott said, as he kissed her on the doorstep. His lips clamped onto hers and his moustache chafed. She steeled herself to reach up and caress the back of his head, knowing that it was the last time this man's touch would be on her.

Lisa watched the taxi turn out of her road with relief. It had been easier than she thought. She changed the sheets on the bed, made herself a vodka and tonic and phoned Ken.

'He's gone,' Lisa said. 'Can you send that locksmith over tonight?'

'I can that,' Ken answered, 'and I'll be over myself at eight. We'll go to that little place on the Moors you like. The one where I pay a fortune for stuff that wouldn't fill a gerbil. It'll get you in the mood for France.'

Lisa's letter was tucked inside Elliott's notebook and he did not find it until the next day. His night duty had passed off without incident, spent patrolling the place of conflict. Like all spent battlefields it now had a forsaken atmosphere, a sad blend of victory and despair which even Elliott's coarse feelings could register. Both sides had been stunned by events and he found few fellow officers wanted to talk about it. For once the nation's cameras had caught a fairer reflection of the fight. Mounted policemen were difficult to keep out of shot and more questions were being asked about the police role in the strike. Not that this concerned Elliott much, for he found Lisa's letter just after dawn as he stood with others at a feeding station.

It took him some time to understand what she was saying. When he recognised the large handwriting on the envelope he was excited, proud that Lisa had written him something to lighten his work. It took three readings for comprehension to sink in. Fragments of sentences drilled into his brain. 'Best we finish,' 'bad for your career', 'I have to go away', something about her mother. He struggled not to shout out in baffled rage as he stomped away from the other officers.

'What's up with Bowles?' one of these asked.

'Christ knows,' another answered. 'He's more than a bit cracked, I reckon. Probably wants more of the heavy stuff.'

'Yeah, he wades in like an idiot, doesn't he? Gives us all a bad name.'

Elliott found a phone and rang Lisa. He let it ring thirty times and with each tone realisation struck him. The loneliness of the unanswered phone was unbearable. His mind raced with clashing ideas. No cow did this to him. He would fix her, smash up the house. No, he had got it wrong, she was only thinking of him, of Susan and the kids. No, she was a fucking slag and had messed him about. He slammed down the phone, chipping off a piece of it. His hand felt for Lisa's house key on his bunch. It was still there. This calmed him a little. She had not taken it. She had kept a link with him, a link to let him back into her life. It was Thursday and Elliott was on tour until Saturday. He had to see her before then and for once his job was a restriction.

Elliott opened the door of the phone box to leave but stopped himself. He used the phone again, ringing his home number. It was instinctive, done before he could think about it. Susan's voice answered.

'Oh, it's you,' she said. 'I didn't expect you to phone today. Are you all right?'

At first he thought she was referring to what Lisa had done to him and did not reply.

'Elliott, are you there?'

He realised she meant the fight with the pickets.

'Yes, I'm fine,' he said. 'How are the girls?'

He hardly heard what Susan was saying. How he wanted to include her in his torment, to somehow blame her for letting him stray. If she stood up to him more things would have been better. As his delusions escalated they whirled him into an unreal vortex, in which Susan was the guilty party. It was the only way Elliott could deal with rejection. It was new to him.

Susan's voice was faint on the phone but it probed him over the poor line.

'Are you sure you are all right?' she asked again. 'Are you listening to me? You sound very strange.'

He regained some control.

'Don't worry. I'm tired, that's all. I'll be back on the weekend. Kiss the girls for me.'

The thought of going back to Susan made his stomach turn. He thought again that it must all be a mistake with Lisa, and he would sort it out. For the first time since the strike began Edwin and the miners were out of his head.

In the aftermath of the colliery engagement both sides drew back. Union leaders urged restraint as they saw their members battered and the police were told to go more softly around the mining areas. Miners' hopes were lifted by the calling of a national dock strike. The help Edwin had prayed for was slowly arriving, but piecemeal.

Elliott managed to arrange a few hours off on Friday afternoon. He had tried several times to reach Lisa by phone but to no avail, so he had decided to go down and wait in her house for her. She could explain things face to face. To be in her house would be something. For two days every permutation of what might be going on ran through his mind and it was hard to keep himself in check. If there was another man he wasn't sure if he could stand it, but it would not do to get involved in a domestic fracas, especially when Lisa was not his wife. The force frowned on that type of thing, though he was by no means the only one to have women on the side.

Elliott sensed the house was empty before he rang the bell but he let its call resound for half a minute. When the ringing was not answered he looked for Lisa's key, isolated it from the others and put it in the lock. It would not turn. He tried it several times, almost snapping the key then took it out and double checked it was the right one. He looked closely at the door to see a few fresh scrapes around the lock. It was a new one. She had changed the locks. The bitch had changed the fucking locks. Elliott kicked the door heavily with his foot, unable to stop himself. He was about to put his shoulder to it when a voice called him. It was Lisa's neighbour craning his head over an adjoining hedge.

'What's your game?' the man said. He recognised Elliott. 'Oh, you're the police chap. I didn't recognise you without your uniform.'

'Nothing to worry about,' Elliott said, fighting for control of his face muscles. 'Just having trouble with the key. I think I've got them mixed up.'

There was a moment's silence and Elliott wondered how much

the man knew. Everything, he felt.

'She's not there,' the neighbour said, with satisfaction. 'Told my wife to stop the milk for her yesterday.'

'Right.'

Elliott had no choice but to go. The man's eyes bored into him, staying on him until he faded from view, thumping his size twelves onto the pavement. He burned, his skin heated by rage as he paced out the two miles back to the station. The curtain that obscured his true self briefly opened. He recoiled, treating this flash of awareness as a traitor - he was not like that. Telling himself this he concentrated on his usual figures of blame – Susan, his parents, Edwin. He used a series of faces as the fault trail of his self-delusion. But this time they did not work.

★ ★ ★

The Bowles' terrace had not changed much in Edwin's lifetime. Modern trappings like television and washing machines had been added to it, but in essence it was the same. The time warp, the air of apathy, was almost tangible for Edwin. The old house spoke the language of his mother. It said why bother, you aren't going anywhere, accept the way things are, take it. Fatalism lived here, and his father had suffocated in it. It was hard for Edwin to accept that his parents had always been equals in lethargy. Something must have happened to them long ago, something traumatic.

He entered the house with the key he had always kept, shouting out his presence to his mother. She answered from the kitchen, a voice that barely broke the quiet. The grandfather clock his father had so wanted dominated the small hall. It sent a solid tick around the still house but had ceased to chime years ago. On the hour there was a confusion of wheels and gears, then it carried on with its tracking of time.

He went into the front room, sat down in the armchair, and picked up the paper there. A picture of Ian McGregor stared back at him. The Coal Board chairman was surprisingly old, with a countenance that might be genial were it not for the steely eyes. 'I am not a butcher,' the man proclaimed, but Edwin knew that was exactly what he was. Thatcher's Scottish-American destroyer. He threw the paper down, making the cat jump and startling Rowena as she entered the room.

'I don't know why you read the things if they make you angry,' she said.

She served tea and his visit took its usual course, her chat washing around him, talk of Elliott and the grandchildren.

'Sarah is almost as tall as me,' Rowena said, 'she's taking after her father.'

There was a westering glow from the window and a last shaft of light cut into the room, adding to the silver in Rowena's hair. Edwin felt the strike was taking place in another world. She picked up her lolling cat and sat it on her lap. They merged in perfect company. His mother distilled a kind of harmony he thought unreal, false even. He knew how hard she had worked to give her sons a start but the die was cast in his view of her. She had spoiled Elliott thoroughly but Edwin could never broach that matter with her: he was too aware of his own jealousy.

'I have to go now, mam,' Edwin said. 'I have a lot to do.'

'Everyone is so busy these days.'

Reluctantly, he stayed for another cup of tea, knowing that Rita Jenkins would wonder where he was. He had planned to meet her in The Merlin.

He left twenty minutes later and hurried down to the pub. Rita was in the midst of her work when he came in through the back entrance.

'Where have you been?' she asked. 'I've been waiting.'

'I've been up to see my mother.'

'How is she?'

Edwin noticed the respect which crept into Rita's voice. Most of them had it when Rowena Bowles was mentioned. They saw another person.

'As ever,' Edwin answered.

'She's been one of our steadiest givers, you know,' Rita said. 'Always fills a box with little things, mainly rock cakes.'

'I knew they would come in handy sometime.'

Rita stood in front of him, hands on hips.

'Go on, then,' she said, 'say something. You might as well, every other bugger have. I've had all the toothpaste and gnasher jokes.'

Edwin looked at her without comprehension.

'You haven't bloody well noticed, have you? Edwin, you've disappointed me, and you being such a one for the ladies.'

It was her teeth he had not noticed. Rita's false teeth were in place, she had a full and perfect mouth which took years from her. She turned to give him a profile and clicked them together.

'I'm getting used to them now, been in two days.'

'They're great,' Edwin said, 'better than my bits and pieces.'

Long trestle tables had been laid out in the back room. On them tinned food and vegetables were piled high, waiting to be sorted for distribution.

'This is taking off, Ed,' Rita said. 'I've got twenty girls collecting now. Food, money, anything we can lay our hands on. We had a parcel of blankets from Surrey yesterday. Perhaps they mistook us for Ethiopia or something.'

'You've really got your teeth into it,' he said.

She dug at him with a carrot.

'Christ, almost a joke, Bowles.'

Rita picked up a food parcel.

'We have standardised it now. This is my usual: eight pounds of pots, tin of corned beef, rice pudding, veg, beans and a bit of fruit if we can get it.'

Edwin let her reel off the list, it was the nearest Rita would ever get to showing off and he wanted her to enjoy it.

'These things look all right,' Rita said, 'but its not much for a family of four or more. It wasn't so bad when the kids could have dinners in school but they're out for six weeks now. Still, more women are coming over to us. I remember my father telling me us women were always on the side of the old pit owners, could always be relied on to nag the men back to work. There's some round here who would like to do that but I think we've been a bit of a shock to the Board.'

'You have, and people find it easier to give to you than the "lawless, overpaid miner". You could cadge a worm out of a crow's mouth.'

'There's quite a bit of money coming in now,' Rita said, 'by our standards.'

'Griffiths said something about that.'

'We've decided to send what we can down the valley to the office. Should be about six hundred quid a week.'

'That's amazing.'

'We're getting better at asking. Anyway, I didn't want to see you about any of this.'

'What then?'

Rita took him by the arm and led him to a quieter part of the room. Women lined up to load the dilapidated van they used for the morning food run.

'This is a bit awkward,' Rita said. 'It's about Susan, Susan Bowles.'

His sister-in-law was the last person Edwin expected to be mentioned here.

'She came down here Thursday morning,' Rita said.

'What for?'

'Said she wanted to help. It went a bit quiet for a minute but the girls didn't say anything. Good job Marge wasn't here or she would have given her a mouthful, because of Elliott. I didn't know what to say to the woman so I told her I'd think about it.'

Edwin's first reaction was one of elation. This was something that would hurt Elliott, but he quickly saw the cheapness of his thought. Susan doing something like this might unhinge his brother, and there were his nieces to consider.

'Taken you aback, haven't I?' Rita said.

'Just a bit. What did she say, exactly?'

'What I said. That she wanted to help and didn't like seeing children suffer. They are the innocent ones, she said. I told her it would be awkward for everyone, her husband being a copper. But she said she was her own woman. That's not how I remember her but she seemed quite changed.'

'Better leave this one with me.'

'All right. I was thinking, it might be good for us, having her doing something. Sort of a victory.'

'You're getting to be a politician, Rita.'

'Leave it out. I don't look that shifty do I?'

She stuffed a few tins into Edwin's pockets and stifled his protests. Rita's sister came over to her when Edwin left.

'You'd think he'd have found someone by now, wouldn't you?' Marge said. 'He's not bad looking, even if he does dress like something out of Oxfam.'

'He's a bit deep is our Edwin, and he's got that sod of a brother of his around his neck. I don't think they'll ever bother with each other after this.'

'They won't be the only ones.'

Edwin walked home thinking of Susan's offer. It was a warm night well into a lasting summer and his duffel coat had long since been discarded. He had a tan, for the first time in his adult life, and the men on the picket line were of the same brown. Most looked healthier than he had ever seen them, ironic when one considered their straitened circumstances. On nights like this Edwin thought of the many miners who kept their heads down and waited out the struggle, neither strike-breaking nor helping. They had all day to tramp the mountains Edwin loved whilst he could only snatch walks, away from the beck and call of the union. The contrary nature of valley life struck him forcibly as he watched the sun turn orange and lose its fire. It sunk down behind the mountain leaving its afterglow as a promise to return. His long spell out above ground brought home the meagreness of his working conditions. No matter how much they modernised and the old men called them soft and pampered, nothing could change the fact that coal was dirty and created a black dust that worked on men's chests until they were silicotic. Miners rarely saw daylight on winter weekdays and technological advancement had yet to change the seasons.

Edwin stopped on the river bridge near his house. From here he could see the railway line he once played on. It was still the main artery of the valley despite the absence of coal trains. As swifts darted about his head in their dusk play he could hear Billy Tucker scream and see the red, screwed up face of Elliott as he pulled him along. Although fewer than in his childhood, the birds seemed to sense the change in the river. It had been cleansed as the valley pits had been stilled. It was almost possible to see the river bed in the faster flowing channels. But a clean river was scant compensation for him. If the government had its way Edwin could see no future. He knew what happened to the older men discarded by the steel industry, the ones who used to be bussed down to the coastal plants. They hung around the village like cyphers, ghosts of their former selves. Edwin knew how slowly time went for them, for they had no skill in dealing with idleness.

He turned away from the road to his house and walked out of the village to the new estate. Elliott's car was not there so he knocked on his brother's door, ignoring the bell with the stupid chime. Edwin felt an interloper here. The new cars parked on drives and the people who polished them in the twilight were from another world, though he recognised one of them from his schooldays. As he turned to leave the unanswered door Susan opened it.

'Good God, Edwin. I was at the back of the house. We don't get many visitors.'

'You wouldn't have got me if his car had been here. I would hardly have been welcome.'

Susan appraised him and he blushed. He had a moment's warning before heat reddened his face but was powerless to prevent it. This happened whenever women studied him.

'No,' Susan said, 'not by your brother. I despair of you two sometimes.'

Edwin shuffled his feet and wondered if his sudden decision to come was a wise one.

Sally stuck her head around the door.

'Uncle Ed. We haven't seen you for ages.'

Her excitement brought her sister to join them, which increased Edwin's fidgeting, as if he was a child himself.

'Oh, don't be so awkward,' Susan whispered, then in a louder voice, 'come on in then, and see your nieces.'

He fumbled in his pockets to give the girls something but his hands came up empty.

'Don't worry about that,' Susan whispered again, 'they've probably got more spending power than you at the moment.'

It had been more than a year since Edwin had called and he could count the times before on one hand. He had helped Elliott move and had visited a few months after that but his first opinion of Elliott's new world proved intractable and his brother soon picked it up. Susan had listened from the kitchen as each man denounced the other's lifestyle, taken aback by the vitriol of the exchanges. She knew their relationship was at a serious point. At this time, although well conversant with her husband's faults Susan shared some of his resentment of Edwin's views. Edwin was in her house and having a go at it and what he said it represented, so this must include her and the kids. Edwin was so much like the father and grandfathers she had grown up with. He seemed determined not to move forward whereas her own man detested anything old. Elliott viewed the past like a disease, something to be forgotten or even denied. When any new gadgetry came out he had to have it, had to show it off before moving on to something else. He led the Joneses on the estate more than kept up with them. They never had a penny put by, despite his endless talk of the future.

Susan made coffee and a quick snack for Edwin, which she knew he would refuse, then eat. Edwin played bashfully with the girls, diligently examining each toy they brought him. Sally was old enough to tease now and like her father she was quick to work people out. She turned her mock surprise into horror that her uncle did not know which doll was in fashion, or had not heard of their favourite television shows. Susan brought in a tray which Edwin placed on his lap after the expected protestation.

'Come on, girls,' Susan said, 'leave your uncle alone. Give him a chance to talk to me. And get ready for bed.' Her daughters reluctantly left them after extracting Edwin's promise to look in on them later.

'They're lovely girls,' Edwin said, 'they make me feel ancient though.'

'You're not used to being around them, that's all. It would be nice if you saw them more often, we haven't much family left between us.'

'Perhaps I will.'

'Perhaps. So, Rita Jenkins has told you, has she?' Susan said. 'I can't think why else you're in this Sodom of a place.'

He blushed again and was grateful to concentrate on the food.

'You haven't changed since school, Edwin, perfect teasing material, you are. We have known each other more than thirty years, and it's not as if I haven't seen you since the fight.'

Edwin knew he was being told to relax but found it difficult. The room screamed out Elliott's personality. It was filled with overpriced tat which he was surprised Susan could stomach. In his sub-conscious he maintained the idea that a marriage should be a perfect mix of moods and interests. In this he was just as much a dreamer as his brother.

'Rita mentioned you went down The Merlin,' Edwin said. 'I hadn't planned to come up tonight, just did it on the spur of the moment.'

'Well, go on then. Ask me what I think I am doing.'

Edwin finished eating, put the tray on the table, and spread his hands. Elliott's hands, though large and strong, were so much softer and better cared for, with rarely a nail out of place. Edwin's hands looked as if they had been re-arranged several times and put back together in a lumpish way. She recognised the scars of his environment. Blue smudges of once torn flesh, a thickening around the knuckles and the fingertips callused into ball-ends. His nails were individuals, each one clashing with its neighbour in shape and colour even though Edwin was in better shape than usual, not having worked for four months.

She wondered at such a stark difference between the brothers. Perhaps each man favoured a different side of the family, people further back in time. They seemed stark opposites, but Susan knew they shared one thing in common – an obsession with the correctness of their viewpoints.

'I was surprised when Rita mentioned it,' Edwin said. 'I feel a bit awkward, to be honest, coming here the way things are between Elliott and me. And I don't know what's going on between you two. I know it's none of my business but –'

He struggled to a halt, his face burning anew.

'Well Christ, something must be up, for you even to be thinking about it. Elliott will go bonkers if you work for us, you must know that. I'm wondering if that's what you want.'

'No, of course not. He's hard enough to handle as it is. Things have changed between us, it's been happening for a long time.'

'Look, you don't have to tell me anything, Susan.'

To lessen his discomfort, he hoped she wouldn't.

'I know your thoughts on how he lives, and all this,' Susan said, waving a hand around the room. 'I thought you were wrong, in fact I thought you were a bit jealous, but now I'm not sure of things myself. I don't know where Elliott is going. What we have is more than enough for me but he never seems satisfied. I don't think I play a part in this future he keeps talking about. He talks about *things*. Bigger houses, bigger cars. And I'm worried about the girls. I'm not sure I can keep this family together.'

Edwin wondered if Susan knew about his brother's long-time womanising.

'I still don't know why you want to join Rita's group,' he said.

'Self respect. I've seen the effect the strike is having on families. Being a policeman's wife doesn't blind me to that, and I work in a school so I don't think even Elliott could fail to understand my link with children.'

Edwin thought for a moment. However Susan dressed it up he knew that Elliott would not be able to swallow this. It would lead to more confrontation and he might be drawn into it. It was a mess he could do without at this time, but he answered intuitively.

'If you are sure it's what you want to do, Rita would be glad to have you. But I don't think you can count on Elliott seeing it your way.'

'My mind's made up anyway. I'll go down tomorrow and get started. Rowena said she'll have the girls. It'll get them out of the house. They seem to have stayed on the estate the whole summer.'

'When's Elliott home?'

'This weekend sometime, he's never sure.'

'Will you tell him then?'

'I'll have to think about that. He'll probably go back after a few days so I might leave it for a while.'

'And the girls?'

'Oh, they can keep their mother's secrets, I've made sure of that.'

'Womens' union, eh?'

Susan smiled and seemed to relax, now that her decision was made.

'Shall I make more coffee?' she asked.

'No thanks,' Edwin said, 'time I was off. Your neighbours will wonder what's happening, me being up here. Their property values might drop.'

'I hardly know their names,' Susan said.

'Aye, a bit different to what we grew up with.'

'I think I liked it at first. It was nice to have some privacy and so much space but before the girls went to school I began to feel trapped here. Elliott wasn't home much, even before the strike. The Overtime Kid, he called himself. Absent father would be more like it.'

'Haven't you made any friends up here?' Edwin asked.

'Not really. The girls play with the other children but I never felt comfortable going into any of the houses. People here think they must behave in a different way.'

'They want to match their surroundings,' Edwin said. 'Maybe that's a good thing.'

'Maybe, but there's more of the village in me than I thought.'

'I'd better not say much about that, you know how my thoughts run on those things.'

Susan let him out. Although only late August there was a touch of Autumn about the evening, a presage of leaves falling that gave the air a nutty quality which reminded Edwin of the garden bonfires that always marked this time. It was one of the lasting sensations of his youth, the smell of the thick, eye-stinging smoke as he helped burn the garden refuse. He had an acute perception of the changing year then but it had dulled as he went underground.

The summer had been a fine one, ironic, he thought, considering the plight of the miners. Each day that proved sunny brought home to him the fact of their poor timing. The strike should have been called in October, with the onset of winter to back it up, yet he appreciated how Scargill felt. If his was a knee jerk reaction it was brought about by the anger that overwhelming odds caused. There had been some patchy success, at the docks and with the railworkers, but it was a gesture more than real support. He saw his class fragmenting before his eyes. What did Elliott used to say, that there was no working class, only an underclass. He started preaching such stuff within a year of joining the police force with all the arrogance of youth, and Edwin felt the same about that as he did about the scab miners. Despair that they could not see what they were doing, anger at their betrayal and at bottom total frustration that they did not share his beliefs. He knew that his would be thought an unreal, unworldly reaction but he could not help it, and knew the miners' president was in the same boat. Just as much a pawn as the men he used.

Edwin walked down Elliott's street. A man garaging his car watched him, noting an alien and checking for any signs of wrong doing. There was a pile of correspondence waiting for Edwin in his office but he was glad to be going home, despite the cracked, uneven pavements and the regular heaps of dog shit. He stopped on the road down from Elliott's estate. The village could be seen at a new angle from here. They had picked the best spot for the new housing, a gentle curve that looked down on the valley. The village loomed dark below, squat, unchanging and old.

* * *

Susan took the girls down to Rowena's at ten the next morning. Sally was a bit disgruntled.

'It's gloomy there,' she said, 'and the telly is fuzzy.'

'And black and white,' Sarah added.

'It'll be a change for you,' Susan said. 'Gran will have baked lots of cakes.'

'Yuk,' Sally grimaced, 'rock cakes with burnt bits on them.'

She helped her sister carry in a box of toys.

It was not an auspicious start and it underlined what few contacts the family had. There was no-one else who could conceivably look after the girls. Susan left them with the slightly baffled Rowena and walked over to The Merlin. She thought it wiser to leave the Volvo in the street. Rita was waiting for her.

'Edwin phoned up earlier, told me you'd be coming down,' she said. 'I'll show you how we operate here. Nothing to it really, even my sister can do it.'

Rita said this to quell the scowl on Marge's face. Within minutes Susan was adept at filling brown bags with food. Rita was right, it was easy but there was something else here, a building on the atmosphere at school. There she had discovered women working together with purpose but here they appeared charged with a mission. There was an enthusiasm in the air that caught her up, although the others were wary of her. She did not expect anything else and she knew nothing of importance would be discussed around her, but there was no hostility shown apart from Marge.

'You'll be useful because you can drive,' Rita said, 'we've only got four girls who can. Do you fancy driving the van on one of our runs? We've got insurance.'

Susan suppressed a smile at this. They would never be able to dismiss her police background.

'Yes, I'd like to,' she said.

'All right, you can come with me this afternoon,' Rita said.

Susan had not expected such a level of involvement so soon and guessed she was being tested. She masked her nervousness the best she could. The height of the van was strange at first but used to driving the large estate she did not find its size a problem, once she had learnt to coax the gears into action. It was an ancient Transit that had seen multiple owners and two hundred thousand miles. She drove it up the valley, heading for the next village. Rita and another woman sat on the long seat next to her. Both smoked.

'Don't mind, do you, love?' Rita said. 'Can't give the buggers up. I *have* tried a few times, but once this lot started I needed them again. Burning up money we are.'

The smoke interacted with the sun that penetrated the vehicle and mixed with the smell of diesel. It was not long before Susan's head began to throb but she knew she was in the world of these women now. Health consciousness did not play much of a role in it. Money was the ally of awareness and they did not have any.

For several hours Susan drove around her valley, making food drops at strategic points. Despite her simple blouse and jeans she still felt her appearance marked her out. She began to notice a certain look in many of the people who received a food parcel.

Cowed and defiant at the same time. She had seen it before, in the poorest children in the school. Children did not dress much differently these days, parents somehow managed to keep up this side but faces could not hide it. By the end of the run Susan was becoming accustomed to it. She saw women who seemed to have gone from thirty to fifty very quickly, as if they rushed to middle age out of necessity, yet these were her own people, living just miles from her. Living on the estate had made her forget quickly, and rather easily. Her viewpoint had narrowed as she had tried to match her husband. In his case it had narrowed to hostile contempt, where poverty and poor opportunities were metamorphosed into laziness and dishonesty. The very sight of the people she now helped usually sparked off an outburst of derision in Elliott, as though their presence made him constantly want to prove his own position. When they married he had influenced her and almost converted her to his way of thinking, but she had resisted his desire to cast off their roots. Susan wanted the benefits they had to be extended to the whole valley and did not know why her husband was so fierce in thinking it should only come to the chosen few. Elliott would be home in a day and Susan had no idea how she would tell him of her new role.

'Miles away, arn' you?' Rita said, as they returned to The Merlin. 'You've done all right today, even if some of the girls think you're slumming.'

Rita laughed at the look on Susan's face.

'Don't worry, just teasing. Part of being the new girl, isn't it? So, what do you think of it, out and about with people like us?'

'I hadn't been to some of those places, ever,' Susan said. 'It was _'

'An eye-opener,' Rita answered for her. 'Aye, it's funny that, how little people get around up here. They know the Costa Del Sol better. Pity, 'cos it gives some the wrong idea.'

'What do you mean?'

'Those morons in London, and much nearer too. Because we don't want to move away they think we don't want to better ourselves. Think we'll take any old shit they'll deal out. It's a very convenient theory.'

Susan parked the van in the pub's rear yard, grinding the gears one last time. She returned to Rowena's tired but satisfied she had made a firm start. As she brought in the ubiquitous tea Rowena shook her head, matching the shuffle of her feet.

'I don't know, girl,' Rowena said, 'getting involved with Rita Jenkins' lot. Her father was in the thick of any trouble going, I remember.'

'How have the girls been?' Susan asked, seeking to divert Rowena.

'Lovely, lovely. Don't think much of my old telly though, do you girls?'

Even so, Susan's daughters were slumped on the carpet before it, Sally trying to get the disdainful cat to play with her. Sarah glared at her mother, a look that accused her of dumping them here. Susan was glad that the new school was just a week away.

'When's Elliott coming home, then?' Rowena asked.

'Tomorrow, I think.'

'Doing so well, isn't he? He's told me about all the overtime.'

Susan studied the old woman's face. Was the outward expression of benign vagueness just a mask? She had never been sure. If Rowena did inhabit a world in which every sharp edge was blunted it might be useful in dealing with the war between her sons, due to escalate at any time.

'We were bored, Mam,' Sarah said, as they drove back to the estate. 'Gran keeps on about the old days, and she says the same thing over and over.'

'And she doesn't know who the Muppets are,' Sally added.

'Is daddy coming back soon?' Sarah asked.

'Yes, tomorrow,' Susan answered.

'Can we all go somewhere?'

'Maybe. We'll see.'

As long as it wasn't that bloody beach.

★ ★ ★

Ceri Griffiths stood in Edwin's front room. He would have preferred him in his makeshift office but Griffiths had called without warning. The man scanned the bookshelves, trying to work out Edwin from the books there. Griffiths was someone who liked to pigeon hole people but Edwin did not fit any neatly.

'This room reminds me of my tutor's,' Griffiths said, 'when I first went up to Cambridge. We didn't have that many books at home and I was in awe when I saw so many of them outside a library.'

Edwin knew this was meant to flatter him, and half-expected

the question "have you read them all?". Griffiths liked to probe a man cautiously, with the promise of friendship in his questions. With the depth of his reading he knew that he had a toehold in Griffiths's world whilst remaining firmly with the rank and file, but he did not want there to come a time when this balance compromised him. He knew Griffiths was giving him a chance to cross over to his clean-handed educated camp, and though he was not blind to its benefits dismissal of new ways was strong in him. In a way he saw Ceri Griffiths as his side's ineffective answer to the likes of Elliott. Softly spoken, college educated, seemingly without temper, Griffiths was a manifestation of a new breed of socialism that some were beginning to adopt and sell. Edwin saw no answers in it for him.

'Do you think we are achieving anything?' Griffiths asked.

Edwin shrugged. 'We knew it would be hard but the things that have happened at Orgreave and other places have surprised even me.'

'This government sees our destruction as crucial,' Griffiths said. 'Emasculating the NUM is the first step of their strategy. They'll have carte blanche to do whatever they want if they break us.'

'That's obvious.'

Edwin noticed that Griffiths did not modulate his language with him. When in The Merlin he went into his 'boyo mode', leaving out the big words, dropping his 'h's' and emphasising the Welshness of his accent. Not that it fooled anyone.

'We have to keep going,' Edwin said. 'Next winter might help, if it's a bad one. The support groups are going well and the strike is rock solid down here.'

'Yes, but is it in men's hearts? Tradition has made it firm, the call of better days. When we went round the lodges in February most of the men were lukewarm about it, especially the older ones.'

'We are a long way from Yorkshire here. Don't forget the executive did not do much to save a valleys pit last year. They didn't want to know and that rankles.'

'I know,' Griffiths said, 'working man against working man. That's manna for the Tories, they think it proves their philosophy. I remember my father telling me about '47, when we nationalised the mines. He worked for Powell Dyffryn and the old pit boss was trying to to be heard over the men. They had all gathered to celebrate the change-over. "Better the devil you know, boys" the man shouted, but the colliers whistled him down and started up the band. God, that must have been such a feeling then, that they were gaining control over their whole lifestyle. And now, if we go through the hoop we'll be back to those days, just about.'

'Nationalisation was not as Utopian as all that. Men still worked for poor wages and in poor conditions. Just like before. And we had to fight for any improvement. Just like before.'

'You sound pretty fed up,' Griffiths said.

'Not really, just tired. There's not enough of us putting in real effort. Half the men are lounging around doing bugger all.'

'That gets me back to my point about February, and the public sees this. We had their support in '74, but not now.'

'We were still close enough to the old days then,' Edwin said. 'Look, I agree with you about this but the men look to us for a lead.'

'Yes, I know.'

'Did you want to see me about anything in particular, Mr. Griffiths?'

'Yes, I did. I'd almost forgotten about that. What are you like as a chaperone, Edwin?'

Edwin's blank returning stare was answer enough.

'That's what I thought,' Griffiths said. 'The thing is, now that it's likely the strike is going to go on into the winter, people are taking more interest in us, especially the more thinking journalists and academics.'

Your lot, Edwin thought to himself.

'A number of people wanting information have been referred to our office. It's been decided that we co-operate with the ones we think might be useful to us, anyone who can speak up for us in their own circle.'

'So what do you want me to do?' Edwin asked.

'A woman wants to come down from London to do some research into the effects of the strike. I have her name somewhere.'

He searched through a folder.

'Right, Kathryn Peters. She seems to be part lecturer, part writer and part newspaper columnist. Have you heard of her?'

'No.'

'Well she's quite well known. She wants to look at what's happening to valley communities, you know the kind of thing.'

Edwin knew, and he did not want any part of it.

'Surely this is your department,' he said. 'I wouldn't know what to do with the woman, and I've got no time.'

'I know, I know, but she's made a point of asking for someone like yourself to show her around, someone who –'

'Is a pleb. I think that's what they call us.'

Griffiths was put out by the interruption.

'Don't prejudge her. She has written some very supportive articles about the strike.'

'Look, I'm about to organise the action down at Port Talbot. Things have got a bit sticky between there and Llanwern.'

'She won't be down for a week, and she has to teach in October so it won't be for long. We want you to do this, Ed.'

'Union directive, eh?'

'It would be appreciated. Right, that's settled, then. I have to go to Cardiff now, arrange a few things with the media. You know Scargill is coming down for a day, don't you?'

Griffiths glanced at the bookshelves again as he left.

'You're perfect for this job,' he said, 'the Peters woman will love all this.'

Edwin was intensely irritated by the thought of another encumbrance and wondered if he might push this unwanted guest onto Rita Jenkins. He put the problem out of his mind as he planned the village miners' next move. A few weeks previously in The Merlin, Griffiths had talked about 'more visual signs to be sent to the British public'. Tom Rees had made a comment about 'them wanting us on rooftops next' which had sparked off an idea in Edwin's head.

A hundred trucks were regularly travelling between Margam and Llanwern steelworks, on the South Wales coastline. It was a ragtag convoy that trundled down the M4 motorway, heavily protected by police vehicles. Transport companies from outside the area had proved adept at using the already weighted law against the miners. The presence of the convoy brought home to Edwin the difference between this strike and former ones. He hadn't been naive enough to ever see much of a link between law and justice but now it was naked in its bias. A number of the trucks were untaxed and unfit for the road but the police were blind to it.

The presence of the convoys escalated bad feeling. So far South Wales had been free of the massed picket versus police scenes of the north. They had managed to achieve a practically scab-free area by talking men out and because of this Edwin had gone along with the cautious approach of his local union. Now the failings of it were apparent to him. The success they had hoped could be achieved with the steelworkers was not forthcoming. Early agreements to limit steel production during the strike had changed into an increase in normal production. Fuel flowed into the plants via the hated convoys. Each time the convoy rolled the miners' lack of real power was brought home to them. Their solidarity was mocked and proved to be ineffective and Edwin knew it was only a matter of time before weaker elements would be enticed back to work. Scabs were rare but their presence burned in the guts of every other miner and the destructive symbolism they provided was meat and drink to their enemies.

* * *

Edwin sat with a small group of men in The Merlin's inner sanctum. Rita's workers were absent and Griffiths knew nothing about this impromptu meeting. For thirty minutes Edwin had listened to the release of the men's frustration, and as they became more agitated they looked to him. Keeping them certain that they would win was a tall order.

'Those bloody steel boys have shat all over us,' Tom Rees said. 'Shat all over us they have. Can't they see we should all stick together in this?'

'Their time came before us, don't forget,' Edwin said. 'Half of them have gone and the ones left have been punched around until they are soft.'

'Aye, my brother worked down Margam,' another man said, 'and he reckons we did nothing for them when they was going through the hoop. I think we should have helped them. And how can we shout the odds now when thirty thousand of our own are working in Nottingham?'

'Yes, but what's the point in bothering with the power workers when they are controlled by the electrical lot?' Tom asked. 'Jesus Christ, they've shown their true blue colours in the last few years. Working class Tories to a man, just like that lot in the Notts' pits.'

'Calm down,' Edwin said. 'I've been talking to a few of the other lodges about an idea I've had. It's Bank Holiday coming up, a good time to try something different. How's your head for heights, Tom?'

'What do you mean?'

'I want a hundred men ready by Saturday, to do a spot of climbing.'

'What the bloody hell are you on about, Ed?'

Six heads came closer together as Edwin beckoned.

'We are going to occupy those cranes down at Margam, sit up on the things. It will get us noticed. The national media have concentrated on Yorkshire so far and it's about time we changed that.'

'They're over a hundred feet high, those buggers,' Tom said.

'A hundred and twenty, to be exact, so you'll have a nice view over the channel, won't you? I want men from each lodge, so the effort will be spread around.'

'They'll arrest us, though, when we come down.'

'We'll be charged with trespass, that's for sure, but they can't do much as long as nothing is damaged. We have to make sure of that. No, they won't want a hundred Welsh martyrs in court, so don't worry about it.'

'You going up yourself, Ed?' Tom asked.

'Of course I am. You don't see a collar and tie on me, do you?'

This lightened the mood and Edwin's group signed up. He bought them drink from his own pocket though he said it came from their picketing allowance. Despite his show of optimism Edwin was not sure how he would fare in this action. He saw those tall cranes waiting for him and struggled to keep the beer tray steady.

* * *

The police Transit dropped Elliott at his local station. No-one answered his home telephone and there was no-one available to give him a lift up to the estate. Fed up, and feeling a stranger in the village he walked over to his mother's house. He wanted to be a stranger, each poxy terrace he passed convinced him of this. They painted them bright colours these days – white, blue and even pink – houses that had been put up by drunken Micks a hundred years ago. It was pathetic the way people stayed in them. To Elliott they were still slum terracing. Even so, he did not mind going to Rowena's. His mother believed in him.

It was mid-morning when he knocked on the door. He had left Rotherham at first light, with the bitter taste of Lisa on his lips.

'Elliott, are you on your own?' Rowena asked, ushering him in.

'Aye. I couldn't get an answer when I phoned the house so I came over here.'

'Susan wasn't sure when you were coming back. She's gone shopping, I expect.'

Elliott walked past her to the back room where he slumped down on a sofa.

'Get me a cup of tea, Mam,' he shouted.

'How about a bit of dinner?' Rowena asked. 'I've got a small chicken this weekend.'

'Go on then.'

Elliott turned on the small television to check on the cricket but could not stand its warped, archaic monochrome.

'Why don't you get another television set,' he shouted into the kitchen. 'You can afford it with Dad's pension.'

Rowena did not hear. She busied herself in cooking for her youngest son, something she rarely had the chance to do. It brought back memories of more ordered days, when there were few shocks or changes in routine. Edwin went to work and Elliott went to school and they came home every evening.

Elliott used his mother's phone, dialled the code for Rotherham, then Lisa's number. She answered, in a sleepy, just-waking voice which jarred him. He had not expected her to be there, so many times had her phone rung to no avail and now he wanted to rage and plead at the same time. Lisa asked who was there again and he put the phone down in confusion. This set the seal on his hate for her. There was nothing in Lisa's voice. She was not suffering and he could sense he had been wiped from her mind.

'Still no answer?' Rowena asked, joining him in the room.

'No, I'll walk up after dinner.'

Elliott sat down and dug into his plate of food. It was what Rowena planned to have herself but this did not concern him. He had never lost his expectancy of servitude in his mother. She had put it there.

Why did Susan's face mingle with Lisa's? He could not keep them apart. Women. They were all trouble, all bitches at heart. In this mood Elliott doubted that even the one thing they were good for was worth it.

'I haven't seen your brother for a while,' Rowena said. She watched with satisfaction as Elliott devoured her food. 'You'd think he'd come more often, living just down the road.'

Elliott struggled to focus on Edwin. Lisa had pushed him from his thoughts for a time, replacing him as the target of his ultimate loathing.

'He's busy planning his stupid little schemes with the miners,' Elliott said. 'Totally useless.'

'Yes, you're both always working.'

What a stupid woman his mother was. It was as if she did not hear anything. Negative comment was filtered through the haze that passed for her brain until it faded away. Elliott wanted to bang the table and shout out what he thought of Edwin, and Lisa come to that, but there was no point. He ate the bread pudding Rowena made every Saturday, scooping it up quickly with his spoon.

'I'm off,' Elliott said. He picked up his holdall and strode to the front door without another word or look back at Rowena.

She realised her sons thought very little of her as a person. Each was selfish in his expectations but she had given them cause when she had let herself slip into the quiet being she was now. She had not always been so, but it had seemed the best way to deal with life after her trouble. Maintaining a secret she had kept from her sons all their lives.

'It's a nice day for a walk,' she said, 'and the girls will have a nice surprise', but her words fell on Elliott's back and his ears were deaf to them.

Rowena began her perfunctory clearing of the table, taking things into the kitchen. She would make this last as long as she could, before facing the rest of the weekend alone. Perhaps Edwin would come.

It was a Bank Holiday, but the village was very quiet. It took Elliott twenty minutes to get to the estate and sweat had gathered in the small of his back and moistened his shirt when Susan pulled up alongside him.

'What are you doing walking?' she asked.

He glowered at her but changed his expression when he saw his daughters in the back. Handing the holdall to the girls he sat in the front with Susan. Sally tried to hug his neck.

'Daddy, are you back for ever? Can we go somewhere? Where are we going to go?'

'Leave your father alone,' Susan said, 'he's tired.'

He did not want to go back to a house with three females. Repulsion welled up in him as Susan opened the front door. It was all he could do not to bellow to the girls to shut up. They squawked around him in excitement expecting presents, but he had none this time.

'Your father has been working, not on holiday,' Susan told the girls, 'so don't keep on.' Then, in a quieter voice to Elliott, 'You look really done in this time.'

'I'm going to grab a shower,' he said, 'and I'm going down to watch the rugby. First match of the season today.'

It was a spur of the moment decision, a means of escape.

'But you've only just got back,' Susan said, 'what about the girls?'

'I'm not in the mood,' Elliott said.

Personally Susan was glad he was going out but she was sorry for the girls. She knew the grizzles now beginning would soon turn into full blown tears.

'We'll do something really nice tomorrow,' she said, as she ushered them to their playroom. What, she had no idea. Good times and Elliott had never gone together much. Now they were opposites. Her eyes blinked when Elliott slammed the front door.

Elliott enjoyed his quick getaway, it gave him the semblance of control again. He drove down to the town whose team he supported. Despite playing police rugby in his early days in the force he did not bother with their games. He preferred the bigger crowds of the leading Welsh clubs.

He parked the Volvo in the members' car park and took his place in the stand. He felt at home here, where once he had stood on the terracing and enjoyed the ribald comments of the crowd. Cigar smoke enveloped him and he smelt whisky as it was sipped from flasks. The field was in prime condition, the grass green enough to look freshly painted. It had not yet been worn down by boots, bodies and weather. As the teams came out he smelled the liniment in the air and for a brief moment regretted his decision to stop playing so early. He had been good enough in his early twenties but other things got in his way and he saw how quickly players aged. The many knocks and wounds worked on faces and, mixed with after match beer, wore men down quickly. They shared this with the miners he detested. At thirty-five Elliott still looked as young as the men playing now. No, he had made the right decision even if he was jealous of the adulation the top players received. Men who had status always interested him for he so craved it himself. As the match progressed Elliott lost interest,

70

clapping robotically to match the applause in the stand. How to get back at Lisa occupied his mind. There must be a way to do so without compromising his career, but he could only think of fantastic things, involving violence and pain.

Someone tapped his shoulder with a flask, offering it to Elliott. He recognised a man he sometimes drank with in the clubhouse.

'Don't blame you for being miles away,' the man said, 'typical first match, eh? All effort and no skill. This bloody lot wouldn't get into the Rags in my time.'

The man had the florid, used-up face of an old forward. Elliott accepted the drink and agreed with the man. He would have more drinks in the clubhouse and go home reeking of it. He felt a great need to cause a row with Susan, but at the moment it was all he could think to do to get back at Lisa, to strike at their faces merged in his head. He was almost used to the headache, gnawing at him behind his eyes.

It was seven o'clock before he got home. Susan expected the worst but she hoped to prevent the children witnessing another rage from their father. Even the sight of her in the hallway niggled Elliott.

'What are you doing watching me?' he said, 'like a bloody school teacher looking out for kids.'

'You shouldn't be driving like this,' Susan said, 'you stink of drink.'

'I'm all right, I know exactly how much I can have,' he answered, though he knew he had passed the limit an hour ago. Drink-driving was something he indulged in. Despite his enthusiasm for his job he had never been able to resist the last illegal drink. He liked the excitement of the risk and gambled that local officers would not stop his well known Volvo. Anything illicit was a thrill to him.

The sight of the girls joining their mother stilled Elliott's tongue.

'Hello loves,' he said to them, kissing them in turn. He picked up each daughter into his arms and draped them over his shoulder.

'Have you got dinner on?' he asked Susan as he took the girls into the living room.

'We've had ours,' Susan said quietly, fighting back tears as her loathing for Elliott tipped over into disgust. She cobbled together a meal from what she found in the freezer, knowing that Elliott would wolf it down without fuss. Food was his one uncomplaining area, as long as it was put before him when and where he wanted it. Often, as she watched him feeding, she thought his eating habits went against the care he took with his appearance, as if a darker side showed itself as he ate.

In their playroom the girls played the television game Elliott had bought them last Christmas. Another first on the estate. It was a device that plugged into the television and turned the screen into a tennis court. Each player pinged an electronic 'ball' back and forth over the net, controlled by a hand set. The speed of the ball could be adjusted and Susan had come to dread the endless beeping as racket hit ball. Elliott stayed on it for hours that Christmas Day. This is only the start, he said, you watch what they bring out soon.

'Mum said we can go somewhere tomorrow,' Sarah said. Elliott was locked in combat with Sally and did not acknowledge her entry.

'We haven't been anywhere much this year,' Sarah added.

Susan could usually count on her daughters as allies but they were also capable of playing one parent against the other and they had her secret as bargaining power.

'Your dinner is ready,' Susan said to Elliott.

'I had something down my mother's earlier,' he mumbled, 'didn't know where you were.'

'You know I always go shopping on Saturday. If you had phoned we could have arranged things better.'

'I might be down for a few weeks,' Elliott said. 'They reckon things are going to quieten down up north. They should do after the hidings we've dished out.'

Susan's heart sank at this news. It would be impossible to keep her support work secret.

Although she had said little about the strike Elliott had a growing sense of his wife's shifting allegiance. Previously, she had only moaned about his long shifts away but now he felt her distaste. Susan was still soft, still harking back to the old days of the village. That was stupid, for the old days for her meant being stuck with looking after her mother until he came along. She had been lucky he had been there.

Elliott wanted and needed to see disloyalty in Susan, it could mix with Lisa's treachery to support his mood. He had never respected women. Now this flared into open misogyny.

72

'You're quiet,' Elliott said. 'Christ, I've only just got back and we have silence.'

'We *should* talk.'

'What's been happening down here, then? Anything exciting in our wonderful little Metropolis? Have they put a statue of my big brother up yet?'

'The usual. The girls have missed having a holiday this year.'

'I've earned enough to take them somewhere special, maybe this winter if I can get the time off. I fancy skiing.'

'I meant we should talk about us,' Susan said. 'About what's happening to us.'

'Not another bloody lecture.'

'Don't swear like that when the girls are around.'

'You know what gets me about women, they either want to talk your head off with rubbish or they do something nasty out of the blue.'

'What are you talking about?'

Susan saw the usual signs of an Elliott eruption, his eyes widening and face reddening as his bad blood came to the fore.

'Women, that what's I'm fucking talking about. Fucking slags. Take, take, take.'

The tennis game had stopped.

'Don't let the girls see you like this,' Susan said.

'No, I fucking won't, I'm going out.'

Elliott stood up and swept plates from the table, scattering gravy and the remains of vegetables across the room. He stormed out and Susan heard the Volvo screech off. For a bleak moment she wished he would crash it into a wall.

Sarah and Sally stood watching her in the doorway, tearful and accusing. Elliott was such a swine but the girls shared out the blame for the rows between each parent. Susan had the guilt of her crumbling marriage to put up with besides the machinations of her husband. The sight of her daughters brought on tears she could not prevent but at least these softened their attitude towards her.

'We'll help you, Mam,' Sarah said.

She organised her sister into getting a cloth and tray and together they hunted for stray bits of food on the carpet. Susan sat down and tried not to lose control completely. Elliott was getting worse, there was no doubt about it, and she did not know what to do about it.

★ ★ ★

Elliott was aflame. He felt the heat on his face and the adrenalin pumping inside him. He had achieved the explosion he wanted with Susan but did not feel any better. It was all Lisa's fault. They could have had it all and she had thrown it away. Even now he could not grasp the finality of this.

He drove the Volvo around the village then along the top road that led over the mountain. At the next village he stopped at an off-licence, where an Asian shopkeeper served him a half bottle of whisky. In a lay-by he took a generous pull and checked his wallet. It was healthy, and the car's tank was full. He drove out of the village, heading north. He would be in Rotherham before he had time to think about it.

As the Volvo ate up the miles Elliott punched the channel buttons of the radio, unable to settle on anything for long. There was little traffic on the motorway, just the headlights of the occasional truck to pick him out. He drove hunched over the wheel, hands white-tight, eyes set somewhere in the distance of his mind. His head thumping, thumping. He began to think of Edwin again. More confusion swirled. The faint traces of a thought that things might have been different between them – better – was quickly crushed. Any positive idea of Edwin that still managed to manifest itself created anger. This was his dilemma. He could not help himself, and it had been this way for a long time. When his mother had let him get away with murder he had liked it, smirked at Edwin, but always in the wake of his spoiling came frustrating emptiness. The more she gave, the more he felt he was missing. A truck blinded him with a full beam and Elliott was jarred out of his thoughts.

'Bastard,' he muttered.

★ ★ ★

Edwin's idea was quickly taken up by other local activists and a plan was formulated. Within days they had the requisite number of men and it was decided that they strike at Port Talbot two days earlier than Edwin had anticipated, on the last Thursday of August, under cover of darkness.

'We'll enter by all five gates,' Edwin told his group, 'that way we'll have more chance of getting in.'

A former steelworker had drawn them a rough map of the plant and the men were filled with a sense of purpose. Edwin himself felt somewhat military as he went through the preparation. He was surprised at the way his idea had flowered, it told him how desperate the men were to achieve something other than solidarity. They were about to strike at an industry miners needed. Power stations and steelworks were their main commercial customers, but having to think of consequences had too often stayed their hands whilst their enemies had no such distractions.

Edwin's guerrilla force travelled down to Port Talbot in ten hired vans, using separate routes to lessen the suspicion of the police. It was close to midnight when they parked up within sight of the steelworks. Anchored at the deep water dock that served the plant was the *Argos*, a Spanish vessel which held 30,000 tons of American coal. 'Scab coal' the men called it, and its presence added to their determination.

'Well, they won't unload that bastard, for a start,' Tom Rees said.

At the gate Edwin had chosen, two bemused security guards tried to stop them. They were bundled aside after a half-hearted attempt at authority.

'Get back in your little shed, boys, and nothing will happen to you,' said Ronnie Jenkins, freed by Rita from his father watch. 'He nagged me into it,' Rita had told Edwin, 'said I had done it all so far, so I let him go. I'm proud of him, I suppose, but watch out for him, Ed. You know how carried away he gets.'

They headed along the dock, past the *Argos* to the cranes. Edwin saw the shadows of other miners moving towards them. It looked as if they had all penetrated the plant successfully.

'It was easy,' one of the other men said, 'we just walked in.'

'Everyone will know about us very shortly though,' Edwin said, 'when those blokes on the gate get over their shock.'

He stood back from the others and looked up at the cranes which loomed out of the darkness, their squat forms silhouetted against the sky. A hundred and twenty feet did not sound so bad until it was in front of you. He knew he had to scale one of these things and thought back to when he used to get shaky standing on the old railway bridge.

The cranes were triangular structures with metal walkways flanking them and crossing through their centres. In the middle of each hung the huge lifting gear, giant scoops to lift out cargo from the boats. Edwin's men grouped around him, waiting for his lead. Faces turned towards him and he hoped his trepidation did not show.

'Right,' Edwin said, 'come on then. Let's climb the buggers and wave to the world. Watch your step, everyone.'

He let Ronnie lead the way, then the men who carried haversacks of flasks and food. They had not given much thought to how they would manage for toilets up above though Jenkins made a few colourful suggestions.

Edwin began to climb. Despite the clement night the metal handrail was cold to his touch. The steps were partitioned every twenty feet by a small platform, then they right-angled upwards to the next section, until the main top platform was reached. Here were housed the crane operator's cabin and the controls.

By the third angle Edwin was suffering. His mouth had dried and he felt light, as if his body might drift away into the darkness. His eyes flicked across to the phalanx of lights from the steelworks, and was caught by the intermittent silver glint of the sea but he did not look down. Ronnie climbed above him, punctuating their progress with his talk.

'Come on, Ed, don't slow down, mun. Eh, do you remember that old film with Jimmie Cagney, when he blew himself up on top of that oil refinery? This reminds me of it. I'm on top of the world, Ma, Jimmy shouted. I might do that – Rita, I'm on top of the world, girl!'

Ronnie spluttered into laughter, but was still able to keep his roll-up cigarette in his mouth. Men further down shouted at him to shut up which only increased his amusement.

For Edwin the climb took an age. He was glad the darkness masked the height from his eyes. When he got to the top platform and stood gingerly on it the thought of descent struck him with horror.

'You all right, Ed?' Tom Rees asked, 'you're swaying a bit.'

Tom put his hand on Edwin's shoulder and led him to the rear of the platform.

'I'll manage,' Edwin said. 'I don't like heights much.'

'You should have said, you could have co-ordinated things from the ground.'

'No, I don't think so, Tom. It'll be swarming with police down there very shortly.'

Taking deep breaths and keeping his eyes from the edge of the platform Edwin steadied himself. Someone passed around a bottle of whisky and they toasted each other.

'Make yourselves comfortable,' Edwin said. 'They can't do anything until it gets light. We'll have to play it by ear. Tom, you're in charge of the radio, keep a check on the news to see how the boys in Newport are getting on.'

Another action had been planned to coincide with the Port Talbot raid. The transporter bridge in Newport was to be taken over. In this way they hoped to highlight the injustice of the convoys linking Llanwern and Margam.

Edwin put his duffel coat against the wall of the crane's operating cabin and settled himself down. The others did the same and even the excited chatter of Ronnie Rees died down after a while. Men began to snore around him but Edwin stayed awake, waiting for the first signs of light to creep over the bay.

Gulls flying overhead proclaimed the dawn. Some examined the men on the cranes, wheeling around them and issuing warning noises, high pitched cries that seemed to strangulate in the throat, militant and far too boisterous for five o'clock in the morning. Certainly too noisy for Edwin's shaken nerves, for the coming of light escalated his vertigo. It encouraged his eyes to stray downwards and a rush of giddiness took hold of him. He cursed himself for his weakness and cursed the gulls too. He had always thought them the most unattractive of birds; unnecessary, bullying creatures, fascists of the bird world.

The men roused themselves, shaking out the sleep from their uncomfortable bodies.

'Who's got the flasks?' Ronnie asked, 'the tea will still be warm.'

He stretched and walked to the edge of the platform. Edwin envied his steadiness and watched as Ronnie pissed elegantly out into open space.

The rising sun turned urine liquid gold as it fell.

'That should scatter a few of them below,' Ronnie said.

Numbers of police had gathered on the dock and Tom's radio confirmed their occupation was dominating the early morning news bulletins. It seemed there had been considerable violence at Llanwern. Edwin was determined his action should be peaceful as he struggled to control his nausea.

★ ★ ★

Elliott pulled into Lisa's road ten minutes before eleven o'clock. He had cut an hour off the usual time by taking advantage of the uncluttered night motorways and not stopping. Driving slowly past Lisa's house he saw it was in darkness. The thought of not making contact again was hard to contemplate for it was the mystery of their sudden end which gnawed at his guts. He had always hated mysteries. His dash north had been a blind rush of anger but now he was cool, and motivated by a harder resolve. Lisa was close, Elliott sensed, and he would wait for her.

He drove down to the nearest pub. It was full of Saturday night punters, well-heeled and well-oiled. Lisa's neighbours. Even Rotherham had its ghetto of wealth. Broad South Yorkshire accents grated on him as he pushed his way to the bar. He was determined to get a pint and a large whisky in before they called time and made it with a minute to spare.

Elliott looked at the lager in his glass and downed half of it in a long draught, enjoying its cool touch and wishing he had time to drink a few more. The whisky chased it down and warmed him. He warmed further when he saw Lisa on the other side of the large room. She was getting up from a table and had her back to him but he knew it was her. With a self-control he did not know he had he stopped himself going over to her. She was with someone, a middle-aged man who draped a coat over Lisa's shoulders. He was heavily built and of average height. At thirty feet Elliott could see the jewelled rings on his fingers and the colourful splash of his tie. Elliott knew it had to be someone like this. The man would have money. Lots of it.

He watched them leave the pub and followed them, far enough behind to escape notice but close enough to catch snatches of their talk. Lisa was excited, he heard her mention something about Paris, and learnt the man's name from her – Ken. He saw the way her body flowed against him as it had done with his own. Lisa had this way about her, a sexual charge that made men jump through hoops. He was still jumping. This Ken was not in shape, his gut loomed over his belt and his face was puffy. When they walked under a streetlight he looked twenty years older than Lisa, at least.

Elliott stood behind the garden hedge as Lisa unlocked her front door. He would give them twenty minutes. Revenge crowded his head as he paced along the pavement, but how to achieve it? The whole gamut of ways to get back at Lisa ran through his mind, he enjoyed thinking about them but in their wake came confusion and pain. He tried to fight down the gut feeling that he still wanted her, that he would swallow all pride to get her back. Then his wounded ego reared up again and he just wanted to smash everything. To fight back.

Elliott saw a light in Lisa's bedroom, which gave him his cue. He walked quietly around to the back door and picked its lock. It was something he had learnt to do in his early days on the force, from a sergeant who told him it might be useful some time. This was the time and the fact that Lisa was not security minded helped. It was a simple Yale type lock which yielded to him after a minute. He stepped into the kitchen, breathing deeply and still not knowing what he would do. For the first time since he had got into the Volvo, Susan and the girls came into his mind. He might be on the brink of ruining his career here, maybe even prison if things went a certain way, but a need spurred him on. Someone was coming down the stairs.

'I thought you had enough in the pub,' a voice said. Ken's voice.

'The tonic's in the fridge,' Lisa shouted down, 'don't drown the gin in it.'

Her voice jolted Elliott, it seemed a lifetime since he had heard it. Now the last shreds of delusion dropped away from him. He noticed the hardness in the voice for the first time, a slightly nasal quality that spoke only of itself and the needs of its owner.

'Jesus Christ, what's your game?' Ken shouted, picking up the gin bottle from a kitchen worktop. 'You stay fucking there,' he told Elliott. 'Lisa,' Ken called, 'phone the police, we got a bloke in the house.'

Elliott saw that Ken had no fear of him. Now that they were close he noted a powerful, streetwise opponent, someone who would not hesitate to use the bottle. He found his voice.

'I am the police,' he said, without the power he would have liked.

'And I'm fucking Mickey Mouse,' Ken answered. He had a Manchester accent.

Lisa was on the stairs, looking into the kitchen.

'Good God, Elliott. I don't believe this.'

She came down to them and Ken looked to her for a lead.

'This is Elliott Bowles, Ken,' Lisa said, 'I told you about him.'

'What's the bastard doing breaking in here?' Ken asked, without relinquishing his hold on the bottle.

Lisa's eyes echoed the question. She had quickly put on a dressing gown but Elliott could still glimpse the body within. It made him feel weak and beaten and his resolve drained away as Ken threatened him. In the force he had usually managed to avoid one-to-one confrontations, apart from the odd hapless drunk bundled into a police van. He preferred the massed actions of strike breaking.

'Well, don't just stand there like P.C. Plod,' Ken said.

Elliot faced Lisa.

'I couldn't get in touch with you,' he said. 'I phoned a number of times.'

Lisa looked at him with a mixture of distaste and understanding. This was typical of the man-boy. She should have known he would not leave it there, but to break in, it was ridiculous. Remembering how much he valued his job she gauged the state Elliott must be in. She felt more embarrassed than angry.

'I ought to give you a right going-over, sunshine,' Ken said, 'it would be apprehending a burglar, wouldn't it?'

He stepped closer to Elliott but Lisa intervened.

'Leave it, Ken,' she said, 'we don't want that.'

She pushed Ken away and took the bottle from his hand. Her power over both men was total.

'Why didn't you accept the letter?' Lisa asked. 'It would have saved you a lot of bother. What the hell were you thinking of, coming in here like this? I thought you had gone home anyway.'

Elliot was unable to answer. He felt his tongue thicken in his mouth, gagging him.

'Look, if he doesn't fuck off I'm going to shift him,' Ken said, 'the man's mental.'

'He'll go,' Lisa said. 'Ken, will you go into the front room, just for a few minutes.'

His face protested but Lisa repeated the gentle push.

'Please Ken, I can handle it.' She gave Ken a peck on the cheek, which made Elliott wince. 'It's probably the best thing,' she whispered, 'him seeing you here.'

'Got a lot of money, has he?' Elliott managed to mumble.

'Enough.'

'I thought we were going places. London.'

'You forgot to ask me. Look love, you are married with kids. I don't want a mess like that. We had a bit of fun for a while, but that's all it was, for me. Don't make out I led you on, you did that for yourself. Get real Elliott, go back to Wales and your life there.'

His 'life there' was a bitter stab in his guts. He stepped towards her but Lisa warned him with a hand.

'Don't be stupid now. Ken is a very rough man, and he has a lot of friends around here.'

'Why him, for Christssake, he must be nearly fifty.'

'That's my business. You have to accept it. Ken can ruin your career and your life if you keep this up. You must go now.'

'Aye, out the back way,' Ken said, rejoining them. 'Don't want the neighbours seeing anything unpleasant.'

Elliott did as he was told, moving his leaden body towards the kitchen door, aware that all he wanted to do and say would be left undone and unsaid. This was the epitome of his defeat.

Ken examined the door as Elliott walked out.

'Not a bad job,' Ken said, 'didn't leave a fucking mark. You are in the wrong profession son, or maybe the right one. Listen, don't ever show you face around here again, this is my first and last warning.'

Ken slammed the door. Its thud reverberated in Elliott's brain and he heard the man's mocking laughter as Ken celebrated his superiority. He walked back to the Volvo with tears of self-pity welling up in his eyes. It was the first time he had cried in long trousers and typically it was for himself. So this was his revenge, to stand in front of Lisa and her new man helplessly frozen, a victim of his own inaction. Another window onto his character opened for Elliott and this time his sub-conscious did not rush to close it. He sat in the Volvo and felt a hundred years old. He stayed like this for an hour, then pointed the car south and drove back to his wife and his 'life there'.

★ ★ ★

It was nine o'clock and the men on the crane improvised a breakfast. One man had the foresight to bring a camping stove with two rings on it and a two gallon water container. It had been set up on the platform and a saucepan of water bubbled over one ring. Jenkins prodded a row of sausages in the small frying pan over the second ring. 'I could make a fortune selling you lot these,' he said, brandishing a sausage on his fork and showily eating it. 'Planning,' Ronnie said, looking down the platform at Edwin, 'that's all it takes, a little planning.'

On the dock at least a hundred policemen had gathered. Their commanding officer had tried to contact the miners as soon as it was light, but answers had been restricted to the waving of defiant hands. As the media woke up so their concentration on the miners' occupation increased. They even had a mention on national radio. Edwin had been successful in this but much of the effect he had hoped for had been negated by the violence at Newport. A radio bulletin stated that there had been hand-to-hand fighting there, and looking around him, Edwin doubted he could control the men here if trouble started. Tom had investigated the crane's controls and had found that the power had been turned off from the ground. Edwin was glad of this, the thought of Ronnie Jenkins getting ideas of using the giant scoop was a worry he could do without. Not to be outdone, Ronnie designated the crane's cabin an official toilet.

The sun was strong, as it had been throughout August. Men stripped to vests or went bare chested, working on their tans, pleased with the way things had gone so far. Yet Edwin could see the younger ones getting restless. What next was the unasked question on their lips. He thought it vital they stay put as long as possible and trust the white collared division of the union to make capital from their media prominence.

His vertigo did not lessen, but he tried to adjust to it like a poor sailor on a long voyage. It was a vague imbalance, which escalated into sickness whenever he got up. They were being addressed again from below. Gingerly peering down, he managed to focus on a high ranking officer with a megaphone in his hand. This effort made his dizziness surge and he held tightly onto the platform's guardrail. Other policemen were an indistinct mass of shimmering black.

'He must be someone big,' Ronnie said, 'I can see his fancy bits shining from here.'

'You men up there, listen to me –'

The officer started with a plea to the miners to come down then added a warning which turned to threats when he heard the derisory response.

'Save your noise, butty,' Ronnie shouted down, but his voice was lost in the wind.

Realising this Ronnie found his haversack, took another bag from it and emptied its contents onto the platform. It contained hundreds of nuts and bolts. He picked up a handful and threw them down.

'Come on, boys,' he shouted, 'this is our ammo. Get stuck in.'

Others joined in and policemen scattered on the dock. For a few minutes it rained metal and the commander with the megaphone heated up his delivery, barking at them to stop, albeit from a greater distance.

'Boys,' Edwin shouted, 'lay off that. Christ, a bolt from this height could kill someone.'

Tom joined in the exhortation and reluctantly the men stopped, Ronnie hurling the last bolt.

'Well,' he said, noting the accusation in Edwin's eyes, 'what's the point in being up here if we are going to do fuck all?'

Edwin sunk back down and the atmosphere calmed. Tom Rees sat with him.

'That's us up shit creek,' Tom said. 'God knows what they'll throw at us after this, attempted murder I shouldn't wonder.'

'Even I'm not that pessimistic,' Edwin said.

He closed his eyes and tried to settle back into some sort of control but this time it was harder. He could not get over the distance he was from the ground. The strain caused by listening to the policeman refixed it in his mind.

'Your heights thing isn't improving, is it?' Tom said.

Edwin replied by throwing up at his feet. He could not prevent it for this had promised to happen since he first reached the top platform. He knew Jenkins would be nudging some of the others and smirking. All external weaknesses were pounced on by miners, with a glee that was a tradition of their profession.

Edwin was ashamed. First police from London had turned him back on his own mountain, now he had incapacitated himself, very publicly. He had willed himself not to succumb to his vertigo but had failed. It had been passed down from his father and he had been aware of it since he was a twelve year old, when he had stuck fast to a tree branch for half an hour before giving in and crashing into the vortex his phobia created. It had cost him a broken ankle, and his father had guessed why he had fallen but kept it to himself. Edwin had to settle for watching his brother prance about the railway bridge and climb trees like a gibbon.

By mid-afternoon restless boredom had taken hold of most of the men. Even Jenkins had slumped into silence, occasionally punctuated by an attempt at a story, which no one wanted. Each time he started with a 'Did I ever tell you about the time I...' he was greeted with a collective sigh that took on an irritated quality as the hours dripped away.

'I reckon we should do something when it gets dark,' Ronnie said, more to himself than anyone else. 'We should go down and get amongst other stuff in this works, like infil... infil... well like fucking wreckers.'

'Shut up, you old fool,' a voice shouted. 'You're getting on all our nerves.'

Jenkins stood up belligerently.

'Oh aye, who says so? I was doing things like this before you was born, son. You should have a clip 'round the earhole. In fact I think I'll give you one.'

Tom Rees put himself between the men.

'Calm down now, Ron. Have one of Rita's sandwiches.'

Seeing that Edwin was becoming more and more detached from the situation. Tom took it on himself to boost morale.

'Listen boys, you heard the radio, they're watching us. We've got to stick at it, don't mind what that copper has been saying.'

Edwin heard Tom's words but they came from a distance, growing faint as they penetrated his head. Yet he was able to smile at Tom's effort. It was standard pep-talk, the catchphrases he had long since learned. Why not tell them the eyes of the nation are upon us, he thought, that's a good one, or Wales expects every man to do his duty. He knew that the police address must have struck home to some extent. Their trespass and damage had been stressed and now there was aerial bombardment. That might be criminal assault and they would all be charged. Edwin knew he would be picked out as a ringleader. He was ready for this if only he could rid himself of this damned sickness. Tom had sat down again but Edwin barely noticed.

'Was that all right, Ed? Didn't mind, did you? I thought you needed a bit of a rest, like.'

'That's all I've been doing since we got up here,' Edwin replied.

He looked at Tom's face, which was close to his own. The worry in it was emphasised by bristling whiskers, which sprouted in uneven patches on Tom's chin and cheeks. Decay was working its way into his front teeth, a brown wave that travelled up from his gums. Edwin had not noticed before but then he had never been so close to the man in daylight. Tom was a mate he had bumped along with underground, since in his early mining days when they still scrabbled along three foot seams, working on their knees. Edwin knew men's eyes best, not the intricacies of their features. Eyes were the most vital points in blackened faces. He had witnessed two fatal accidents underground. A man crushed by a tram and two others smothered in a roof fall. The light went out of their eyes as they turned to a glazed blankness. Like jelly. These had been times when Edwin's duality had rushed to the fore, when he hated his foul, unyielding, profession but loved its closeness of belonging and hurting and feeling until he blubbed like a kid.

Tom tapped his shoulder.

'You should try to eat something,' Tom said, offering a sandwich in which a piece of ham complained about the sun.

'No thanks,' Edwin said, 'it will only come back up in half an hour. I'll have a cup of tea though, before that gas thing runs out.'

Jenkins approached them, alerted by the tea preparation.

'Look at them down there,' Ronnie said, pointing to the police. 'I bet they're more bored than I bloody am. They'll be changing 'em soon. This lot will be off to feed. Feeding like pigs, that's a good one.'

Edwin directed his groan inwards.

'So, you feeling bad, are you, butt,' Ronnie continued. 'I knew a bloke couldn't stand being cooped up, they got a big word for that. He didn't last long down the pit.'

Ronnie laughed, an invitation to the others to join him, but there was no response.

'Let us know when you decide to do something,' Ronnie said.

'That man is a pain,' Tom said, 'no wonder Rita let him come. Perhaps she hopes he might fall off this thing.'

Jenkins was an irritant but his jibes stayed with Edwin. It was true, his leadership had dissolved as soon as he had put a foot on the first step of the ladder.

Night fell. They had been on the cranes for twenty-four hours. Edwin's tortured senses had some respite when the view was taken away, though police lights had been put in place to shine up at them. Tom positioned men on the walkways, in case the police tried to make a night assault. Occasionally a voice of encouragement shouted from the other cranes. Feeling free of Edwin's diminished presence men dropped the periodic missile down, but vertically and well away from the shadowy policemen.

'Any signs from the other cranes?' Edwin asked Tom.

'No-one has moved off them, I'm certain of that. It's a pity we didn't have one of them walkie-talkies.'

'What about the radio?'

'Nothing new. We have showered the police with murderous objects, shown a complete disregard for property, we can only worsen our cause, etc, etc. You know it all by heart now, don't you?'

'Just about.'

'It's getting a bit nippy up here,' Tom said, checking his watch. 'Almost midnight. It'll be September in a few minutes.'

'Season of mists and mellow fruitfulness,' Edwin murmured.

'What's that?'

'I said I could do with a bit of fruit, can never get enough of the stuff, especially apples. Real apples, not these tasteless green things they shine up in supermarkets. We could never afford much when I was a kid, but I remember Mrs Pugh's big bowl of the stuff next door. Like a still life permanently on her front room table. I never saw her eat any of it.'

Edwin's thoughts matched his physical state. They were light and disorganised, floating around his head at random. Childhood merged with the present to form a kaleidoscope for him to peer into, to be a witness to his own life. He felt he was trapped in his sickness forever and thoughts of himself had taken over from his union duties, an invalid self-consciousness that made him question the worth of all he had tried to do. Jenkins had been more perceptive than he realised when he mentioned the Jimmy Cagney character. He too felt he was on top of the world and about to explode. His hearing had never been so acute. It was as if his blurred vision had enhanced this sister sense and now, as he tried to sleep, the night made a multifarious impression on him. Sounds from the steelworks. Hissing, belching, clanking, the moving of men below them, a periodic shout or the cough of a vehicle being started up. Every few minutes there was a lull and he could hear the sea punching the dock. The platform occupants settled down for the night, their water for tea having run out. Rations would be meagre the next day.

* * *

Elliott's trip back to Wales was the antithesis of his dash to Lisa. He dawdled, letting the car idle at sixty. It was the slowest he had ever driven on a motorway but he did not want the journey to end. To arrive meant decisions. What to do about Susan. How to live. At thirty-five years old this problem was just entering his mind. So far he had mapped out his life to suit himself, with little thought for his family or their needs. He thought that Susan should be grateful he had married her, and that he, Elliott Bowles, was very special. So strongly had his mother ground this attitude into him that he would never root it out. He wanted Susan to be the continuation of Rowena Bowles, an evanescent presence who worshipped him as the family figurehead, but without bothering him too much. He could not change for he lacked the strength to know himself for long. The closest he came to it was at times of extreme stress, but he could not bear the guilt these brief insights caused him.

Elliott turned off the motorway and headed up to the valley. In four hours of driving he had not resolved anything. It still did not seem possible that Lisa could have rejected him but he knew it was for one reason. That bastard Ken had money, the money he had always lusted after. He was no longer sure he had made the right choice of profession. The attraction of power had been even greater than his greed and it had directed him into the force, but perhaps he should have gone into some sort of business, the financial stuff he heard so much about these days. He wanted it all, power, money and women, each facet of his desire needed the other two components to make his life whole. A kernel of ridiculous optimism had been placed in the centre of his mind, giving him the capacity to believe that everything and everyone would fall into his lap. Until Lisa nothing had shaken this belief.

He parked the car in a lay-by on the road into the valley, the same one in which his brother had been stopped by the police. It was going to be another fine day, the night sky was edged with light, pink streaks that emphasised the blackness of passing clouds. He tuned to the local news and heard that miners were still occupying cranes at Port Talbot. He wished he was there, waiting for the bastards to come down, or better still, getting them down. That was the easy part of life. Visualising Edwin up there, he clenched his fists in anticipation. He did not want to go north again. Fuck the overtime. He wanted to stay local, to have the chance to come up against his brother.

Elliott pulled into his drive but the house he had been so proud of did not welcome him now. He saw its neatly trimmed boundaries as boring, its matching neighbours as evidence of other people chained to mortgages and trapped in awful, well-paid jobs. It was not much after six in the morning but, on a whim, he knocked on his own front door. To announce his presence.

Susan answered immediately. She was dressed.

'What are you doing up?' Elliott asked, annoyed his performance had been thwarted.

'I'm not going to ask you where you've been,' Susan said. 'I would have phoned the police, but that would have been stupid, wouldn't it? I've been sitting up, but don't think I've been worried about you.'

This was not what he had envisaged. To be let in by his sleepy, grateful wife, to sink into a warm bed and have the children come and wake him at tea-time would have been more to his liking. He followed Susan into the kitchen.

'Are you making coffee?' he asked.

'You know where it is.'

He switched on the kettle and looked for milk in the fridge. The food there made him want breakfast, a plate piled high with anything that could be fried. After Lisa, he particularly needed Susan to be subservient.

'Do you think it it clever, to bugger off like that?' Susan said, 'driving half bloody pissed.'

'Don't swear,' Elliott said, 'I don't like it.'

'I don't know what's worse, your hypocrisy or your childishness.'

Elliott made his coffee, making as much noise as he could with the crockery.

'Childishness,' Susan murmured. She was determined to conceal her worry from Elliott. If he had been stopped or been involved in an accident his career would be over. For herself she would not have minded this, it might present an avenue of escape, but there were the girls to consider. This was one reason she despised Elliott now. He always made sure his daughters were used as a buffer zone. He would be a difficult man to divorce, though she knew many reasons could be found. Good reasons.

Susan was different, Elliott realised, she had been all summer. He could not reduce her to tears so easily, and she was no longer timid. She still had good legs, they were the first things he had noticed about her. He moved over to his wife, feeling an echo of his old desire.

'Oh, for God's sake,' Susan said, 'you stink of whisky and Christ knows what else. I've had a gutsful, Elliott.'

His fetid breath enveloped her and his arms grabbed, as if they were mechanical claws and she a fairground prize. Elliott gave up and pulled away from Susan.

'Fuck off, then. You don't turn me on anyway.'

A car door shut in the drive next door. They heard their neighbour call to his son and saw him bundle fishing tackle into the car's boot.

'Boring bastard,' Elliott muttered. 'Jesus, fishing. It must be like watching paint dry.'

'What do you do, apart from making everyone's lives a misery?' Susan asked.

Elliott spun round and Susan tensed for the blow but Elliott contented himself by throwing his mug against the wall.

'Well done,' Susan said, 'first the dinner plate, now the mug. The girls will be down any minute.'

'I've had it up to here with you,' Elliott said. 'Do you know how boring you are? I shouldn't have stuck around this dump, doing the same as everyone else.'

Susan made an instinctive decision to bring things out into the open. She sensed a vulnerability in Elliott not evident before. It was as if he was exhausting his deep fund of malice, and cracks were appearing in the elephant hide skin of his vanity.

'Things gone wrong with your latest girlfriend, then?' Susan asked.

Elliott did not answer but she knew he had heard her.

'What did you say?' he said, after a long moment.

'You heard me. Come on, you don't think I haven't worked that out long ago. I've had plenty of opportunities. You've had only a passing acquaintance with our marriage.'

Elliott was at a crossroads. The initial need for denial was great, his life of sly lying insisted on it but the need for relief was greater. Anything to ease the vice which clamped his brain. He paced the room, hands in pockets and Susan prepared herself. Their relationship had reached a watershed.

'All right, I'll tell you, if you think you can stomach it. There has been someone, someone with more excitement in her little finger than you could ever have. She had vision, she didn't want to be stuck in all this shit.'

He kicked at things around the room and Susan heard movement upstairs, but could not stop Elliott now. It had to come out.

'She was someone I met up north. You don't know what the pressures are like with the pickets. She was there for me, made me feel that tall.'

Elliott reached up a hand to the ceiling. 'She wanted me to leave you, to go to London. I could have transferred to the Met, but I couldn't do it to the kids. I've finished it. Do you know what that took? And to be like this with you now, I'm thinking for what... but I know my responsibilities....'

'What was her name?' Susan asked.

'Never mind what her fucking name was. It's none of your business. I don't want to talk about it ever again. But if you want to keep me here you'd better shape up. Do something about the way you dress. Do something. Anything.'

He slammed his way out of the room and went upstairs. Within ten minutes she knew he would be snoring in their bed, a bed she could never share with him again.

Susan felt a curious absence of emotion. She was cold, despite the early sun penetrating the window. Cold with revulsion. She could not guess how much of what Elliott had said was true, he probably did not know himself. He had confessed too easily, she knew that much. He had been unhinged since the fight with Edwin, that had sparked something deep within him. Her husband's life had been one of easy progress but he had convinced himself that it had been hard won and that the world was against him. Perhaps this was a good definition of someone spoilt rotten. Sarah and Sally crept down the stairs, fearing a continuation of the previous night. They came into the front room and sat either side of their mother.

'Is daddy back?' Sally asked.

'Yes.'

'Is he going to take us somewhere?'

'I don't think so, not today. He's tired. Look, it's too early to get up. Go back to bed and I'll call you later.'

Susan cleared up the coffee but did not do much to rid the wall of its stain. She would leave it there, the mark of Elliott, to remind her of this morning. She was uneasy about his confession, not knowing which way he would jump now. The one thing she did know was that she had to get away from him, and hope the girls would come through the trauma. She knew Elliott was capable of using his daughters any way he could and that was her great worry.

The phone next to Susan rang, startling her from her thoughts. It was Rita Jenkins.

'Sorry to phone so early, love,' Rita said, 'but I've got to get down The Merlin early. The boys are still up on them cranes. Have you been following it? They been on the telly. I'm sure I saw our Ronnie dangling his fat arse on one of them.'

Susan had not thought much about it, though she knew the occupation had been Edwin's idea.

'Look,' Rita continued, 'are you coming on Wednesday, you said you had a half day then.'

Rita wanted her to go on a fund raising run to Cardiff, and the girls would be back at school. At least Elliott would have less time to get at them.

'Yes,' Susan said, 'I'll be there.'

'Good, we'll go down in the van.'

Susan's work with the support group would be her next battle with Elliott, but she did not flinch from it now. Fear had drained from her. His shouting rages had lost their effect and she gained strength as she sought to break free of the life he offered her.

Susan looked in on Elliott mid-morning. It was as she thought, he slept face down, snoring into a pillow. When he woke he would expect her to adjust to his confession, and would blame her if she did not. He would make a fuss of the girls and spoil them, as he always did after one of his explosions. Only this time Elliott had gone further, he had brought his cheating out into the open. What Susan had known since their early days together was now fact.

She left Elliott in the bedroom and turned on the television to catch the local news. Talking to Rita brought other issues into her mind. Her timing was impeccable; on the screen was the Port Talbot docks.

'...early this morning a man came down...' a voice intoned.

Susan saw a figure being helped down the metal stairway of a crane, police running towards him and grabbing him. It was Edwin, a white-faced, almost trance-like Edwin, but it was her brother-in-law. She could not believe it, to see him like this, beamed into the house while the brother who hated him slept upstairs. No-one else came down from the cranes and the commentator did not clarify things. In his present state, she knew the television set would join the dinner plate and coffee mug if Elliott saw his brother gaining so much publicity. Edwin was leaving his

91

mates on the cranes. She did not understand this. Something must be badly wrong with him. She knew something was badly wrong with Elliott. The Bowles family was disintegrating before her eyes. She allowed the girls to sleep late then got them up quietly, quelling their demands for their father by doing a bit of spoiling herself. She announced they would go out and enjoy the sunshine, letting her daughters choose the place.

When Elliott woke he called down to Susan in vain. Searching the house and seeing the car gone he fumed for a few minutes, then took a pack of cans from the fridge and settled in front of the television. He felt easier, now that he had mentioned Lisa. Let his bitch of a wife stew on that piece of news. The beer soon attacked his empty stomach and he saw Ken's gloating face as that man showed him Lisa's door. He began to burn again, and his headache stuck fast.

* * *

Edwin had slept fitfully on the platform through Friday night. Not more than thirty minutes continuous sleep. Most of the time he seemed to float somewhere between sleep and consciousness. His stomach crying out for food it was unable to retain. He checked the radio periodically. He was anxious that the dockers' strike would firm up in their support but he knew how fragile this alliance was. Dockers earned good money and had gained a degree of autonomy since the war. Nationalisation had given them high wages and short working hours. Privileges that disturbed him.

Tom saw Edwin stir and stretch. Their leader was ashen-faced, like a ghost in the pre-dawn. Tom was worried. Edwin was in no state to continue his occupation.

'Ed,' Tom said softly, 'can't sleep, eh?'

'Fits and starts.'

'Look, Ed, I've been thinking. I know you're not going to like this but shouldn't you go down? There's no shame in it.'

'No shame,' Edwin muttered. He attempted to stand but had to lean against Tom. The lightening skies revolved around his head. Banked clouds etched with the red glow of the plant. The steelworks and its associated industries were a lattice-work of metal structures, tall, squat, angular, and seemingly endless from Edwin's vantage point. Sculptures of twisting pipes, chrome, steel and darker metals, a complexity of forms punctuated by smoking, steaming outlets. Yet not noisy, like the pits. There was a subdued throb here, a confident beat that made Edwin's world seem old. And a kind of ordered beauty, each necklace of lights joining with the next to continue the display. His eyes were not blind to this, despite his sickness.

'Ed,' Tom said, shaking him gently. 'Look at you, mun. You hardly know where you are. You can't go another day up here, specially when the sun gets up. It's going to be another fine day, by the look of it.'

Tom encouraged Edwin towards the walkway, gesturing to the two men stationed there.

'Help me get him down,' he whispered to them, 'a bit at a time. He's had it up here.' And to Edwin, 'It will be better in the dark, you won't see the drop.'

Edwin had vague recollections of his descent, arms either side of him to steady him, the age it seemed to take to get to the ground, more revolving sky and the challenging voices of the police to welcome him as he neared the ground.

Tom was saying something to him.

'We've got to leave you here now, Ed, or we'll be arrested.'

To the shadowy figures approaching Tom shouted, 'this man is very sick,' and in a flash of inspiration, 'he should be rushed to hospital.'

Tom thought if he stressed Edwin's state his friend might avoid arrest. He scrambled back up the walkway to the platform, where Jenkins and the others had been alerted to what was happening.

'Best thing for the boy,' Jenkins said, in conciliatory tones, 'he was no good up here. I had a butty, see, couldn't stand being cooped up...'

Edwin staggered into the arms of two policemen.

'What's up with you?' one of them asked, digging Edwin in the ribs, 'pissed?'

'His bottle's gone, more like,' the other said.

Edwin was dragged to a senior officer.

'We've got one of them, sir,' a policeman said, 'seems to be something wrong with him.'

The Inspector shone a torch in Edwin's face, though natural light now competed with it. He flipped through a sheaf of photographs.

'Ah yes, Bowles, Edwin. Lodge official. You've been very stupid, Bowles. What's the matter with you man, lost your stomach for it?'

Edwin did not answer, but he already felt the benefit of being on level ground.

'I am charging you with assault and trespass with intent to cause criminal damage,' the Inspector read him his rights. 'Put him in a van and take him away.' And as an afterthought, 'phone the doctor to come and take a look at him when you get him in a cell.'

The Inspector walked over to a car just arriving on the dock. In it was the Assistant Chief Constable of the transport police, now in charge of the operation.

'One of them is down, sir,' the Inspector said, 'they should all follow shortly.'

'Maybe. The lawyer will be here soon, to serve them with a writ. We'll see what that effect that will have. Anyone hurt?'

'No sir. We've had things thrown down at us but the men stay well out of range.'

'Right.'

The commanding officer got out of his car and walked along the dock, sniffing the air like one not used to it, with the Inspector dutifully in tow.

'I'll tell you what,' the more senior man said, 'the shit's going to hit the fan about the way they got in here. Walking in just like that, be buggered. Well, I'm not carrying the can for it. That's down to you local boys. Go and deal with them.' He pointed to the gaggle of newsmen on the fringes of the dock, being kept back for their own safety.

By the time he arrived at the police station Edwin felt considerably better, well enough to weigh up his miserable situation. He was the first man to come down, he would always be known for that. Edwin Bowles, the one who abandoned his mates.

After being formally charged Edwin was put into a cell, but no stray boots or fists helped him on his way. The police could not take a chance there might be something seriously wrong with him. A miner dying in custody was the last thing they wanted.

He sat on a thin, stained mattress and read the graffiti on the cell's walls. 'The world is dead' someone had scrawled, in a heart. By the time the doctor came all traces of his weakness had gone.

'It was vertigo,' Edwin told the doctor, 'I've always had it. I feel better now.'

The doctor chuckled as he conducted a routine check.

'They were a bit worried about you,' he said, 'didn't want you croaking in the station'

He shone a small light into Edwin's eyes.

'Well, you seem all right now. Fear of heights usually evaporates very quickly when you remove the cause. In other words, don't piss about on high buildings. Right, that's it then. I'm off for a day's fishing. Bleeperless.'

Edwin still felt sick but it was from the emptiness in his stomach. He had been tempted to ask the doctor to get him something to eat but retained enough pride to refrain. He fell into a deep sleep on his bunk, something he had not achieved in two nights on the cranes. When noise awakened him he thought he had been asleep for many hours, but it was just two, in fact. The noise was made by Tom Rees, Jenkins and the others. Edwin sat up as he recognised their voices, the blood rushing to his head in mimicry of vertigo, only this time it cleared in seconds. His cell door opened and Tom and Jenkins were pushed inside.

'You two in here,' a sergeant said, 'your mate's keeping the place warm for you.'

Other men were placed in the cells next to them.

'What's happened?' Edwin asked.

'We're down, that's fucking obvious, innit,' Jenkins answered.

Edwin ignored him and looked at Tom.

'We were served with a writ,' Tom said. 'They got their lawyer to do it not long after you left. The man was threatening all sorts of things if we didn't come down. What he said seemed to trigger things off in the boys' minds, what with the food situation and everything. We took a vote on it.'

'I didn't fucking vote for it,' Jenkins shouted, 'we should have fought it out, covered them cranes with blood. We could have kept our heads up then.'

'The majority wanted to jack it in,' Tom continued, 'and they started to come down from the other cranes anyway. We made a statement like you said, Ed, brought the dock strike and the imported coal business into focus. And you needn't worry about coming down yourself, we were right behind you.'

Edwin did not know what disturbed him more, Ronnie's empty, blustering words or the quiet empathy of Tom. Both grated on his pitiful performance.

They subsided into silence and sat quietly for half an hour until the door opened again and they were all taken to Afan Magistrates' Court, where a special session had been arranged. One hundred subdued men stood together, caught up in the anticlimax of their action. Unshaven faces smudged by weariness and worry. Most thought about their futures now. Seeking to defend jobs and the lifestyle of his community Edwin thought he might have driven another nail into its coffin.

With all his comrades charged with criminal damage and trespass his plan seemed vainglorious in retrospect. The dock strike they had hoped to support was crumbling, broken by the likes of the Barry dockers, who were deaf to the pleas of their colleagues at the other Welsh docks.

The court proceedings were cursory, the magistrates anxious to get through their heavy workload and be gone. The dishevelled group of men herded into court were treated as one, their individualism crushed by proceeding. It brought to Edwin's mind tales and imagery of the past. Thoughts of hanging judges and banishment to Australia. Things were less raw now but it did seem the country had taken a firm step backwards, to the days when working men had no power, or influence, and precious little hope.

All the men were bailed to re-appear in court in one month.

'At least they dropped the assault charges,' Tom said, as they filed out, 'they knew they couldn't make that stick.'

The police had bussed them down to the court but they had to walk back to their vans. It was a long walk but Edwin and Tom managed to detach themselves from Jenkins, and Edwin's stomach was salved by a bar of chocolate he bought on the way.

'Try to imagine we are on one of them hunger marches they had in the old days,' Tom muttered.

'They didn't work either,' Edwin said.

Tom clasped his shoulder.

'Ed, you take too much on yourself. I'm glad we did it. All the men are, deep down. Once we get a good night's sleep they will all be back on the picket lines. It was worth it but it's lucky I don't believe in fate though.'

'Why?

'That police boss they sent down, do you know what his name was? Ian bloody MacGregor. Another one. Can you believe that?'

Edwin felt he could believe anything as he mechanically put one foot in front of the other. When they reached the vans there was a further delay as some of them had been disabled by the police. He arrived back at the village on Saturday afternoon, while his brother was waking a mile away. Two flawed characters battling against bitter experience.

Edwin was glad the village was quiet. The muted goodbyes were almost inaudible as he was dropped off outside his house. The men tasted their defeat and some, like Jenkins, would be straight down The Merlin to wash it away. He imagined what the man would say down there, his description of the events colouring as the ale took hold. Edwin's performance would figure prominently.

He was tired, more so than after the most gruelling shift underground. He craved a bath but realised he could not have one. His house lacked the modern timing devices he knew others had, he still burnt what he mined and his immersion heater would take at least an hour to heat up the water. After the few days he had spent on the cranes this should have been a trifling irritant, but he felt it keenly. A sour end to a poor time.

He tried not to capitulate to depression, making himself a pot of tea, reading his mail and then snoozing in a chair. Light washed over him as the sun made its way west, helping him to relax. The phone rang but he ignored it, knowing it would be Griffiths or someone like him, demanding a report on the occupation. The phone rang twice more but did not penetrate his oblivion. The fourth time it rang it did rouse him but only to go upstairs to the bathroom, where he ran himself a deep bath and sank into it. The water eased grime away and its heat soothed him until he nodded off again, with his nose just above the water line. Edwin's meditative nature turned off to allow him a sensual enjoyment of the bath. For a brief time he did not care about anything.

The phone would not give up, it called him back from sleep several more times and he regretted not unplugging it. After an hour in the bath, when his skin was puckered and he had used all the hot water he got out and answered the extension in his office. It was not who he had expected.

'Susan,' Edwin said, 'you don't often phone here.'

'No, I know. I saw you on t.v. It was you, wasn't it, at Port Talbot?'

He felt himself flush. He had not even considered this, that his humiliation could be made so public. Elliott came into his mind instantly and he burned the same way his brother had.

'Edwin, are you there?' Susan asked.

'Yes, sorry. I've just got out the bath. Yes, it was me. What did they say, on television?'

'Nothing much, just that a man was coming down from those cranes. Are you ill?'

'No, I'm all right. It was the height we were at, I've always had trouble that way.'

'You shouldn't have done it if that's the case,' Susan said, 'but you've certainly got publicity. It's on the front page of the *Western Mail* as well. Rita Jenkins was on the phone earlier, Ronnie was with you, she said. She's quite excited about it.'

'Aye, Jenkins was there all right.'

He was not sure if Susan was humouring him or if paranoia had him in its grip.

'Where are you?' he asked, 'I can hear a lot of noise.'

'Porthcawl. I hate it here, but it's where the girls wanted to come. They've pigged it all day and been on all the rides.'

Susan answered his unasked question.

'Elliott is back. He's been back twice, in fact, came, went, and came back again.'

Edwin was thinking more of himself on television. Perhaps they would not show them again, perhaps the papers would not name him. God, that was pathetic, Jenkins would make sure the story would be around all the pubs by closing time.

'He's worse than ever,' Susan continued. 'I don't know how to handle it any more. That's why we are down here, to get away from him. I left him in bed.'

Edwin wished he could be selfish. He did not want to deal with this now, he had more than enough problems yet he fought down the temptation to wash his hands of his brother's marriage.

'Is there anything I can do?' he asked finally.

'No, not really, not with the way things are between you two. I just need to talk, that's all.'

'I don't know what to say. Perhaps I'm not the one to pronounce on Elliott.'

'Look, can I come round later? I'll drop the children at Rowena's and come over.'

'Do you think that's wise? That car of yours is noticeable in the village.'

'I'm past the wise stage. I'll come about seven.'

No sooner had Edwin replaced the phone when it sprang into life again, and this time it was Griffiths.

'I've been trying to phone you for hours,' Griffiths said, 'you've not been in.'

The conversation that ensued had an element of unreality about it. Griffiths probing in the sly but insistent way he had, full of understanding for Edwin's predicament yet stressing how little had been achieved by the occupation. Fortunately Griffiths had already been briefed by Tom Rees so he was spared the ritual of a detailed explanation of events.

'How will the charges affect us?' Edwin asked.

'I'm not sure yet. Our legal people are looking at it, but you'll have to keep a low profile with regard to picketing. It's a great pity about the missiles but the fact no-one was actually charged with assault is something. And you weren't on Coal Board land. It was nothing like what happened at Llanwern, it turned into a riot down there, and we lost two good men.'

'What! You don't mean people have been killed?'

'Not the way you mean, but two miners were involved in a road accident. From what I've heard they were so dazed with events there they drove straight into a truck.'

'That wraps up a great weekend,' Edwin said.

'The situation they've had up north is spreading down,' Griffiths said, 'especially with the younger men.'

'They want a result,' Edwin said, 'the younger you are the more you lose if they shut down the pits.'

'You sound totally done in,' Griffiths said. 'Look Edwin, I know you'll not want to think about this just now but that woman from London is coming down Tuesday, remember? Kathryn Peters.'

This plunged his mood to further depths. He just wanted out for a while, to walk over the hills and grab whatever fleeting respite they might offer. Now he had two women to contend with.

'I'll let you get some rest now,' Griffiths said, 'don't feel too bad about what happened. No-one can blame you for having vertigo.'

Aye, but they all will, Edwin thought, as he replaced the phone. Each time people tried to be understanding he felt his failure more keenly. He preferred the open derision of men like Jenkins.

When Susan knocked his door promptly at seven he had eaten and cleaned himself, though sleep was still badly needed. He had never slept well, his mind found it hard to turn off at night and five hours of fractured sleep were his norm. Two days on the cranes had cured this, if only temporarily. He anticipated the pillow and a quick fall into the void.

Edwin showed Susan into the front room, which he had quickly tidied.

'You've got it quite cosy in here,' she said, sitting on the couch he offered. 'I'd forgotten how many books you had.'

Her eyes strayed along the bookcases, in the way of all Edwin's visitors, but soon lost interest. Susan's life was too practical to ever have the time or inclination for books, but she did recognise them as a facet of Edwin's difference – weirdness, some of the girls in Rita's group said.

'I'll make some tea,' Edwin said.

'I'd rather coffee.'

In the kitchen Edwin hunted for a rather old jar of instant coffee, for which he had never acquired a taste. When he took a tray back in Susan was examining her hands, pushing cuticles back and absorbed in her thoughts. Edwin felt the tension in her and knew who had put it there. He determined not to be too derogatory about his brother. It would not help matters.

'Girls all right?' Edwin asked.

'Yes, considering what they've been hearing lately. They are a tough little pair but I'm glad they're not a few years older, when they could work out the rows better.'

'Does Elliott know about the support group?'

'No, not yet, but I'm not giving it up. I just don't want to be with him any more, Ed. I really think he's round the twist. He seems to live in another world, a dream world where his family don't exist. Then he pops back into ours with his vile tempers. He expects me to put up with all this and his womanising.'

Edwin knew of his brother's affairs, most of the men in The Merlin did. Before the rift between police and worker was complete Elliott occasionally drank there and talk of his sexual prowess was always around him, an aura that other men admired, especially as Elliott was married. Edwin had felt for Susan and, from an avuncular point of view, had worried about his nieces. But he had kept well out of it. Now he knew Susan was about to draw him in.

'He's finally come clean about his playing around,' Susan said. 'There was a terrible scene this morning and I don't know how much the girls heard. He's been with some tart in Yorkshire. God, it's so pathetic and I hate myself so much for letting it go on for years. And the way he came out with it, boasting to me about that woman even as he confessed. And he thinks I should be grateful to him for telling me, the bastard.'

Edwin drank his tea and thought of his response. Over Susan's shoulder he could see a sliver of mountain, softened by evening sun. He wanted to help Susan, sympathised with her, but what did he know about relationships? What people invested in them he could only imagine, and the countless times he had read of the tortuous pitfalls in his books was no substitute for experience. A ten minute fumble with a woman in Paris, when he had gone on a rugby trip with The Merlin crowd, was the sum total of his experience. If Susan knew this it did not matter to her. It was his pliant ears she wanted.

'I've got to get away from him,' Susan continued, 'but I don't know what he might do. The way he is now he is capable of anything. I'm not afraid of him for myself any more but I fear for the girls. I'm not even sure if the thought of buggering up his job restricts him any more. This strike has warped him. When he comes back from his tours, as he bloody calls them, it's like he's describing a war.'

'When's he going back?' Edwin asked.

'I don't know. He said he's finished with that woman up there, for the sake of us. Jesus, what a joke that is. I can't believe anything he says. Edwin, was he always like this, a liar, a cheat, a complete sod?'

How he wanted to shout yes, but he restrained himself. It would not have been true anyway. Elliott had always been difficult but he could not remember him being malicious or devious early on. He had changed so much since their father had died. Some kids might have gone into their shells but Elliott seemed to gain another skin, a layer of hard showiness and self-interest. And their mother helped preen and nurture this, mistaking it for promise. Not that Edwin blamed her too much, for Rowena had also been traumatised by her husband's sudden and early death. She had never recovered from it and they had never talked about it as a family. They never talked about anything, which was the great failing of the Bowleses. Elliott had become Rowena's *raison d'être* and she had steadily ruined his character, saturating it with one-eyed affection while her eldest son began his working life underground.

He wondered what he now felt for his brother. If the tables were turned Elliott would gloat at his problems. Being stuck at a hundred and twenty feet with his brain floating in some strange ether had shaken him to the point where he felt the need to examine everything, and with this went a certain desire for security. He got none from his immediate family. He was fighting a losing battle for the miners and lacked the solace of a home life to compensate. Ironically, the more Susan described her failing marriage and its horrors the more this fact was brought home to him. Lately his books and the hills and a commitment to a cause did not seem enough. Life might have been better if he had remained close to Elliott. He had failed just as much as his brother.

'Are you listening?' Susan asked. 'I know its difficult for you but you're the only other person who really knows Elliott.'

'I'm not so sure I do, now. I could see some of the signs years ago, but other things, they seem to have come out recently. When I slapped him we were nose to nose, and I was looking at a stranger.'

'Evil,' Susan said.

'I don't know about that. To be honest, Susan, life has changed so much around here since the strike took hold. I'm not sure about a lot of things. You think you know someone, a group of men, and they change before your eyes, behave in ways you would not have thought possible.'

Now they both wanted to talk, but about different things.

'Is there no-one you could stay with, for a while?' Edwin asked.

'No, not really. My father still thinks the sun shines out of Elliott's arse, like he never thought much of you miners, remember? And Shirley in New Zealand is not much use, is she? We get a card from her at Christmas, that's it, not even any presents for the kids. She got out early with that English bloke.'

'I'd forgotten all about that,' Edwin said, 'must be over twenty-five years ago now. New Zealand is not a bad place, they say, plenty of space and a damn sight better government than we have.'

'To put ten thousand miles between me and Elliott is a nice thought, but it's a pipe dream, as well you know.'

'Aye, I can't offer any solutions. They say these problems should be worked at but what can I say? Me, the bachelor.'

Susan managed a smile.

'Yes, I don't suppose you make the perfect agony aunt,' she said.

Edwin felt her thoughts turning towards him and deflected them before the inevitable questions about his single state came.

'So what are you doing next with Rita's lot?' he asked.

'Fund raising. They don't want me in school until Thursday. I'll get the girls settled into the new term Tuesday and then it's off with Rita.'

'Well, if you want to bring things to a head with Elliott that will do it. If things get too much Rowena will have the kids, she's a better grandmother than she ever was a mother.'

Susan looked at him closely for the first time since she had sat down.

'You sound bitter,' she said.

'No, not about that. But these times we are going through set lots of thought in motion. Bad thoughts usually. I'm just disillusioned about the way the strike is going.'

'And I'm adding to it,' Susan said. That's the trouble when you are on your own, isn't it? Everyone else uses you. You said you can't relate to marriage as a bachelor but what do I know about your world? You come home to an empty house every night.'

Susan saw the look on Edwin's face and quickly added.

'Rita told me that all the men look up to you and value your opinions.'

Edwin shrugged. 'I think you'll have to say used to from now on. It's getting dark, Susan, don't you think...'

'Yes, it's time for me to go. I can't put off going home any longer. Perhaps Elliott has been called back to work.'

He showed her out and stood at the side of the car. Susan wound the window down.

'Thanks, Ed,' she said, 'I don't feel so het up now.'

'I've done nothing.'

Edwin leaned into the Volvo.

'Posh, isn't it,' he said.

'Why haven't you learned to drive?' Susan asked.

'Why? I'd never buy a car.'

As Susan turned the key in the ignition Edwin touched her arm.

'Elliott is never violent with you, is he?' he asked.

'No, it's all words with him,' she lied.

She drove the large car down the street and Edwin noticed there were other eyes on it. He shut his door and went straight to bed.

Edwin woke ten hours later, a personal record of uninterrupted sleep. It was another fine day. The weather had been so good, as if it was perversely mocking the efforts of the strikers. He ate a quick breakfast, put a few apples and a chunk of rather hard cheese in his rucksack and was through his front door before the phone called him.

It took him twenty minutes to get to the top ridge but he did not stop at his usual spot looking down on Elliott's estate. He strode out along the spine of the ridge, scattering lazing sheep and swinging the badger-headed stick he had collected from Rowena's shed. His short stature kept him close to the ground, and he covered it quickly.

Fortified by rest his equable nature began to reassert itself. He tried to re-evaluate his performance on the crane and laugh at the tittle-tattle of men like Jenkins. Tomorrow he would be able to deal with that unwanted woman from London, plan the next course of strike action and perhaps even think up something to help Susan. Today he wanted to walk ten miles up the valley, have lunch in the small town there and come back down on the train.

Cumulus rippled the sky above him, competing with bands of blue. Fat white bolsters piled atop each other stretched down to the far coastline of the Bristol Channel. He could see over to Somerset, to its gold and green squares of neat farmland. He had never been there. Going to London was his sole experience of England. That was in his rugby-following days, when he did not see much more than the insides of Twickenham and pubs on the way to it. His knowledge of the world at large was second hand, gleaned from pages – other peoples' experience. But he felt his village environment gave him a good grounding in people. Until recently he had thought this enough but he knew what the likely end of the strike would be and worried about the longevity of his working life. What would he replace it with – professional hill walker? In his ideal world there would be room for such people. Like Elliott, he could dream.

He covered four miles in an hour. He knew the landscape so well he was able to enjoy it without changing pace, noting what he liked in each familiar profile. The way the bare stone ridge sloped down to meet the gentler lower hillside curves pleased him. It had never changed, for he walked above the interest and influence of man. On rough turf, and old weathered rock of great age.

Walking on what was not needed in the modern world.

Now that he had reached a time when his livelihood was being displaced he felt a great affinity with his land. Wales was a place of curves, in its nature and its people. When he studied his country's history he saw this clearly. The delicate symmetry of Celtic art had been replaced with squat Roman, then Norman architecture, four square and solid. Made to last. To dominate. That the minds of Welsh folk were also curved might explain their strange blend of unreliable romance and the ability to plunge into dark despair as if it was a refuge, 'Welshing' on their strengths and responsibilities. He knew he had a measure of it in him, but on days like this it exhilarated him. Secure in his national identity and wanting to maintain it, despite the many warts on its subjugated psyche.

He stopped at one of his staging posts and munched the apples, watching the miniature cars wind up and down the valley road. Sometimes their noise drifted up to him, then they were dumb, beaten by the keening wind which was ever present at this height. He could hear the chimes of an ice-cream van, a cracked and distorted 'Somewhere Over The Rainbow'. A car detached itself from the main artery and made its way towards his perch, using a lane that ascended the lower slopes of the hillside. It stopped and reversed into a side cutting, pushing as far as it could get against the undergrowth. It was a young man's car, proclaiming its owner's youth with backscreen stickers, an oversized aerial and multi-coloured panelling, culled from scrapyards. A pulsing radio combined with a geriatric engine. It was modern music that Edwin could not recognise, and did not want to. Legs and arms began to appear in various positions in the car and before long it began to rock on its suspension. He would have been disappointed if it had not.

He walked on, until it was time to descend to the café that awaited him, one that was open on Sundays. Here he ate, and drank tea for half an hour, and read a newspaper. A few kids sat opposite him, competing in coke-slurping and in a corner an old man conversed with himself. Edwin recognised a fellow miner's hands as they clasped around a mug and saw there was a tremor in them that matched the man's nodding head. Perhaps he was still underground somewhere. The café and town had the same derelict air of his own village but it did not depress him, in fact he often loved this sonambulant, locked-in-time atmosphere, which probably qualified him as mad in some quarters.

After a few hours watching the television and three cans of lager Elliott was restless. He wanted his car. To be without it was like losing an arm and to have to walk anywhere was a nod back to impecunious times. He especially hated Susan using it. If it hadn't been for the kids he would have bought something more sporty. A two-seater which Susan's extra salary would have paid for, but at least the Volvo was large and imposing. It made a statement and was a car driven by people he admired.

He heard Susan pull into the drive and the girls tumble out of the car and run to the door. He let them in and they crowded around him, showing him what they had bought from Porthcawl.

'Why didn't you come, daddy?' Sally asked. 'We had a great time.'

Susan stood behind them. They glanced at each other, each tensing for an outburst, but nothing came. Their wrath of the morning was replaced by a cold mutual indifference.

'I'll get the dinner on,' Susan said, knowing that this was the most likely statement of appeasement. She hated saying it and knew that Elliott would misinterpret it, but she thought it necessary to protect her daughters from further scenes. He opened the last can and went back to the television, making sure the girls sat either side of him on the floor. Whilst Susan was in the kitchen he let them sip from his can and they were his once more.

'I might not be going away anymore,' Elliott said, 'you'd like that, wouldn't you?'

Susan heard the game start up, it pinged its way into her head as she peeled potatoes. She thought of Edwin's house, a loner's world but calm and ordered. There were no tensions waiting there to rip one apart and she envied its peace.

★ ★ ★

Heartened by his walk Edwin ventured down to The Merlin on Sunday evening. He knew that the longer he left it the harder his re-integration with the men would be. Most of the crane occupiers were there. They usually were, even if they had no money for beer. For most the pub was an oasis of liquid dreams, for a sad few a place that offered a few hours oblivion, if one drank enough. Tom Rees came over quickly, before Edwin could buy a drink.

'I'll get that for you, Ed. Nice to see you looking right again.'

'It doesn't last once I'm on level ground.'

They sipped their pints and there was a minute's awkward silence. Jenkins could be heard leading the conversation at a table but Edwin did not look around.

'Well, what have you been doing?' Tom asked, clapping his hands together.

Edwin looked his friend in the eye.

'You don't have to be so cheerful, Tom. That's supposed to be my job, remember. Are you surprised to see me in here?'

'I'm glad you're here.'

'Has he been shouting the odds?' Edwin asked, dipping a shoulder in Jenkins' direction.

'Not particularly. I think everyone has been set back by that outing we had, especially as we're all on bail now.'

'They'll have to stay off the picket line until we go back to court,' Edwin said, 'we can't afford to get into any more trouble.'

'Ronnie won't like that.'

'He doesn't have to like it. I'll have a word with Rita, she'll have him housebound again by tomorrow.'

Edwin drank his beer slowly, savouring its bitter freshness.

'You been walking, haven't you,' Tom said, 'you always do when –'

'Things get fucked up. You know me too well, Rees bach.'

'Not really. I don't think anyone in the village does. My missis says you are as deep as a well.'

'As long as I haven't run dry I don't mind.'

Jenkins joined them.

'Hiya butty,' he said, 'all right now, are you? I'm having another pint then I'm off, before Rita gets her tongue out.'

He put his glass on the bar and made a play of searching in his pockets.

'I'll buy you that,' Edwin said.

'Oh, ta.'

Was this all it took, thought Edwin, to pay off an irascible old man?

'We was on the telly,' Jenkins said, 'specially you, Edwin. I wished I had one of them video things, could have kept it then, sort of a memento, like. But we showed the bastards a thing or two, didn't we.'

He emptied his glass in two long draughts.

'Lemme know when you want me again, boys,' Jenkins said. 'I got the taste for it now, and that bail nonsense means fuck all to me.'

He walked out with an inebriate swagger.

'A true Welshman,' Edwin murmured. 'Glorious in defeat.'

'See,' Tom said, 'it's all forgotten.'

Edwin knew it never would be by himself but he appreciated Tom's support. It had never wavered in all the years he had known him and he knew the man would be without work within two years, whatever was being said now. This made him determined to battle on but he was not sure how. Perhaps men like Jenkins were right. Why not go all out to fight back, knowing they had little to lose? What if he had been at Llanwern, would he have lost control, like others had? There was an increasing chance of any massed action by the miners would end like this, and he had been shaken by the ease in which men had started throwing things from the Port Talbot cranes.

His thoughts began to churn. Ideas, worries and frustrations. It had been so easy to strike his brother. Until then he had not thought himself capable of violence. Now a dark edge gnawed at him, as it had always gnawed at Elliott.

He stayed in The Merlin for an hour then went back to his house without dread. When his spirits were on an even keel his home had a comforting privacy that no-one breached. His small mortgage had been paid off, so at least it could not be taken it away from him. Edwin, man of property, he told himself wryly, as he turned the key in the front door lock.

* * *

The visit of Kathryn Peters to Edwin's house was a rare occurrence for him. Apart from family and the occasional woman he saw through union work there were no female callers. He thought about this for a few moments when he heard cars arriving. Opening the door to Griffiths' knock he found himself facing a woman of his height. Her auburn hair and blue-green eyes reminded him of his mother, when she was younger. He took her proffered hand and shook it hesitantly, although the returning clasp was firm. Imposing, that was the word people would use to describe Miss Peters, Edwin thought, if she was a Miss.

'This is Ms Kathryn Peters,' Griffiths said, as if reading

Edwin's thoughts. He gestured towards him. 'And this is the redoubtable Edwin Bowles, one of the linchpins of our struggle here.'

Shut up you prat, Edwin hissed in his head, willing himself not to blush.

'Come on through,' he said, showing his guests into the front room.

'I've filled Ms Peters in on a few points, Ed,' Griffiths said. 'I've got to get down to Cardiff now so I'll leave you both to it.'

Edwin showed him out, glad that the ordeal of two of them had been halved.

'I met her off the motorway and she followed me in this,' Griffiths said, pointing to the car parked behind his.

He could not believe it. Another Red Volvo stood outside the house, older and not so bright as Elliott's, but the same voluminous estate.

'Remember, we need any good press we can get,' Griffiths said as he left.

Edwin busied himself in making coffee, which the woman wanted black and sugarless, then he watched her drink it, concerned that she might guess its age. She was expensively dressed, even he could tell that. Stylish black boots hugged her ankles, matching her black skirt and jacket. She wore silver earrings but no other jewellery and her hair was cut short to highlight the fine features of her face.

There was a few minutes of polite nothingness. She described her trip down, and they both commented on the fine summer.

'It's my first time down here,' Peters said, 'though we went to North Wales on holiday when I was a child.'

The English middle classes usually went north, he'd noticed, away from the dirty work that made his country tick.

'I'm sorry that you've been lumbered with me,' Ms Peters said, 'I wouldn't blame you for resenting it, another outsider poking her nose in.'

He shrugged, regretting it at once.

'I don't mind,' he said, 'as long as you are here to help us. What exactly do you want?'

'I'm doing some articles on the human side of the strike, how it's affecting communities, marriages, that sort of thing. We've been slow to pick that up in the national press, but stuff is being written about it now.'

'Now that it's lasted more than a few weeks. Do you know anything about mining communities, Welsh ones?' he asked.

'Nothing hands-on. I don't come from a similar background, if that's what you mean, but I've been up to Nottinghamshire, to try to compare those working there with the strikers. It was a strange atmosphere, very defensive.'

'What did you expect? They must be suffering from a massive scab complex, never mind what they spout in the papers. That lot have made it nigh on impossible for us.'

Edwin was on the defensive. He had resolved to try to treat this woman as fairly as he could but he was aware of his working class snobbery. The strike brought it out. This was another white collar before him and he had to work out if the woman just wanted to use them, or that she really could offer something more than distant sympathy.

'Mr Griffiths said you could introduce me to the women's group here. You know their organiser quite well, don't you?' Ms Peters asked.

'Yes. I can do that. Perhaps its best you spend your time with them.'

'Amongst my own kind, you mean.'

'Oh, they certainly aren't your kind, Ms Peters.'

'Have you worked out "my kind" so quickly, Mr Bowles?'

He knew his face was flushing. The more he told it not to the more the heat came – stupid bastard. Next his tongue would thicken and stick to the roof of his mouth and his words come out in an indistinct muddle, a flaw from schooldays that occasionally still surfaced. Stress and strangers brought it on, strange women more so. He was able to discern a fragrance in the room now, delicate and unassuming, nothing like the overpowering scents of The Merlin women. This must be a sign of intelligent money, he thought. No showy jewellery, clothes of muted colour, teeth that looked quite perfect. He felt for the gap in his own with his tongue and closed his mouth even more when he spoke. He knew he was behaving in a way this woman probably expected but he could not help it. She did not press for a response to her question.

'Before meeting the support group do you think you could show me the valley?' Peters asked. 'That would be a start, I'd like to get a feel of this place.'

Oh aye, in a few bloody hours, he told himself.

'You'll have to drive,' he said. 'I don't have a car.'

'Don't worry, mine's outside. Shall we go, then?'

Elliott came floating into Edwin's mind as he sat in the Volvo. This car was not tidy like his, notepads and bits of paper were stuffed in recesses and he noticed the car had clocked up almost a hundred thousand miles. It did not match Peters' elegant appearance.

'Horrible thing, isn't it?' she said, 'hopelessly too big for London. My father gave it to me when it got too scruffy for him and I needed the room at the time. I was going back and forth to Greenham Common and there were always people who wanted lifts, tents to stow and so on.'

Griffiths had mentioned to him that Peters had written a lot in support of the women there. It was not something he had taken much notice of but he knew Rita and others had picked up on that protest as their own awareness grew. This woman might be a heroine to them but Edwin could not see her ever being on any front line.

He took her up the valley, pointing out the pitheads that still remained and the many sites that had closed down.

'It's easy to spot old pit sites by what they've left behind,' Edwin said. 'Look for the mounds of spoil or slag heaps as we call them around here. That's one, a lump on the mountain, as if someone has just thrown it there. Some of the old sites have been redeveloped, most have been left with just a minimum of landscaping.'

They stopped on the road out, where they could look back down the valley for some miles, not that they could see much. The good weather of August had changed into something more autumnal. A soft drizzle fell and mist hung low over the valley slopes.

'This is the best weather to get a feel for this place, as you put it,' Edwin said. 'The summer we have had was unnatural to us but this,' he swept a hand around the view, 'this is the valley, soggy and grey. It just lacks the smoke of the old days to go with it.'

'Do you mind if I make a few notes?'

Kathryn reached for one of her many pads and started writing. 'What are you putting down?' Edwin asked.

'What you said about scars. You don't mind do you?'

He was not sure if he did but gave his assent anyway. He felt easier now they were out of his house. There he was too naked,

111

his books betrayed his life too easily and Peters would have taken in his range quickly. She probably took in everything quickly, analysing succinctly without much personal involvement. A professional.

'Have you lived here all your life?' she asked.

'Yes.'

'What about family?'

'Mother, brother.'

'I get the impression not many people do move away. Look, can I call you Edwin, it would make me feel less of an interviewer. And please call me Kathryn.'

'All right. But you're wrong, a lot have gone. The valley population is probably half of what it was fifty years ago. The pit and heavy industries are dying on their feet, or being murdered, more like. Surely you know that?'

'Of course, but life still seems very steady here.'

'Are you sure you don't mean stagnant, us ignorant proles yoked to tradition, living in a backwater and so on.'

'No, I meant steady.'

She tightened her hands on the wheel and he noticed her facial colour moved closer to the hue of her hair. They had this in common, at least.

'We'd better drive back down,' he said, ignoring any attempt to draw him further into conversation. He was aware of his rudeness but could not stand this woman giving him the benefit of her two hours' valley experience.

Kathryn Peters did not seem much affected by the atmosphere.

'Look, can we stop somewhere to eat?' she asked, 'I'm starving.'

It was the last thing Edwin wanted but he felt the obligation.

'If you want,' he said. 'Will a pub lunch be okay?'

'It usually is.'

He directed her to a pub which served food, and where he was not well known. On their way to it they passed the entrance to the other valley pit, with a token force of pickets outside it. Kathryn wanted to stop but he urged her on.

'Best not to,' he said, 'if you want to catch that meal. They don't serve them all day here.'

It was all he could do to prevent himself from ducking down as the pickets gave them a cursory glance.

The Golden Age was a refurbished and renamed public house, a place that had been gutted of its true past and replaced by a

Victorian 'theme'. It was open plan, which Edwin hated and its plush red wallpaper looked like cloth to him. A few local business men glanced at Kathryn as they entered, noting her as a stranger and wondering what she was doing with someone like him.

She ordered a chicken salad and a glass of white wine and he felt obliged to have something too, though he balked at the prices. At least by concentrating on food he hoped to still Peters' probing questions but it was a vain hope. They kept coming as his guest tried to build up a profile of him.

'So, you're a Lodge Official, are you? I think I've worked out the structure of the NUM now,' Kathryn said.

'Aye, that and a miner.'

'Have you ever done anything else?'

'No, never felt the need.'

'And your brother, is he in the industry too?'

'No.'

He excused himself, spending a few minutes in the toilet to divert this line of enquiry. Whilst he was there Kathryn wrote down a few comments in her pad.

'Edwin Bowles – fortyish going on eighty; loquacious he isn't.' She thought people in this area would open up more easily than they had in Nottinghamshire but this Bowles man used words as though each one was a personal enemy. He would be a challenge and she hoped the women's group would be more forthcoming.

Kathryn finished her meal and glanced around at the setting. It was awful, as if the pub's designers had a brief to be particularly phony, tasteless and crass. Yet the place was somehow perfect, this pathetic outpost of modern tat highlighted the dereliction outside by its determination to oppose it. And the name, The Golden Age, was laughable. When was that?

Despite her repeated trips around deprived regions of Britain she had never got used to the poverty of some people's lives and, worse, of their expectations. This gave her an uneasy relationship with her chosen career. When she went to college in 1970 sociology had been the fashionable course, the science to ally with a decade of innovation and the dismantling of convention, which had changed Britain for good, she believed then. She had been an eager advocate of the new feminism drifting over from America, and thought it the way forward for her. Her fundamental views had not altered but life had clouded them. Broken relationships with men still hurt and as the eighties developed and began to restrict the freedoms of her campus she had to maintain her career with considerable in-fighting. This was part and parcel of the new times and she had developed a hardness to deal with it, though she worried that it would get worse, as this decade sought to snuff out the one that had so shaped her.

What had focused Kathryn's mind in the last ten years, career advancement, academic credibility and the women's movement, seemed a long way from what she had seen in the miners' strike. She researched a crumbling man's world, with women as addendums, so closely tied were they to the fortunes of their men. It was a world that was archaic and restrictive to her own sex yet she still felt for it, for it was fighting against the monstrous con that was being worked on the country at large. The dominant philosophy of the age rushed people headlong into a shallow, mercenary world with nothing to ground them and smashed the lives of those who did not want to join, like the man taking a leisurely piss in this pub, and thousands like him. Edwin rejoined her and she put her notebook away.

'Recording your observations, are you?' he said.

'Par for the course for sociologists.'

'Right, are we ready then?'

Kathryn noticed that Edwin had left most of his food but did not comment on it. They drove back to the village and Edwin relaxed a little. He tried to be less defensive, pointing out things he thought might be of interest. They passed the Top Pit.

'That's where I work, or used to work,' Edwin said.

'There are so many old sites around the valley,' Kathryn said.

'Aye, the place is riddled with them. A rabbits' warren of old workings, with waste scooped out on top to mark them. They're a part of the valley for me. Been here for generations.'

'You don't think they've damaged the environment.'

'Of course they have. But they've also given work. Good choice, eh? Dirt or poverty, or both. But if it wasn't the pits it would be something else. That's progress, isn't it?'

Kathryn looked at Edwin with interest. He was not as tongue-tied as she thought, and she liked his line in irony.

Elliott's estate loomed above them on the hillside.

'That looks a bit out of place,' Kathryn muttered.

'Our pocket of affluence. People with a bit of brass like to live together. Cut themselves off from us rabble,' Edwin said. 'Where are you staying?'

'At a pub – The Merlin. Ceri Griffiths organised it for me. He said it was at the heart of things here.'

'He's right. The women's group have their headquarters there. You'll be Davidson's first guest in years. He's a Scot by the way, but we don't hold that against him.'

Kathryn parked in The Merlin's rear yard, praying it would not be anything like The Golden Age.

'I'll see you in,' Edwin said.

'No, it's all right, I can manage. I always have.'

'Right. What are your plans now?'

'Mr. Griffiths is meeting me later. I'm going to one of your regional offices with him, to see how things work there but will you introduce me to some of the women tonight? I'm told they meet on Tuesday evening.'

'Yes. My sister-in-law is involved there.'

He was glad to say this, it lessened the dread he had of revealing what Elliott did, and what he was. This woman would surely find that out. It would be a useful nugget of information to brighten her research. He watched her go in the back way, carrying a small weekend bag and a briefcase. She reminded him of the woman who came to see them after his father had died, the one from the welfare, confident and determined to distance herself from the family in need. That one also asked a lot of questions.

* * *

Elliott stressed the needs of his wife and family to get himself taken off the list of officers being sent north. After the four days' leave he had accrued he would be back to policing his own patch again. He hated losing out on the overtime but Yorkshire meant Lisa, and he wanted to crush that bitch out of his thoughts. With the kids going back to school, and Susan with them, he would be able to spend time on his own, getting his head together and planning his next move. It was only a matter of time before he bumped into Edwin, whom he had not seen since that time in Rowena's kitchen. His brother's punch had started off his run of bad luck, since then Lisa had fucked him up and his wife had gone through some weird character change. He had always ruled the roost with her, if ever she stood up to him a sharp burst of temper made her give in quickly. That was how it should be, it kept their marriage on the straight and narrow, but now, it was as if he did not know the woman at all.

He took Susan and the girls to school Tuesday morning, so he could have the car. Susan was maintaining her sullen silence and he let her get away with it, for now. He had not been outside the school gates in a long time. Amongst the mothers were a few old flames who had thickened up and aged quickly. He avoided their glances over to the Volvo. Making a show of kissing the girls and ignoring Susan, he sped off from the school and drove down to the local leisure centre, to work on the weights there. Pumping iron had once been a keen interest of his but he had let it go with his rugby. Now he planned to retrain, to get super fit again. He spent an hour in the gym, going at it too hard but not caring, sweating and steaming until his limbs screamed at him to stop. The exertion did not offer the release he sought, instead of calming him it fired his ill humour. The faces of Susan, Lisa and Edwin revolved in his head; three traitors. He finished his routine, showered and checked himself out in the full length mirror of the changing rooms. He had gained a few extra pounds on his gut but otherwise not bad, better than most of the new police recruits.

He put the Volvo through a car wash and went back to the village, driving slowly around its streets, something he had not done in years, off-duty. What a knackered dump it was, uneven terracing clinging together with hardly space to swing a cat, a few shops out of the Ark, others boarded up. What the fuck were people here fighting over? He could not see it. Clowns like Edwin talked of community spirit but the only spirit here came out of bottles down at The Merlin. And the great traditions of the past, as their father used to say. All the past said to him was abject poverty and misery – where was the tradition in that? He wished he had been born somewhere else, somewhere within shouting distance of London, without the stink of Welshness on him. It held you back, was a useless thing that everyone laughed at outside the country, and often inside. Now they were starting up Welsh-speaking schools all over the place. Pathetic.

'Taffy was a Welshmen, Taffy was a thief', and to that the English added idiot, wanker, loser. He agreed with them but it still made him burn. If he had gone to London with Lisa he would have shed his ancestry like a snake its skin. He had worked for years to minimise his accent but those Met boys could still spot it. This was why he had always taken care of his body, so he would not be like the rest of them, runtish, bony little men or fat-gutted, bandy-legged boozers.

When he got home he continued his exertions. He waxed the Volvo and vacuumed the interior, polished everything in sight and cleared out the junk of his family. When it was time to pick up Susan and the girls the car gleamed. He had restored it to show-room condition, as he would his own chassis in a few weeks. At no time during his energetic day did his mind stop grinding. It went through its own assault course, jumping through the hoops of his malice and focusing his thoughts increasingly on Edwin. Lisa was gone, Susan was a problem but Edwin was a simple target, close and reachable.

He parked the Volvo behind the group of mothers waiting at the school gate and sounded his horn when he saw his daughters stream out with the other children. They ran towards him, eager to show him and the car off to their friends, and Susan followed behind, canvas bag under her arm, pretending she was a teacher, stupid cow. She sat in the rear with the girls, not saying anything and taking a great interest in whatever they passed.

He wished his timing had been better. If he could have got leave a few weeks earlier he could have spent some time with the girls in their holiday, counteracting their mother's influence. Now they were back at school and she was there half a week with them. He felt his exclusion.

'Did you have a good first day?' he asked the girls.

They competed in their telling but he let it wash over him and watched Susan in the rear view mirror. This was how she want-ed to play it, building up a wall of silence between them and treat-ing him like a stranger. Well let her, for now. He did not want her around him much anyway. She was going nowhere, had nowhere to go. There was nothing much in the bank account and then there were the kids, she would never leave them. No, Susan would always be around, this would blow over and she would go back to being how he wanted.

As Susan prepared dinner he played with the girls. They usu-ally helped their mother in the kitchen but he made sure they kept close by him this evening. He let them win and told them glori-ous tales of his exploits.

'It's great now Daddy's home again, isn't it?' Sarah said as Susan came in with the plates.

'Go and get the cutlery and let's have that game off now.'

Susan felt Elliott's jealousy rubbing off. She could not prevent it surging over her when she saw how easily he won over their daughters and how unfair that was. She wanted to dash a pan of boiling water into his face to ruin its handsomeness, and was not ashamed of her thought. The more Elliott cavorted on the carpet, so phony, the more she wanted to hurt him, yet she knew she could never show this to the girls. Elliott wanted her to fight him for them and they did not deserve to be in the middle of a battle. The women she worked with seemed to have caring, supportive partners, who did their share of work around the house and did not treat their wives like chattels or chase other women like over-sexed schoolboys. She had drawn the short straw in Elliott, a man who could no longer tell the truth even to himself. 'That village lot are going nowhere,' he was apt to say. But neither was he. And she still cooked dinner for him.

* * *

Edwin switched off his radio. The TUC conference was on this week but he could not bear to listen to it. He knew the 'problem' of the miners' strike would be passed around like a rugby ball, various factions would make a show of running with it before letting it be booted into touch by the majority.

Resignation that they would receive only token help had settled into his mind months ago. They would have to fight on alone, like they did in '26, more in stubborn hope than good judgement.

He finished his meal and prepared to go down to The Merlin. For this he changed into what he thought were his better clothes and gave his hair a brush, having bathed earlier. He told himself this had nothing to do with the Peters woman but it was not his usual preparation for a Merlin session. It was raining heavily as he shut his front door, though a fragment of blue sky was still visible over the mountain, echoing the summer now well and truly gone. Kathryn Peters was sitting at the bar when he got to the pub, talking to Ken Davidson.

'Hullo,' Edwin said, 'are the girls in the back, Ken?'

'Aye, some of them. I think I heard Rita's dulcet tones just now. I told Kathryn here to go on through but she wanted to wait for you.'

'Do you want a drink?' Kathryn asked.

'Yes, all right. A pint of that muck, please.' He pointed to a bar pump. 'It's our local brew.'

Davidson left them to serve, though Edwin noticed his eyes lingered on Kathryn. Her attractiveness stood out in this environment.

'How did it go with Griffiths?' he asked.

'Very well. Ceri is very enthusiastic, a finger on the pulse type, I'd say.'

Edwin was glad the man was not with them, for then he would be squeezed between two formal educations and might feel the lack of one of his own. Though he hid it well he often wondered how it would have worked out if he had done better at school. In his days no-one in the secondary modern thought much further than leaving at fifteen, and teachers encouraged them in this belief. Like the pupils they were deemed of insufficient quality for the top rank. He might have taken up study in night school, in the time honoured tradition of his profession but his father's death and his instinctive distaste for the educated working man put paid to that. Men like Griffiths seemed to him to have been dragged away and distanced by what they had learnt, remoulded until all the sharp edges of their beliefs were blunted into safety.

'That beer must be good,' Kathryn said, 'you're miles away.'

'Am I? Come on through to the girls' den. Rita has taken over Ken's storeroom. It's her bunker now, so to speak.'

He led her through the pub, ignoring the winks of the drinkers in residence. Thankfully Jenkins was not about. He had been put back on hold by Rita, back to his father watch. Pushing open the backroom door the talk was stilled as Edwin ushered Kathryn inside and introduced her.

'Nice to meet you, luv,' Rita said. 'I hope Edwin here has been treating you right. He's hell with the women, you know.'

He edged towards the door and stood there for a while, letting his guest get on with it. Kathryn mixed in easily with Rita's group. Like Griffiths she had that air of concern in every question but also had something more. An ability to say 'I am one of you' when she patently was not. Perhaps female solidarity was less distrustful and competitive than the male version. By the time he ducked back into the bar the women were in animated conversation, Rita enjoying the flattery of outside interest.

Tom was in the bar, with a few other crane veterans.

'That woman from London is here, isn't she?' Tom said.

'Smart piece, Ken says.'

'Aye, I suppose she is. Griffiths has asked me to show her around.'

'Lucky bugger. Don't want help do you?'

'I could do without it, Tom, what with all the work we've got on here.'

'I wanted to see you about what Griffiths said, that those on bail can't take part in any more direct action. It don't set right with some of the boys. They want to have a go at those coal convoys. They are rolling a few times a week now, forty or fifty bastard trucks each time.'

The thought of another action probably ending in violent confrontation coming so soon in the wake of the Port Talbot business made Edwin wilt.

'I don't know, Tom. If any of us get arrested again it will be bad, you know that.'

'Well tell them that at the next meeting, I'm just passing on the general mood. In the meantime enjoy yourself with your girlfriend, nice bit of stuff like that. Show her your socialist credentials, they love that. Don't know fuck all about anything real but they like to get involved, as they call it, identifying with the plight of the worker and all that.'

'You seem well informed,' Edwin said.

'Of course, I seen it on the telly, heard them going on on those discussion programmes. You know, that actress woman, Workers Revolutionary Party and so on. Laughable.'

Tom saw the blank look on Edwin's face.

'No, you probably don't. I was forgetting you don't have the telly habit. Christ, that really does make you strange, you know Ed. Go on, get in there with that woman, you can be her bit of rough.'

'I'd better buy you a pint to shut you up,' Edwin said. 'You've become a talky swine since you were up on the crane.'

Kathryn rejoined them in the bar half an hour later, with Rita in tow.

'She probably wonders how we can afford to drink,' Tom whispered, as the women approached, 'and this is only my second pint in a week.'

'Kath is coming with us tomorrow, on that fundraising run,' Rita announced, putting an arm around her new friend.

Edwin remembered that Susan was also going on that and

wondered how much talk would pass between her and Kathryn.

'Do you want a drink?' he asked.

'Yes, but I'll get them,' Kathryn answered, dismissing protests with a waved hand.

They took their drinks to a table where they were joined by others. As the evening wore on it seemed to Edwin that Kathryn integrated herself into the group. Her accent no longer stood out and she pressed all the right buttons of support to impress Rita and Tom. By closing time they were firmly on her side and he knew his doubts would not be heeded. He kept his own counsel and wondered if his friends would be similarly received in Kathryn's London world.

'Here,' Rita said, when Kathryn left the table, 'you've come up with a good 'un there, our Edwin. She really cares what's going on here, I can tell. And she knows a lot too. That's the difference, see, when a woman gets some learning inside her.'

'I didn't come up with her,' Edwin said, 'She was Griffiths' idea.'

'No matter. Kathryn is going to write about us, put our side of things.'

'So she says.'

'Oi, glumface, you're not still moping about that Port Talbot thing, are you? That's gone now.'

'No, I'm not.'

'What is it, then? Oh, not sure about Kathryn, are you? Look, you know me, I always make my mind up quickly about someone but how often am I wrong? She's all right and I tell you another thing I've found out, she haven't got no fella around at the moment. Between traumas she told me, whatever that means.'

'Reet, stop it, I've had enough of that off Tom. Bloody hell, has everyone turned matchmaker around here. I'm only showing her around, for Christsake.'

'That's a wonderful colour you have, Ed.'

Kathryn's return stilled any further comments though Rita occasionally dug an elbow into his side. The impromptu party broke up at closing time and Kathryn went to her room above the bar. Edwin walked home with Tom.

'I noticed you shared the drinks bill with that London girl,' Tom said, 'but I know you too well to feel guilty about that.'

They stopped to urinate from the bridge into the river, the traditional piss-point for men returning from The Merlin.

'They say this sludge of a river is getting cleaner as the pits go,' Tom said. 'Maybe we'll have to stop doing this, for the environment, like.'

'If it does run clear one day that will be the end of our work, Tom.'

'I know it, but there's talk of us becoming a tourist area. We could have rich Yanks down here, stuff like that. You could do bed and breakfast, Ed, you'd look good in a pinny, or you could be one of them guides, like they have in Greece and places like that. Part of the service industry, I think that's what they call it.'

'Have we ever been anything else? Jesus, that would be from the frying pan to the fire, but I don't think it will ever happen, Tom. Our grim reputation is too well established.'

'Aye, established by outsiders and suffered by us.'

'Are you coming back for a night-cap? I think there's a few bottles somewhere.'

'Don't tempt me. No, I've got to get back, I told the missis I was only popping out for an hour. Go to bed, and dream about that Peters woman.'

He walked on alone, a fine rain cooling his beer-heated face. Unwittingly, he did think of Kathryn, and the way she so easily gained the confidence of a bunch of strangers. She had style and charisma, there was no doubt about that, but this only added a tinge of jealousy to his initial caution. Even so, it kept her in his mind.

* * *

Susan's breakdown in communication with Elliott made it easier to get away from him on Wednesday morning. His bulk remained turned away to the wall in the bed she had no option but to still share with him. He grunted when she told him she was taking the girls to school and pulled the blankets more closely about him, a lump of male flesh she never wanted to touch again. Elliot had made no demands on her body since his return, and had not done so for several months. She prayed this would continue and realised that silent disdain was her best defence. It might bring her more punches but she did not think he would stoop as low as rape.

She got the girls ready as quietly as possible, drove them down to school and went on to The Merlin, parking the car in the rear yard, away from prying eyes. She would pick up the girls after school and go home with them. Elliott might rage about being deprived of the car but the girls would be her defence against his shouted questions.

Rita was waiting for her.

'The van's ready,' she said, 'will you drive again? Marge is coming, and a few others. We have a guest supporter with us, too.' She ushered Kathryn forward.

'This is Kath Peters. Down from London, to write about us. Susan is married to Ed's brother,' Rita added, to Susan's discomfort.

'Hello, Edwin has mentioned you,' Kathryn said.

'You've met, then?'

'Oh yes. He's been my guide around the valley.'

'Really?'

Susan could not think of anyone less suited than the taciturn Edwin. She hoped he had not worn his duffel coat. Kathryn Peters was a striking woman, tall, in her early thirties, with none of the excess weight of the women around her. Her complexion was clear and well groomed, and her eyes were a cold blue. They did not waver when they stared into Susan's.

'Aye,' Rita said, 'Kath is trying to tell how it really is down here. We can do with a bit of truth, can't we? Come on then, girls, let's go down to Cardiff and hassle the shoppers there. Don't look so worried, Susan, we'll be perfect ladies.'

Susan cursed under her breath as she ground the van's gears. She felt self-conscious with the London woman, felt her cool appraisal and knew that questions about Elliott might come at any time. Kathryn sat in the front alongside Rita, her long legs elegantly clothed in expensive jeans and matching denim jacket, imitations of working clothes.

The van was parked in a central car park, after much direction from Marge and Rita.

'It's not a bad day,' Rita said, 'at least the rain's stopped.'

They had prepared sealed plastic buckets with slits for the money cut in the tops, outsized money boxes which they hoped to fill. As they tumbled out of the van Kathryn was so much better dressed than the anoraked, rotund women of Rita's group that she looked like a teacher taking a bunch of deprived kids on an outing. Rita made sure they all had their stickers on. They carried no legal weight but were a way of bonding the group together.

They fanned out along Queen Street, now conveniently pedestrianised. Susan was relieved that Kathryn walked on Rita's side. At first she shook her bucket rather timidly towards passers-by, letting Marge do the shouting, which she did very effectively. Her 'help the miners' families' translated into 'you must help' and Susan was amazed at the number of people who could not resist her.

'You gotta make your presence felt,' Marge said. 'Come on, woman, it's no good just standing there.'

Susan found her voice, hesitantly at first, then louder as she grew more confident. Her own bucket began to take on weight.

The group joined up at the end of the street.

'This is going great,' Rita said, 'they'll always give more to us girls. Men are useless, they just stand there and look glum. You got to involve folks, tell them it's for the kids.'

Rita noticed Kathryn's notebook.

'That's right, luv, you put this down. Thoughts of chairwoman Rita. Come on, let's work our way down St Mary Street, we can have a cup of tea then.'

The collection continued to go well, and there was the occasional donation of bank notes. One man thrust five pounds into Susan's bucket. He wore a mohair coat with a fur collar and she smelt the remnants of a cigar on him.

'The miners are behaving like yobbos,' the man said, 'but I don't think children should suffer.'

Kathryn had switched to Susan's side now.

'You haven't got a bucket, then,' Susan said to her.

'No, I'm not an official collector, and Rita wanted to keep things formal.'

'Uh uh.'

'You are part of a good family effort,' Kathryn said, 'Edwin is doing a lot for the strike, Rita tells me.'

'I haven't done much,' Susan said, 'just this and a few food drops.'

'Does your husband work at the same pit as Edwin?'

Susan shouted almost as loudly as Marge and pretended she did not hear Kathryn's question. She saw two policemen approaching. They stopped in front of the women. How was it said, that you are old if coppers begin to appear young? These two hardly seemed acquainted with a razor, they were clear eyed youngsters, with helmet straps pressed against boyish faces. Rita crossed over quickly from the other side of the road.

'Nothing wrong, is there, boys?' she said. 'We're only collecting for the miners' families.'

The officers looked at each other for guidance. Rita's group had not been hindered by the authorities so far, but others had.

'Well,' Rita said, giving one officer a little dig, 'aren't you going to give something?'

Her attempt at friendliness did not have the desired effect.

'Thing is, you are causing an obstruction, aren't you?' the policeman said. 'Marching down the pavement three abreast, shouting like hell. I saw a woman back there had to wheel her pram into the street to get past you.'

'That's a bloody lie,' Marge shouted, 'we made room for them.'

A number of people had stopped, their inquisitiveness alerted by police uniforms.

'So, what are you saying,' Rita said, 'that we can't look for donations?'

'Are you a registered charity?'

'You know we're not.'

Marge's face glowed a solid red.

'Don't expect any change from them, Reet,' she said, 'they might be only kids but they got all the necessary qualities needed for their work.'

She thrust herself forward and shook her bucket.

'This is money for bloody children,' she shouted, 'where's the harm in that? Perhaps you want some of it, how about a few quid, butt?'

'Behave yourself, Marge,' Rita said.

'Perhaps we'd better go,' Susan suggested, noting that Kathryn had moved to the rear of the group.

'Why should we go?' Marge said. 'I'm not being chucked off the street by these two fuckers.'

This gave the policemen the green light they sought.

One of them talked into his radio.

'Right,' the other said. 'You've pushed a police officer, used foul language and are refusing to stop your obstruction.'

'Good Lord, you are not arresting us, are you?' Rita asked.

'This lady we are,' the policeman said, putting a hand on Marge's arm.

'Fuck off me,' she yelled, swinging her heavy bucket at the man. She connected with his shoulder, making him stagger into the road. There was now a ring of watchers. Perhaps a hundred people, delighted at this break in their routine. All keeping a strict neutrality.

Blood thickened and Rita tried to help her sister, kicking out at the men and wielding her own bucket effectively. Susan and the other women looked helplessly on. A police van pulled up and the Jenkins sisters were bundled inside, two policemen struggling with each of them

'Get in, all of you,' a police sergeant said, 'we'll sort this out at the station.'

As soon as they got inside the police station the thought of Elliott came to Susan, inevitably so given her surroundings. But where once she would have felt abject panic at his reaction to this now there was just resignation in her. It was as if fate had conspired to cement the wall that had been thrown up between them, with an incident that had happened so fast.

After a long wait in the station's reception area the Jenkins sisters were dealt with by the desk sergeant. They were charged with causing an affray, and 'using foul and abusive language'.

Kathryn stood behind them with Susan.

'This is a new experience for me,' Kathryn said. 'I've been in plenty of police stations but never as a customer.'

'None of us has,' Susan said.

'No, I suppose not. Don't worry too much about this, Susan, they can only charge the rest of us with obstruction and that will never come to court, believe me.'

'Can't we do anything to help Rita and Marge?'

'Not at the moment, but perhaps even their case won't be taken further, they might not think it worth their while when they weigh it up. Those policemen were a bit too young and a bit too keen. This will be part of your battle stories, something to show off to your husbands.'

The other women were cautioned and had their details taken down, but were not charged. It was mid-afternoon by the time they were released.

'Oh God,' Susan said, 'the children. I've just realised, I'll never be able to get back in time to take them home.'

'Can't your husband be there?' Kathryn asked.

Marge heard this. 'Bloody hell,' she said, 'she thinks your old man is on strike. A striking miner, that's a laugh.'

'Shut up, Marge,' Rita said, 'you've got us in enough trouble today. Phone the school, Susan, it'll be all right. Someone will run them home for you.'

'Yes but Elliott might be anywhere, he might...'

Rita took her to one side.

'So, you haven't told him what you are up to. I thought not. Look, you can't keep a secret long in our place, he might as well find out now. Not about this police business, but just the fund raising. The girls will keep quiet, I'll make sure of that.'

Susan phoned her house first to check that Elliott was there, putting the phone down when she heard his voice. Then she arranged for a teacher to take the girls home. As she drove the van back to the valley she was deep in thought.

She heard Marge going on about their fracas but it did not register. How to deal with Elliott occupied her mind. If he received the double shock of her work with the women's group and their arrest he might become unhinged completely. As she pulled into The Merlin's yard she decided to take Rita's advice. She detached herself from the group quickly, before Kathryn could follow up Marge's comment.

Elliott was waiting for her on the drive when she got back. The fact that he had been deprived of the car for a day would have fanned the flames of his anger. She felt it as soon as he wrenched open the car door.

'Get in the house,' he said, his face more white than red. 'What the fuck have you been up to, you stupid bitch.'

'Are you going to do your bully act,' Susan said.

His hand flexed into a fist.

'Get in that fucking house before I knock you in.'

Despite her new found resolve she was afraid. Elliott was a large, powerful man. Not in control. He pushed her into the house, pulling the car keys from her hand. Slamming the front door behind them he spun Susan around and bunched up her jacket in his hand.

'Elliott, don't. Where are the girls?'

'In their playroom, and they'll stay there.'

He hissed through clenched teeth which was more menacing than his usual bellow.

'I've just had a phone call,' he said, 'from Cardiff. It was a bloke in the force I used to work with. He recognised you, as you were being charged in his fucking police station. I thought he was winding me up until that teacher brought the kids home. It's true, isn't it, you been messing around with those fucking loonies.'

'I wasn't charged,' Susan said.

The first blow came, a stinging slap that jolted Susan's head backwards. It was impossible to get away from his grip and he slapped her several more times until she tasted blood at the corner of her mouth. From a distance she heard Sally's voice, a screaming voice that urged her father to stop, but he did not. She was pushed into the living room and kicked onto the sofa.

'You did this to get even with me,' Elliott shouted, 'just to pay me back, you cow. Do you know what this will do to my career, my fucking wife mixed up with that rabble, a policeman's wife for fuck sake.'

She wondered why the girls did not come down. Despite the shame she wanted them present. Elliott might stop then. He read her thoughts.

'I've locked them in their room,' Elliott shouted, 'they can't help you.'

'You don't know what you're doing,' Susan moaned, as slaps turned into punches.

'You have to learn,' Elliott said, but more to himself than her. He was truly mad. Susan knew this before she lost consciousness.

★ ★ ★

Elliott sat down on a chair and watched Susan's inert body. He could hear his daughters crying upstairs. But quieter, more of a whimper now.

Susan stirred and moaned. There was not a mark on her face, it was a bit red from the slaps. That was all. He was proud that even at the end of his tether he had still exercised caution. What he had inflicted on Susan had been necessary, she was so far out of order it was not true, trying to undermine him, betraying him like that other cow. No, she would learn from this. She had to learn, and there would be no more nonsense from her. He got up and stood over her, satisfied by the terror he saw in her face as she focused on him.

'Elliott, stop,' Susan gasped.

'You've had your punishment. I think I've got my point across, don't you?'

He pulled her upright, making her shudder.

'It's hard to breathe,' Susan said. 'I think there's something wrong with my ribs.'

She bit her lip as she tried to control the nausea the pain caused. Each breath was like another blow from Elliott. She was dazed by it all, by the suddenness. She had become another battered wife statistic. This was the worst day of her life. As she heard the girls crying she knew this was the worst day of her life.

'Let them out, Elliott, for pity's sake.'

'All right, I will, but you listen first. We were just messing around, right? You went to go upstairs and you tripped and fell. A nasty fall.'

He pressed his head close to hers, brushing her face with his moustache.

'Right?' he repeated.

'Yes' she agreed, with defeat in her voice.

Elliott went upstairs to free the girls.

'It's okay, gang,' he said, 'I was just playing a joke, but it went a bit wrong. Your mother has fallen over, she's shaken up a bit but it's nothing to worry about.'

The girls stepped away from him. They wanted to get past to go down to Susan but dared not approach him. For the first time they sensed something bad in their father. Fledgeling instinct battled with natural trust.

'Come on,' Elliott said, 'why are you looking so frightened? It's only a little accident. Come on, we'll go down to Cardiff, to that burger place you like.'

There was no response.

'Well, go down and see your mother then.'

He stood aside to let them pass hesitantly.

Looking out of the playroom window he saw the valley curving away. They had a good view of it from their hill, not cooped up like the terraces below. He hummed to himself, feeling easier in his mind than he had for ages. The chances were that Susan's misdemeanour would go unnoticed by his superiors and he had nipped any further action in the bud.

There was a small clump of oaks still left on the estate, he could place them in the woods that had made way for the housing. How he had loved to climb the trees there, swinging round the branches like a monkey whilst Edwin watched below, always on the ground. He had liked to show off to his older brother then, especially as his father took little notice of what he did. It was back from the pit, eat, and in the chair for his old man. Rowena was left to take care of everything. Edwin had watched over him when Dad had died, bossed him around until he got too big, and then mocked him when he joined the police force. When he had been dealing with his wife he had been punching his brother as well, and also Lisa. That bitch he could never get back at now but Edwin's time was approaching.

When he went back down the girls were nestled against their mother, the three of them crying quietly together.

'Come on Sarah, Sally, don't take on. It was only a little fall your mother had, wasn't it, darling? She'll feel better soon.'

He tapped Susan lightly.

'Does it hurt anywhere in particular?' he asked. He knew that she was desperate for him to be elsewhere but could do nothing about it. The master had regained control over his own household and asserted his power, which was how it should be. His headache was receding.

'It hurts when I breathe,' Susan answered.

'Try to get up,' Elliott said, holding her hands.

She did so shakily, but stumbled back onto the sofa, bringing a fresh bout of tears from the girls.

'Right, I'm taking you to hospital. You're probably just a bit bruised but we can't take any chances,' he said.

Susan was taken to casualty where a cracked rib showed up on her X-ray. Elliott enjoyed the process, being with his family, in charge, organising tea and soft drinks, talking to the girls constantly, the concerned father anxious to allay anxiety.

A doctor came to chat with Elliott.

'She's in rather a lot of pain, Mr. Bowles, but we've given her some strong painkillers. As long as she doesn't want to play squash or anything like that for a few weeks there should be no problem. The rib has not been pressed into the lung.'

'It was a bit of loose carpet on the stairs,' Elliott said. 'I feel bad about it, but I've been so busy with this miners' strike I didn't notice it.'

'Well, it could have been a lot worse,' the doctor said, 'houses can be dangerous places.'

'Is everyone sure they don't want a burger?' Elliott asked, as he drove away from the hospital. 'Come on, Sal, you love 'em.'

'I don't feel like it, Dad.'

'Sarah?'

'I just want to go home.'

'Okay. Are those pills working, Susan?'

'Yes.'

She sat in the back, drowsy from the strong medication. He would have no more trouble with her, now it was just a matter of winning back the girls. They would believe the story about the stairs by the time he went back to work. The three pinched faces behind him made his head start up again. He was never free of it for long these days. Flashes of guilt tried to break in and although he pushed them back his sense of power and control was evaporating. It was as if someone else had beaten Susan. Someone he didn't know, someone he could not bear to look upon. Small insistent needles probed behind his eyes. He had tried various pills from the chemist's but the pain was resilient. And it came on so quickly after he felt good, cheating him of the mood.

* * *

Rita had persuaded Davidson to open up the bar for them.

'Well, today didn't exactly work out right, did it,' Rita said, 'but we got them buckets filled despite it all.'

As The Merlin was officially closed they emptied the buckets onto the bar, showering it with coins and the odd note. They counted it.

'Must be about three hundred quid,' Davidson said, 'not bad at all.'

'Get your hands off it,' Rita said, 'it's not going in your till. In fact this drink should be on the house. These girls have been fighting the good fight.'

Davidson held up his hands.

'Okay, okay, it's on the house, but don't tell anybody. I'm letting down the reputation of the old country.'

Kathryn stayed with the group. She had not forgotten what Marge Jenkins had blurted out earlier and when Marge went to the toilet she saw her chance to talk to Rita.

'What was that about Susan's husband?' Kathryn asked. 'I didn't quite understand.'

Rita finished her half of lager and thought for a moment.

'It's Susan's business but I 'spose you might as well hear it from me, it would be more awkward for her or Edwin.'

'Why all the secrecy?'

'You assumed that Elliott was another miner, didn't you, but there are other jobs around here and he's got one.'

'So?'

'He's a pig. A copper. Boy in blue. A police officer.'

'You're joking.'

'Nope, that's why things are awkward for Susan.'

'I should say. What sort is he, does he support what she's doing with you?'

'Hardly. He doesn't even know. No, Elliott Bowles is a swine of a man now, though he seemed a normal sort of bloke years ago. At least I never saw no harm in him. But he changed when he turned his back on the village. Whether the police force done that to him or there's other reasons I wouldn't know. These days it's hard to believe that him and Edwin come from the same stock. I wouldn't like to be in Susan's shoes if Elliott finds out what happened today.'

Kathryn realised the possibilities here, that the tensions in this family triangle must be great. It partly explained Edwin's reticence. The local union leader with a policeman for a brother.

'How about the two brothers?' Kathryn asked.

'Don't talk now. They hate each other. Things wasn't too good between them before, not since their old man died, but the strike has put it all in a nutshell. I don't think they'll ever bother again. Course, Susan is in the middle of it all and she's got two lovely kids as well.'

Kathryn went up to her room anxious to write up her notes and muse on this information. Davidson had brought up a table from the bar and set in by the large bay window for a desk. A touch of late sun penetrated the room and cast a sepia hue over the valley, making her think it even more anachronistic. If the mines failed she could see little future for it. This had long been an area for London-based politicians to make empty promises over, a place where industrial progress had turned in on itself and collapsed like a lung. Yet it fascinated her. So many walking clichés lived here, evincing a strange mix of Celtic gloom and defiance.

But there were other qualities present, the burgeoning awareness of the women in Rita's group, all the more sharp for its rawness, and the single-mindedness of men like Edwin and Tom Rees. They had a kind of stubborn honesty she had forgotten could still exist, so alien was it in her world. The village was trying to cling to a way of life that was ruthlessly being taken away. She felt a little guilty that she might be using the situation here, as Edwin had suspected. Taking her research back to her lucrative jobs and preparing a eulogy for the inevitable outcome of the strike. Never to return.

Kathryn did not identify with any class other than her own, which was comfortable and educated. With liberal, professional parents every advantage which had been denied the likes of Edwin Bowles had come her way. She thought Edwin would make a great portrait, a figure to mould her piece around. The loner miner in a book-lined house, self-educated and dedicated to the cause. She laughed at her thoughts. That was the stuff of films. Edwin singing his way through his once green valley. But the man was real. His concerns and beliefs were real.

It was well into the evening when she finished writing up her notes. On one page she drew a simple chart and placed Edwin, Elliott and Susan Bowles in columns, with notes on each one. She had been handed two perfect symbols of polarised viewpoints in the brothers, and Susan was the buffer zone between them. But it could never be this simple. Already she had seen enough of Edwin to sense complexities lying beneath the surface. Tension and conflict abounded there and she guessed he may have adopted a role set out for him by the village and hidden the true man from everyone. Even himself. And his brother Elliott. Surely he must be more than the one-dimensional sod Rita described. All sorts of things might float to the surface.

* * *

Edwin heard about Susan's accident from Rita.

'She phoned me yesterday,' Rita said, 'told me she had fallen down the stairs in her house. She'll be off work for a few weeks and won't be able to drive the van. I don't know what to make of it. It happened right after our brush with the law. He was home, wasn't he?'

Rita stopped, not wanting to directly suggest that Edwin's brother was capable of beating his wife.

'Thing is, Ed,' Rita continued, 'it's awkward to go there, until Elliott goes back to work, at least. I don't suppose –'

'Out of the question, I can't go there. I don't know, Reet, even I find it hard to believe he could have done that to her, but I'll find out, as soon as I can.'

'Another thing, Kathryn knows about Elliott. It came out

Wednesday, I thought it best to tell her sooner rather than later.'

'It's a nice titbit for her. She phoned me up earlier, wants to see a picket line this afternoon. I suppose I'll have to take her, so she can assess how the natives perform.'

'Don't be so defensive or I'll be thinking you're as bad as my husband. Chauvinist, that's the posh word for it, man is a better one.'

'I'd feel the same if she was a bloke,' Edwin said, trying to convince himself.

'I'll believe you,' Rita said. 'Eh, does this phone line sound all right to you?'

'Why?'

'I don't know, I think I'm getting paranoid after that Cardiff do. I'll see you, Ed.'

Later that day Edwin walked down to The Merlin, through a village much quieter now that its children were back at school, not that they had had a complete break from their places of education. Throughout the summer holidays miners' children had been able to have their main meal at local school canteens, if they wished. That had been wrung from the authorities, at least. Edwin grinned as he thought how he would have hated that. He had been a reluctant schoolboy, always eager to get away to the woods or his own books. That was ironic, the well-read man shunning an education system that had shunned him. It was the confinement he had not liked, being made to stay amongst large groups of people. Yet he had gone against this instinct in his choice of working life, in close proximity to many other men, men who now looked to him for a lead. He was no longer sure this course had been freely taken. Perhaps he had followed a route tradition and his own vanity had mapped out for him. Being around Kathryn Peters confused him, she heightened his commitment and identification with his narrow world but she turned his thoughts towards what might have been, to other things he might have done, and the places he might have gone. Dreams.

Kathryn was in the bar with Rita.

'You are starting early, aren't you?' Edwin said.

Rita answered by raising a glass to him.

'Now you watch there's no trouble up at the pit, Ed,' Rita said, 'though I can't shout, can I?'

'Have you heard any more about Cardiff?'

'No, but Griffiths said he'll get Marge a good solicitor when she goes to court.'

'I still don't think it will come to that,' Kathryn said, acknowledging Edwin with a brief 'hello'.

'There won't be any trouble at the Top Pit,' Edwin said. 'No-one would ever scab around here.'

Kathryn drove them up to the pit, stopping several hundred yards away from the entrance.

'I don't know what you are going to learn,' Edwin said, 'you'll probably find it boring. A few men sitting around watched by the odd copper. Sometimes they have a delivery driver to question, something like that. There's a maintenance crew working in every pit and the management are still in there, though God knows what they are doing. Planning revenge, I expect.'

'It's important I see every aspect of the situation,' Kathryn said. 'I want to hear the views of the men.'

He was right. It was not an inspiring scene. Half a dozen men standing or sitting around a makeshift shelter adorned by NUM placards. Two kicked a football back and forth, their right legs swinging at it mechanically. They stopped when they saw Kathryn. Most of the village was aware of her presence now. He introduced her to the men and stood aside as she asked her questions.

The day was dull but a pleasant warmth to the air made Edwin think of his autumn garden routine. Taking down bean rows and burning off the remains of summer vegetables, the dread at the back of his mind at the thought of another winter underground. A true night world if ever there was one. He was fighting for a job that had no attraction in essence. It was the community built upon it that was important. The work itself was disgusting.

One of the younger men detached himself from the others and walked over to Edwin. Lyn Morgan was tall, sunburnt and clad in a rugby shirt, and like many of the strikers he had never looked better. He had seen more sun this year than his father had in his working life. He was the son of a man who had guided Edwin through his early coalface experiences.

'That's a good looking piece,' Lyn said, 'you've struck lucky there, Ed. Are you shagging it yet?'

He looked up at Lyn's open and as yet unscarred face and felt old.

'Am I supposed to?' he said.

'No 'spose about it,' Lyn said, 'if it's there take it and if it's not try for it anyway, that's what I say. It's not as if you're married, is it?'

Edwin remembered when Lyn's father died, disembowelled by a tram that crushed his guts against the black wall. That was twenty years ago when Lyn bawled in his pram; yet it might have been yesterday. And he was still being ribbed about women by a Morgan.

A police van pulled into the opposite lay-by.

'Aye aye' Lyn said, 'here's the pig wagon. Sometimes they send someone up, sometimes they don't. Look, when we going to do something else? We haven't followed up that crane thing and those convoys are still running down the motorway...'

'We'll talk about that in the next meeting. Go and chat to Ms Peters now, and watch your language.'

He had cut the young man off because Elliott had come into his vision. The van had deposited him on the other side of the pit entrance, and they stared at each other across the road. It was the first time they'd had a clear sight of each other since the fight.

Edwin walked across to Elliott, in an attempt to prevent him coming amongst the pickets whilst Kathryn was there. He stopped a yard away.

'You're working back here, then,' Edwin said.

'Looks like it, doesn't it?'

Elliott looked over his shoulder, to Kathryn.

'Who's that woman, and what's she doing here?'

Edwin thought it best to be frank.

'She's a lecturer from London, researching the strike.'

'Oh aye, some bra-burning lesbian is she?'

'I wouldn't know.'

'You were behind Susan working with that women's rabble, weren't you?'

'I knew nothing about it, until she told me,' Edwin said. He realised his mistake at once.

'So the bitch has been talking to you, has she? I'd like to –'

Elliott stepped forward and Edwin tensed.

'Look, calm down for Christ's sake,' he said. 'We don't have to be like this. I know I hit you, but there are other people to consider. Mam, for one.'

The muscles of Elliott's face twitched as he struggled to control himself.

'Leave our mother out of it. You'd like me to thump you here, wouldn't you, in front of all these witnesses. Ruin my career. No,

I'm going to bide my time.'

His hand went to his eye and rubbed around it.

'You're trying to break up my family, you jealous bastard. You can't get anyone for yourself, not even one of the village bimbos.'

Edwin saw there was no reasoning with his brother so he said nothing more. Part of him knew the strike was the catalyst to ignite his long smouldering differences with Elliott. Another part still did not understand how they had come to this. It wanted to cool things down, talk rationally, perhaps even go back to something akin to brotherhood. He wondered if his brother had similar divisions within him. At the moment all he offered was a black-eyed stare of malice.

Elliott stood amongst the men as provocatively as he could, with no fear for his safety. He knew them all from his schooldays.

'All right boys,' he said, 'still wasting your time, I see.'

'Christ, it's Ed's brother,' Lyn said. 'Back from the wars, are you butty?'

Elliott ignored the question and stared at Kathryn. She was nothing like he expected. He saw a tall, well dressed woman with a figure very much like Lisa's. He stood as erect as he could, willing his frame to make an impression on her. Kathryn heard what Morgan said and matched Elliott's look. This story was being delivered into her hands but she was not sure if she wanted it. The air crackled with the tension between these two men. Elliott was very good looking there was no doubt about that, but in a vacuous way. Peacock-like posture, archaic grooming and a face that betrayed a tin soldier mentality. His eyes were glazed with a darkness that almost obscured them. Edwin was framed over Elliott's shoulder, a stocky, shuffled-up man with clothes hanging randomly from him.

'Who are you, then?' Elliott asked her, adjusting the strap of his helmet.

'Kathryn Peters.'

Elliott cocked a black eyebrow and waited for more.

'I'm from London, doing some research.'

'On this lot,' Elliott said, waving a dismissive hand about him. 'On their side, are you luv?'

'That's none of your business and I'm not your "love".'

'People like you should be talking to all sides.'

'Perhaps I will, though there are plenty of people who are talking to just the police and government side.'

'What do you think of my brother then?' Elliott said. 'Fine

figure of a man, isn't he, like that Worzel Gummidge my kids watch on t.v. Edwin hasn't got any kids, hasn't got a wife either.'

'Why don't you just fuck off, Bowles,' someone muttered.

'Aye, go back to your side of the road,' another added.

Elliott grinned broadly and went back to his position, satisfied by his foray. Kathryn walked over to Edwin, who had remained detached from the other men. She could almost taste his embarrassment.

'Well, now you've met my brother,' Edwin said.

'He's very aggressive.'

'Especially when he's around me. Look, have you got what you need from the boys? I think it's best I don't hang around here.'

'Quite.'

They walked back to Kathryn's car.

'How about coffee at your place?' Kathryn asked. 'The Merlin gets a bit tiresome after a time.'

'To be lodged there is the idea of heaven for most of the men here,' Edwin said.

As Kathryn drove to the terraces Edwin wondered what questions she might ask about Elliott. He had never talked to anyone about his family before. Perhaps it was time.

'Go through to the front room,' Edwin said, as he opened his front door.

'No, I'll come into the kitchen with you,' Kathryn answered. She sat on the lone kitchen stool as Edwin busied himself with his small jar of instant. He had to hide the inevitable streak of sticky coffee down its side.

'You two are not exactly alike,' Kathryn said.

'Who? Oh, Elliott and me. But brothers are often like that, aren't they? Too much rivalry down the years.'

'You sound as if you're trying to convince yourself.'

'Maybe. It's the sticking together bit we don't conform to. When the chips are down Elliott is more hostile, not less. *Our* blood is not thicker than water. Don't ask me why.'

Having made the coffee without too much mess, he led the way to the front of the house.

Kathryn wondered that large families once lived in houses as small as Edwin's. His front room was box-shaped, not much larger than his antique kitchen, complete with antique coffee she thought as she sipped. A random stacking of books. Mainly decaying hardbacks which gave off a musty smell. Edwin sat opposite her and began to talk, without prompting. She could almost hear his tongue unlock.

'Our father died when Elliott was still in school. I had just started down the pit. Looking back, Dad going like that affected Elliott more than we thought at the time. He began to spend a lot of time with Rowena, our mother, and I think he began to see me as a father figure. He even started to rebel against me, stuff like that. I had to clout him once. Elliott went to the grammar school but didn't do that well. Passed a few 'O' Levels. Most of the time he spent playing rugby and sending for forces' brochures, army, air force, anything which had uniforms in it. Where that came from God knows, there's no military strain in the Bowles family. The old man spent his war underground. Elliott ended up joining the police force – got in no trouble. Rowena's been proud of him ever since but that just widened the gap between us, and it's been growing larger.'

'There doesn't seem to be any physical resemblance between you.'

'Beauty and the beast, eh?'

'I didn't say that.'

'Rowena says she can see a likeness. Perhaps it's right we should look so different, for we are so different the way things are now.'

'You share one thing, at least. From that short experience of Elliott I should say he's absolutely sure his views are the right ones.'

'Yes, we're an opinionated pair of bastards.'

Kathryn drank her coffee and sized Edwin up. This was the most freely he had communicated. There was a latent warmth in the man but he needed someone or something to bring it out. She wondered what her reaction might have been if Edwin's character was superimposed on Elliott's body. That might have been a man to rekindle her interest in the male sex. In the last ten years they had been a sad disappointment to her. Edwin would benefit from a different environment. He was like the many mature students she had taught from working class backgrounds. Men who arrived with a chip on the shoulder, wanting to kick at the world they sought inclusion in. Sometimes they metamorphosed into more open individuals, with a lot to give.

'Where does Elliott live?' Kathryn asked.

'Just outside the village, that modern estate up on the hill. I pointed it out to you, that day we toured the valley.'

139

'I remember. I'm surprised he hasn't moved away, thinking like he does.'

'It would have been bloody better for everyone if he had. Yes, I've wondered about that, but he did spend a lot of time with Rowena, until this strike started.'

'You often use your mother's first name, that's unusual here, surely.'

'It's something we've always done, she encouraged it after Dad died.'

'Now that I've met Elliott I'm impressed that Susan joined the women's group.'

'We all are, though God knows what strains it's putting on her marriage.'

'Rita told me that Susan had to go to hospital.'

'Aye, something happened that day you came back from Cardiff. I daren't go there, or even phone. It will only make matters worse.'

'But I can call on her. Now I've met Susan there's no reason for me not to inquire after her health.'

'I don't know about that.'

'Don't worry, I'll be discreet. I'll go now, whilst we know where Elliott is.'

With some reservation Edwin gave Kathryn the address. He was losing his self-consciousness with her and as he saw her out his eyes strayed to the line of her hips and thighs. Dreams, boyo, he whispered to himself. Just dreams.

* * *

Kathryn located the house, parked in its empty drive and rang the doorbell, gazing around her as she waited for an answer. She had been born in the genuine period housing Elliott's estate sought to ape. The mock Georgian facades and ridiculous black and white Tudor paint schemes had been the real thing for her. Her eyes fixed on a collection of gnomes in the garden opposite. Garishly painted, they depicted a working theme and carried picks and shovels. The door finally opened.

'Hello,' Kathryn said, to a disconcerted Susan, 'I was just about to go. I thought no-one was in.'

'Oh, it's you Kathryn.'

Susan was pinch-faced and frightened. She held herself stiffly and there was an air of defeat about her.

'I heard about your accident,' Kathryn said. 'I thought I'd drop by to see how you were. Edwin and Rita are concerned about you. Can I come in?'

Susan held the door open and Kathryn stepped inside.

'Come on through, then,' Susan said.

She led her to the kitchen, which looked out over the valley.

'So you are all right?' Kathryn asked.

'I cracked a rib, that's all. A stupid fall.'

'I met your husband today,' Kathryn said.

'How? What happened?'

'Nothing happened. He was on duty at the pit entrance, watching over the pickets. Edwin took me there.'

'Oh God, was there trouble, did they....?'

Susan was trembling.

'Don't get worked up. Like I said, nothing happened. We all had a brief chat, that's all.'

'You must know how things are between them now.'

'I have some idea.'

'Will you tell Rita I can't come anymore?' Susan said. 'It's just not possible now, with my job and getting the girls back and forth to school.'

'I see.'

There were a few moments of silence. Susan stirred her coffee incessantly, digging at it with a spoon.

'It's a great view,' Kathryn said, 'you can follow the curve of the river. This must be quite a change from the village.'

'I hate it here,' Susan said quickly. 'I never did think much of it but now I hate it. The people here come from all parts and I don't know any of them. All that's here is space. Look, it's very difficult for me at the moment. I should never have got involved with the women's group. It was unrealistic.'

'You don't have to explain anything to me, Susan.'

'Give me a bit more credit than that. You are here to analyse us, test out your theories on us, but when you are back in London I'll still be here, in a situation I don't know how to handle. And this village is a very small place.'

'I really don't want to pry,' Kathryn said, 'shall I just leave and tell Edwin you're all right.'

Susan began to sob, she tried to prevent it by cupping her hands to her face but only succeeded in distorting the sound.

'I'm not all right, if you must know. I have a husband whose views I detest, who has become a liar and a cheat, or perhaps has always been. I live in a house I hate and which I don't see any way out of, and I have two children to consider....'

She broke down completely making Kathryn feel awkward and helpless. The Bowles' family waters ran very deep. Kathryn placed her hand over Susan's and pressed gently.

'You didn't fall down the stairs, did you?' Kathryn said.

'No, it was him. When I came home that fund raising day he was waiting for me, and he knew all about my arrest. He laid into me like a man possessed – I couldn't believe it was happening. Things like that happen to other women, not the wives of police-men. And do you know what plagues my mind? *I* feel ashamed, not him. Ashamed I could ever stay with someone like that.'

'I'm so sorry,' Kathryn said.

'It's just that I don't know what to do,' Susan continued. 'Elliott is not the kind of man you can just walk away from, and there's nowhere for me to go anyway.'

'The fact that he is a policeman should be in your favour. I got the impression he's very much into his job, and this type of behaviour must jeopardise his career.'

'I could never tell the police about it, I'd dread what he'd do.'

'Do your girls know about this?'

'They know about the rows but they were upstairs when he attacked me. He had locked them in their playroom. That's what makes my blood run cold. It was premeditated.'

'You have friends in the village and Edwin obviously thinks a lot of you.'

'Yes, but that doesn't change anything. Edwin makes it worse in a way, being so different to Elliott.'

'Don't be ashamed,' Kathryn said, 'about marrying Elliott or what he has done to you. I've lived with a few men myself and it's not until then that they show themselves in all their glory.'

There was the sound of another car pulling into the drive.

'Oh Jesus,' Susan said, 'that's Elliott. He pops home at all times now he's back in the village.'

'Don't worry, I've just come to see how you are, remember. Dry your eyes quickly.'

Elliott smiled broadly at Kathryn when he entered the room.

'I thought I recognised the car,' Elliott said. 'Last time I saw it my brother was in it. So, we meet again, Miss Peters.'

He stood behind Susan's chair and stroked her shoulders, pressing into their contours with his large hands.

'I came to see how Susan was,' Kathryn said, 'I heard about her fall.'

'Aye, she's always rushing down the stairs, takes no notice when I tell her about it. Do you want another coffee, a drink perhaps?'

Kathryn saw the surprise on Susan's face. She had expected a very different entrance and Kathryn herself was taken aback at the change in character. The belligerent, mocking man of a few hours ago had been transformed. If she knew nothing about him she might have been attracted by him now that he had changed out of his uniform, falling into the trap of looking at the handsome mask rather than what lay behind it. Her intelligence had not prevented her from doing this in the past. She felt Elliott's eyes probing her, checking out each part of her body, sifting through her clothing to what lay underneath. Susan looked twenty years older than him and Kathryn pitied her.

'Yes, Susan is getting over it well,' Elliot said, 'she'll be her old self again in another week. Then she can concentrate on being a mother again and working down the school. That's a worthwhile little job and I'm proud of her. Are you sure you don't want a drink, Kathryn? How about joining us for dinner?'

He slipped into first name usage very smoothly and Kathryn wanted to be away from him, but this thought was accompanied by a more uncomfortable one, that she was abandoning Susan. She could only hope that her visit might have instilled caution into Elliott's head.

'No thanks,' she said, 'I have to be off.'

She tried to put as much support as she could into her parting glance at Susan, but once Elliott shut the door on her Susan was on her own. Elliott showed her out, guiding her familiarly towards the front door. How she would have liked to turn and kick the man in the balls, tell him what a bastard he was, but she was powerless.

'I'll move the car for you,' Elliott said, 'and don't forget, that offer to talk about our side of things still stands, as long as you don't use my name.'

'I'll bear it in mind,' she said.

Elliott touched her again as she got into her car.

'Do that,' he said, 'you might find I surprise you. I don't doubt

Edwin and company have been eager to tell tales about me, but perhaps I can prove them wrong. We could meet for a drink.'

Elliott swung his car into the road and offered her a final smile as she left.

Kathryn phoned Edwin later that evening and confirmed what they had feared.

'So, he has sunk to that, has he?' Edwin asked. 'I'd like to get Susan away from him, but how?'

'Yes, I felt helpless when I was there,' she said, 'but it's no one's business but their own, at the end of the day. Susan must make her own decisions and I think she will ask for help if she wants it.'

'I feel like bringing out into the open what he's like, telling his bosses.'

'Susan doesn't want that.'

'It should have been me,' Edwin said, 'not Susan. Elliott has been itching to hurt someone since I slapped him in our mother's kitchen.'

'I didn't know that.'

'I'm not proud of it but that's the way things have gone between us. Thanks for going along there, Kathryn. Perhaps I'll see you in The Merlin tomorrow.'

Kathryn put down the phone more concerned than ever. She knew that once men started beating their wives they found it hard to stop, and what Edwin had told her exacerbated matters. She could not imagine Elliott's passive acceptance of Edwin's blow. He was not a man to let anything like that rest so his assault of Susan might be just a warm-up. It would be prudent if she detached herself from this situation. She had enough information and experience of how the strike was being conducted in the valley to write effectively about it, and there was much to do in London, with the new term only weeks away.

* * *

Edwin's burden of worries was growing larger. The miners were balked by the forces ranged against them, and what passed for his family was savaging itself. It was with some relief that he chaired the unofficial gathering in Davidson's back room the next night. This was a world he understood. He had bowed to the pressure to tackle the problem of the coal convoys feeding the coastal power stations. Griffiths knew nothing about the meeting and would have prevented it if he had. Most of the men present had been bailed after the Port Talbot affair, but looking around at their faces, Edwin saw that they were ready for further action, and did not care overmuch about the consequences. Even Tom Rees, his ally in steady counselling, had changed.

'We've had boots ground against our necks since this business started,' Tom said, as they stood at the bar. 'If it's a question of fighting on we might as well use the same tactics as the other side.' Tom lowered his voice. 'You and I know it's pretty hopeless but what else can we do? The cards were fixed long before Scargill called the strike, that's obvious now, but I don't want to look back and think I just lay down and took it.'

Edwin felt obliged to support Tom, and put consequences out of his mind. Whatever happened he would not suffer to the same extent as the married men, he had no mortgage to pay off, no kids' futures to worry about, and no wife to disappoint.

He let the men talk freely, noting the return of some of the enthusiasm lost in the wake of the debacle of the cranes. They had tempered this with an appreciation of the odds stacked against them. They knew they could not rely on much tangible support from other British workers and were fighting a lone fight. Yet this had the effect of pressing them together into an even closer unit. He wished Kathryn was there, to witness this solidarity.

'Where's Kathryn?' he asked Davidson.

'Down Cardiff, I think.'

'Has she said how much longer she is staying?'

'No, but I'm surprised she's still here. People like her usually have a quick look round then buzz off sharpish, back to what they call civilisation.'

A date was set in late September for Edwin's group to lend their support to other activists who planned a major attempt to stop the convoys.

'You know that we all have to be back in Afan Magistrates' Court the week after, don't you,' Edwin said. 'Everyone sure of the risks they are taking?'

A solid 'aye' settled matters.

* * *

September weather fluctuated from echoing the fine summer to the grey, dank days endemic to the valley. Edwin was caught on the hillside by a squall that got up from nowhere, a thin drizzle insinuated its way through his light clothing and made his stick feel cold in his clammy hands. It was his first walk for some time, a few snatched hours that ended with a dash back. He decided to stop at Rowena's when he took his stick back to the shed, to dry off and ease his conscience with a visit. He had not seen her since Elliott had been back for he did not trust his tongue. It would be easy to pour out his true thoughts of his brother when he had to endure Rowena's blind praise of him.

She was how he expected, how he had always seen her. Hunched up over the open fire, clicking at her knitting and directing the odd word to the cat. He wondered how she had ever brought them up, if one could describe his childhood as an upbringing. It was more a loose period of house sharing. It was hard to remember Rowena ever doing much with them. She had sometimes cried off from their rare holiday day trips with a headache or other ailments, leaving their overworked father to traipse around with his sons on his own. Yet she had always been in the house, to put food on their table at the right times and clothe them to a slightly better standard than the village average.

Rowena's lack of involvement was on the emotional side. Edwin felt she had never given much of herself, not to him at any rate. It was as if husband and son had been happenings that came upon her, and had nothing to do with her own volition. Even her fondness for her grandchildren was passive, Edwin could not remember her walking up to the new estate more than a few times.

Rowena inclined her head as he entered.

'You're a stranger,' she said, 'and a wet one.'

'Hello Mam. I was out for a walk and got caught.'

'I can see that. Put the kettle on, make yourself some tea.'

He made the tea and brought in a tray, beckoning the cat onto his lap as he sat down.

'How old is this thing?' Edwin asked, gouging the loose fur around the cat's neck.

'Must be fourteen, at least. She's an old woman, like me.'

'You're not that old. Had any visitors lately?'

'Only her next door, and I could do without that. A woman with too much nose, even for this place. I haven't seen much of

146

your brother but then he's busy, isn't he? I'm right enough on my own.'

The room was a haven of quiet which should have appealed to him but in this house it meant a deadening of the senses, with few good memories to counteract the atmosphere.

'How is this strike business going then?' Rowena asked. 'I don't know what your father would have thought of it. It didn't get them anywhere in the old days.'

Edwin would have liked just one gesture of support from his mother, even at this late date. What Elliott had been offered throughout his life. It was always why are you reading books, bothering with that union, walking out in all weathers?

'It's going to go on a lot longer,' he answered, 'through the winter.'

Rowena's ears had already lost interest. Edwin took a closer look at her. Her age would have been difficult for a stranger to estimate, between sixty and seventy was the safest bet. She had settled into a sedentary mass, overweight but of a size that matched her armchair and seemed right. Impervious to illness and unknown to local doctors. Edwin wondered how long she might carry on. He had a dread thought of trying to sort out the house with Elliott, perhaps fighting from room to room whilst their mother was laid out in her bedroom. She would die intestate, refusing point blank to make a will. 'Sort it out when I'm gone' were her final words on the matter.

'Do you know about Susan's accident?' he asked.

'Aye, Elliott phoned. That girl should be more careful, rushing around all the time. Seems the whole world is rushing around.'

But not in here. He felt like saying that cholera had broken out in the village, the pit had sunk into the ground and dogs ate babies in the streets, to see if he could get a reaction. But no, Rowena's bland mentality was an institution, and could not be breached. Not now.

He began to steam as the fire warmed him, and Rowena dozed, her cup and saucer balanced precariously on the arm of her chair. Edwin put down the cat, quietly removed the crockery and took himself home, filled with the usual vague dissatisfaction a visit to his mother brought on. His presence was never encouraged. Rowena exuded a certainty that she did not need anyone, and that saddened him. As the rain turned heavy and swept down off the hills to gust along narrow streets he mused on the rum bunch that were the Bowles family. Perhaps they were all losers and the die cast a long time ago.

* * *

Wednesday, the twenty-sixth of September was the date chosen for a major attempt to disrupt the movement of the coal convoys. These were now seen as the most serious threat to the strike, a running sore that festered with the anger and humiliation of the miners. Transport companies had taken full advantage of the weighted laws to frustrate the strike whilst lining their pockets with the fat profits available. There were more than a hundred trucks travelling between Port Talbot and Llanwern, with little hindrance from pickets. They had heavy police protection, kept in military formation and slip roads were often closed while they were running. To see these Juggernaut trucks laden with coal incensed men and the frustration caused by their hands being tied incensed them even more. Unlike many British steelworks Llanwern relied exclusively on local coal, drawn from the five pits near to it. If it was forced to shut down it might never re-open, threatening the jobs of thousands of miners. They were caught in this dilemma, yet when Edwin looked around him at the increasingly bitter faces of men he worked and lived with, he knew that restraint was weakening. The convoy was being increased to 130 trucks, many driven by Transport Union members hired by English firms on the Welsh borders, whose bosses would become millionaires in the course of the strike, whose drivers taped their wage packet details to the windscreens to taunt the pickets, knowing full well they were cosseted by the police.

How could Edwin tell them to stomach this injustice when his own gorge rose? He was hardening daily. Perhaps he was becoming an extremist, if extremism meant the inability to control oneself in the face of great provocation. At this time in his life it felt normal. And right.

The convoy trucks were loaded at Port Talbot, the coal scooped out of boats by the cranes they had tried to immobilise. It was decided to concentrate their attack at this end of the motorway before the trucks had a chance to take on speed. Once again, men travelled down from the valleys to the coast, hoping that the element of surprise would be with them. At least this time Edwin knew he would not be higher than a road bridge.

To coincide with a massed picket at the steelworks entrance, men would be stationed at strategic points along the motorway, on bridges and roadside verges. Many would have pockets filled with missiles. Edwin knew this but had said nothing about it. He saw the danger of real injuries occurring whilst the instigators of the convoys would be well away from the front line. Like all generals.

Rita had let loose her husband again. Jenkins sat on the floor of the van, behind Edwin's seat, humming to himself in the gloom. He was calm and his tongue was still. All the men were quiet. The boyish excitement of their first incursion had been replaced with an awareness of the forces ranged against them. The strike was slipping away and men like Jenkins now wanted to inflict damage and be blind to the consequences. Edwin did not blame any of them. They were all trying to hold onto self respect.

Edwin's men deployed around a motorway bridge, close to the slip road the convoy would use. They were joined by men from the other mining valleys, about a hundred in all. It was cold enough in the early morning for them to clap their hands together and cup roll-up cigarettes against the wind. The inadequate clothing of earlier engagements had been replaced by heavy donkey jackets and boots. Bruised bodies had learnt from the long summer. A few men wore crash helmets in shabby mimic of their opponents.

Edwin leant carefully over the parapet of the bridge, able to handle this modest height. He shared his flask of tea with Tom.

'Christ, I think you'd bring a flask to your own funeral,' Tom said. 'It won't be long now.'

'No. This is a bit different from the cranes do, isn't it? We had a solid plan then, but now, look at that lot down there.' He pointed to the clusters of men either side of the road. 'Ready to ambush the convoy. Like bloody bandits. This is what we have come to.'

'No, this is what we've been forced to.'

There was a chipping sound, metal striking against stone. Edwin looked cross the bridge to see Jenkins and others trying to raise curbing stones from the pavement.

'Go and stop that, Tom,' he said. 'Something that heavy will crash right through the roof of a truck. They're only made of fibreglass.'

Tom walked over to Jenkins as Edwin's attention was caught by something else. The sounding of horns, the type he had heard in the American films of his youth, husky, wheezing air horns that blasted the quiet. He saw lights emerge out of the half-light of dawn. Police motor-cyclists acted as outriders for the convoy and behind them came Landrovers, heavily reinforced with crash bars and steel meshed windows.

'Get down everyone,' Edwin shouted, 'and let the front lot pass.'

Men ducked down behind the parapet and flattened themselves into the grass verges. The trucks passed under the bridge, almost close enough for Edwin to touch their roofs. They were huge vehicles, the type used on the hated opencasts. With their illicit loads gleaming, their chunky, oversized tyres and filthy, obscured exteriors they looked very menacing, and they seemed to stretch in a line to infinity. There was no need for him to give any orders. After a dozen trucks had passed under the bridge the men below jumped up, raining stones and nuts and bolts at drivers' cabins. Men on the bridge threw or dropped whatever they had brought with them. A truck windscreen shattered and its driver swerved across the road, causing the vehicles behind to break sharply. A shower of coal slewed over the road, raising a cheer from the miners. Police sirens sounded as escort vehicles raced to the scene. Jenkins struggled with the curbing stone he had continued to dig out, raised it up to his chest like a weight lifter, and let it drop over the side of the bridge. He did this nonchalantly with no prior sighting. The stone struck the damaged truck squarely, crashing through the cabin roof, but not on the driver's side. The convoy had been halted and the miners cheered anew their initial success.

There was a sudden influx of police. Several vans and Landrovers disgorged officers in riot gear, who immediately closed with the miners on the motorway verges. There was no attempt to reason or talk on either side. Men went down under the batons and shields of policemen. Others managed to grapple officers to the ground. For once they were not hopelessly outnumbered. Jenkins ran down from the bridge to join the fray, charging into the police head down. Edwin could feel the man's happiness from thirty yards away.

'This is going to get hot,' Tom shouted. 'Look, there are more vans coming.'

Two police vans sped up the slip road towards the bridge and policemen burst from them to rush at the men on the bridge. Edwin pushed his way out of trouble and made his way down to the road, where he thought he would be less of a target. Jenkins was being held by two men and pummelled by another but was exacting his own damage by kicking out with his steel capped boots, yelling all the while with joyous incoherency. His bulging eyes caught Edwin's and he knew he had to help the man.

'Edwin, get these bastards off me,' he shouted.

So, he would join the violent men, a split second decision that caught hold of him and drove him on. One that had been coming since the strike began. There was no other way to go. Edwin kicked at one of the men restraining Jenkins and heard him gasp, but he did not relinquish his hold around Jenkins's neck. He closed with him, pulling at his helmet and working his fist under it into the man's face. I'm assaulting a police officer, he thought. He had the man down and Jenkins was free, throwing the other policeman away from him and wrestling his baton from him with great strength.

'They're not fighting boys in fucking daps with me,' he bellowed, seconds before he was struck in the face by another stick. His nose disintegrated but this did not slow him down. He lurched around, slashing at anyone blue and whilst Jenkins was on his feet there was a a chance that they might win the day. The police saw this too and Jenkins was finally overwhelmed by four officers. They managed to carry him, a limb each, into a van, pounding him with their sticks until he lay quiet.

Now that the police had grouped together into a formation, they were gaining control, herding miners into a knot in a smaller version of their Yorkshire tactics. More bloodied men were being thrown into the backs of vans. Edwin blocked blows as he moved through the fighting bodies, glad of his multi-layered clothing.

'Come on,' Tom shouted in Edwin's ear, 'this has gone too far. Let's get out of it while we can. With other men they broke away from the police and scrambled back up the motorway banking. Many were bailed men who sought to avoid another arrest. Edwin regained the bridge with Tom and it was their good luck that no police officers had been left there. They had all joined the fighting mass that he now looked down on. He felt he was viewing a film on a living, three dimensional screen, watching things that happened in other countries, in Chile or South Africa, anywhere but here, in safe Wales. He took a last look before heeding Tom's pleas to get away. A figure caught his eye, a figure he knew despite its disguise of helmet and riot gear. Edwin wondered that they had not found each other earlier but perhaps it was not yet time, despite their paths being increasingly crushed into one.

'Come on, Ed, for Christsake,' Tom urged, dragging him by the arm.

They ran over fields to the lane where their vans were hidden. Amazingly, these had escaped police attention, and they were away in minutes.

'My brother was there,' Edwin gasped.

'Bloody hell, are you sure?'

'Aye.'

'Well, that's us fucked, then.'

'I'm not sure he saw me, but even if he did he won't say anything.'

'What do you mean? Of course he will, as things stand.'

'No, he won't. I'm sure of it. It's too hard to explain right now, but trust me, we'll hear nothing from him. Get us home as quick as you can and come down the valley by the mountain road, through the forestry. We'll all have to give each other alibis – all that got away.'

'I can't believe that back there,' Tom muttered. 'We stopped that convoy, anyway.'

'For half an hour maybe. Now we'll have all the animal and thug stories about us in the papers. Those crooked bastards in control will be rubbing their hands and cheeping I told you so. But what's new about that?'

'Right enough, but perhaps some of them truck drivers will have second thoughts now.'

'I'm sure they will, Tom.'

Edwin did not have the heart or the energy to point out to Tom that there were many drivers available. When he saw the black line of trucks coming out of the gloom he had felt like a native of the old American Plains, powerless to stop railways ploughing change into his world. He too ran around metal monsters throwing ineffective missiles, waiting for his turn to be shot.

'We have to keep going,' Edwin said, to all the men in the van, the battered remnants of the morning's action.

'You're indomitable, Ed,' Tom said proudly, 'indomitable.'

They regained the village without incident and Tom dropped him off at his house, before speeding off to his own, where his wife would swear he had been all morning.

Edwin sank down into his armchair and the silence of his home welcomed him back. There were few children at his end of the street, just old people drifting through their last days. Even Saturdays were quiet. Retired miners did not last too long as pensioners, many went within five years of their release from the pit, used-up men with lungs like the dust bags of vacuum cleaners. Their widows abounded in the village, some living a further twenty years past their husbands.

His thoughts turned inwards. He had fought to preserve a way of life that ruined men's health, a fight that came naturally to him. But where was it leading him? The books that surrounded him were now accusers, and each row he scanned made him question himself. His character had been moulded by a series of antitheses which had not been tested before. He had a built-in suspicion, antagonism even, towards those formally educated, yet books were his backbone. The arrival of Kathryn Peters had tested this bias. He diligently represented working men but knew their frailties only too well, for every Tom there was a Jenkins. His was not a romantic socialism, that was a middle class ailment. If some force took the village up and cast it down in Surrey, gave it clean, well paid jobs and spacious housing, would his people reject this lifestyle and trail back to the valley? No, only fools like himself would do this. He was a die-hard who had nothing of his own to die for. The '74 strike had been won with little fuss in the valley. This was the test that counted but it was time to think past it. His job might last another two years at most. Talk of closure had been rife at the Top Pit for years. They would be moved down the valley to another pit until that too closed.

The phone rang. It jumped to life on the table beside him, squawking ten times for his company before he answered it.

'So, you're back, are you, you bastard?'

It was his brother's voice.

'I'm glad you got away,' Elliott said, 'we arrested forty of your cronies but I'm glad you weren't one of them. I want you for myself.'

Elliott's voice was strange, a distorted quiver.

'What, don't you have anything to say to your little brother?'

Before he answered Edwin thought of Susan and the girls. Care was needed.

'What are you talking about?' he said, keeping his voice as steady as he could.

'Don't piss me around. You know I saw you, but I don't care a fuck about that. You're just a prat playing losers' games.'

'What do you care about, Elliott? I don't know you anymore.'

'Climbing on your high horse, are you? Jesus, you're a smug bastard, always were, and you never did know me, pal. When you hit me in Mam's kitchen the penny finally dropped. We have nothing as brothers, that's just an accident of birth.'

'Don't you think this has gone far enough?'

'Getting the wind up, are you, afraid of what I might do to you?'

'You don't scare me, as you said, you're my little brother. You can never change that.'

This was not a wise thing to say. He knew that if Elliott was in the room he would be at him now, and there would be a resolution to their conflict. But it was true, he was not afraid of him. In fact he knew he would always have his measure, despite the difference in size. It was what he might do to others, what he had done to Susan, which was his real fear.

'It's been a nice little chat,' Elliott said. 'I'm marking your card, boy. It won't be long now, not long at all.'

The phone went dead. Reconciliation would be even harder. If not impossible. The Bowles men had dug a hole, grubbed it out over the years with their stubborn hands until it lay deep and dark, with an invitation to fall into it. Edwin had run twice, from the cranes and the convoy, perhaps he should make it a hat trick of flight and take himself away. Let Elliott have the victory, for the sake of Susan and her daughters.

He walked around his small front room considering this, glancing out at the browning hills and sucking in air between his teeth. No, he could not do this, his pride was firmly rooted and as selfish as Elliott's malignancy. Stress pricked at him and he thought of his two escapes, the hills and his books. The former was pulling him and he put on a coat and prepared to leave the house. Walking would not solve anything but it was all he knew.

Someone knocked the front door. Cautiously he peered around a curtain to see Kathryn looking at him. He let her in.

'I've heard what happened this morning,' Kathryn said. 'I've had Rita Jenkins on Davidson's phone. You kept that quiet.'

Edwin shrugged.

'I haven't seen you for a while,' he said, 'and the less people who knew about it the better.'

'So, you're acting as a lone wolf now. I was with Griffiths last night. He was worried about things like this happening.'

'He would. White collar against blue, when you come down to it. Do you think I was wrong to take part?'

'I don't think I've got the right to pass an opinion.'

'Diplomatic as ever. Have a seat, I'll get you coffee.'

His jar of instant had finally given out and he was not a man to think much ahead with his groceries.

'It'll have to be tea,' he shouted from the kitchen.

He took a tray into the front room, having found some biscuits which did not look too stale. Kathryn was sitting in his favourite chair. She always looked good, no matter what the weather or time of day. He was almost used to her now.

'Rita's husband was arrested,' Kathryn said. 'Rita is enraged but she expected it, she says.'

'Jenkins went down with one purpose in mind,' Edwin said, 'a lot did.'

'Was it very violent? The radio is talking about a battle.'

'Hah, the battle of the convoy. Sounds like good stuff for modern Welsh folklore. Yes, it was a bit hairy.'

Kathryn was staring at his hands and he realised he had not washed or changed. He stood there bloodied.

'God, are you hurt?' Kathryn said, standing up.

'No, nothing to worry about.'

'I never thought you would get involved in anything like this,' Kathryn said.

'I'm not sure how to take that,' Edwin said.

'I mean you are too careful, too aware of what the consequences might be.'

Edwin smiled and sat down himself.

'That's a kind way of putting it. Perhaps I've been too cautious in my time, missing the boat. But please Kathryn, no research today.'

Normally she might have ignored this request and developed a subtle line of questioning, but this time she thought better of it for she had come to tell Edwin she was returning to London. Time was pressing and common sense had finally over-ridden her interest in the Bowles family. If it was about to tear itself apart it was best she was not in the midst of it. She was an interloper despite the bridges she had built with Rita's group, and interlopers were easy targets for all sides.

Kathryn had grown fond of Edwin and sensed that he was tolerant of her presence now. His blunt honesty was so apparent it was almost ingenuous but it still impressed her. She had looked for signs that he might be bogus, but there was no side to him.

'What will you do when it's over?' Kathryn asked.

'It'll never be over for the likes of me. The strike will end, yes, but the questions it's raised will still be valid, they have been for centuries. For ever, maybe. I suppose I'll continue to ask them, but I'm not sure in what way.'

'Do you see a change of direction for yourself?' Kathryn asked, sensing that Edwin wanted to talk.

Edwin hunched his shoulders.

'I don't know where my place will be. Most of the men will take the redundancy money on offer and evaporate. I'll be due a lot of money myself, as a twenty-five year man. See, I'm falling into the trap already. It will be two years wages, that's all, and after that a drift into poverty for most of the men. That or some Mickey Mouse job.'

'Have you thought about going to college? You could get in easily as a mature student. I'd help you.'

'Nah, I wouldn't fit in – wouldn't want to fit in, to be frank.'

'You can't be sure of that and who says you have to, anyway? Take what you want from the system, it might be a watershed for you. Christ, you're only forty, that's not ancient.'

'No, but it's a set age. I don't know, I have a lot to see out here.'

'Why don't you come up to my college in a few weeks, when the new year has started. Have you ever been on a campus?'

'No.'

Suddenly Edwin felt shy. He glanced at Kathryn whilst pretending to concentrate on his tea. She was so elegant. Most of the women he knew looked like lumpy peardrops. Stress lines had not been carved into her face and he doubted they ever would be.

'Getting away would be difficult,' he said, 'but I'll think about it.'

A police car went by outside. He tensed and waited for it to stop, but it kept on.

'All the boys have alibis,' he said, 'if the police do come.'

'I'll say you've been with me all morning,' Kathryn said.

'No, don't get involved. It's all right anyway, I won't hear any more about it, not officially at least.'

156

'How are you so sure?'

'I just am. So, you are going back.'

'Yes, my bag is in the car. I've said my goodbyes to Davidson and Rita and whoever was in The Merlin at the time. I'm sorry I can't see Susan before I go.'

'You're best out of that, though I'm sure she appreciates your help. As do I. Things will settle down there after the strike finishes.'

He lied and Kathryn knew it. It was certain that matters would worsen in the Bowles family.

'So, what have you learned from us, Doctor Peters?' he asked.

'I'm afraid I might sound patronising if I say anything,' Kathryn said.

'Go on, spit it out, I'm interested, and it might be the last chance we get to talk.'

Kathryn saw that the taciturn man of a few weeks ago had changed somewhat.

'The women have been great here,' she said. 'They don't seem to suffer from the same complexes as some of the men. I haven't met a woman who feels inferior because she is Welsh and lives in a mining community. They recognise my difference but don't make me feel awkward, I'm treated as an equal and nothing more.'

'And us men?'

It was Kathryn's turn to shrug.

'The ones that have resented me the most are the most fearful. They see their way of life crumbling, their women usurping their authority. Wales is a different country, no doubt about that, but I've seen this in other mining areas. I think it is a question of coal not race.'

Kathryn coloured and came to a halt.

'Sweeping statements with the benefit of a fortnight's observation,' she murmured.

'That's all you are likely to have, isn't it? I'm surprised you talk of Wales in the context of this valley. I've always thought we are far from "Wales" in this village. You won't find much affinity with nationhood around here, or anywhere else in the valleys, except when we're playing England at rugby of course. We're all boyos then. No, amongst the men I've worked with interest in anything Welsh varies from nil to a real disdain of the language and the people who speak it. Perhaps it's more of that fear you talk about.'

'How do you feel?'

'Confused. I tried to learn Welsh for a while, in my early twenties, and I read my way through our history. The real history, not the bits and pieces of mythology they tossed us at school. That fired my nationalistic side, you might say.'

'But you don't speak Welsh now, do you?'

'No, it fizzled out. I didn't know anyone who spoke the language and I wasn't sure of my own position anyway. Part of me wanted to jump right into it, be swallowed by my roots. Welsh was the language of my grandparents. The whole valley was Welsh-speaking not much more than a century ago. But the other part of me took the standard socialist view. That it was an archaic language dying on its feet, hijacked by the middle classes for their own ends. Even my grandfather said that the language should have been allowed to die out. We might have been better off as a country without it. Look at Scotland, you won't find much Gaelic there, but they've regained so much more than us. Same with Ireland. There's no language to divide them.'

Edwin stopped, somewhat abashed as his rush of words.

'Going on a bit, aren't I?' he mumbled.

'Not at all.'

Kathryn glimpsed a different man, one bursting for an audience. She sensed he had a wealth of views and ideas locked up inside him, trapped there by his own character and the isolation his intelligence reinforced.

'You really should come up and look around the college,' she said. 'We have plenty of mature students.'

'I haven't been anywhere in ten years.'

'Then it's time you did. You might get a different perspective on life here.'

Kathryn got up to leave feeling that Edwin opening up like this might be a step forward for him. It might be the spur he needed. She hated to see potential wasted.

'It's a change not to talk about the strike,' Edwin said.

He showed her out to the car. On his front step she brushed his cheek with her lips.

'Look after yourself,' she said, 'you're an endangered species.'

The Volvo's horn sounded as she drove down the street. Three short, confident toots. Edwin watched the car disappear before going back in. Back to his small, enclosed world. He looked at his blood-smeared hands and went up to the bathroom.

* * *

Elliott saw his brother early in the motorway engagement. His first reaction was to rush over to him as something inside cried out for violent union. But he forced himself to keep away from him, and even prayed Edwin would not be arrested. He wanted a much more personal retribution. When it was obvious that Edwin would get away he enjoyed letting his brother see him.

It was coincidence that he was at the scene at all, a last minute call for reinforcements from a neighbouring force. With Edwin gone he contented himself with wading into his fellow villagers. The miners knew who was knocking them senseless. It was a good way of breaking links. These were not his people and he wanted no part of them. When the strike was over he would move to another area. Where Susan would behave, and his life would move forward again.

As he watched Edwin clamber up the grassy incline his thoughts on him became clearer, despite the pounding in his head. It was increasingly easy to behave as he did. Lisa, and his brother's slap, were swords that pricked at his pride until it festered. He convinced himself he was still the captain of his ship and that all around was under control. He would soon be able to strike out at the black pain that gnawed at him and remove it with his fists.

Elliott was home by early afternoon. Susan was alone, the girls staying with a school friend. He was glad he had her to himself. She was afraid to be around him now and he sensed her fear. He liked it. It was part of her rehabilitation process, her coming back to heel. He knocked on his own door, to make Susan answer it.

'I've had fun this morning,' he said, pushing past her. 'Get me some food on. I'm going up for a shower.'

He examined himself in the full length mirror in the bathroom. One small bruise where his shield had been pushed against his shoulder. Nothing more. He might get back into the gym in the winter, tone up his muscles. He flexed them, and smiled at himself.

Susan had something ready for him when he came back down, clad in his new black tracksuit.

'You're quiet,' Elliott said, eating his food as noisily as possible. 'Not still moping, are you?'

159

When Susan did not answer he thumped his fist on the table, making pasta jump and Susan shudder.

'Well?'

She shook her head, murmuring 'no'.

'Christ, you're never satisfied. I'm back, aren't I, no more going north. We'll have no more nonsense and things will get better. Just sort yourself out.'

It was comforting to raise his voice. The tension in his head was released for a moment. It was increasingly easy to behave this way. Whatever was rushing him on he no longer wanted to fight it.

Susan watched her husband slobber over his food. Being with him now was like floating into a dismal void. His wild eyes were wilder, and there was a stiffness in the way he walked. As if he was permanently on parade. He even seemed oblivious to the girls' increasing fear of him.

Kathryn had phoned Susan earlier, to say goodbye. It had increased her panic, and she envied Kathryn's freedom. For days her head had reeled with tales of battered women. She remembered television programmes she had watched on the subject. How she had always wondered why they did not get away. How she fought down the feeling that these were hopeless women for having tied themselves to such men. She saw it very differently now, and knew if Elliott was given the excuse he would beat her again. They always did. And he was capable of anything now. Some control mechanism in him had snapped and his mind had decayed to the point where it could justify his actions.

Susan edged away into the kitchen where the glint of a bread knife caught her eye. She thought to take it up, run into the dining room and plunge it in his chest. Women who did this often received only short prison sentences, but their victims were not policemen with exemplary records. Her hands strayed to the knife, fingers running along its keen blade. Its touch chilled her and she knew such action was beyond her, whatever Elliott might do.

He came up behind her so quietly, encircling her with his arms. She fought against the impulse to go limp in his grasp, to play dead like some small, wild animal. That would only annoy him. Her relationship with Elliott had disintegrated to this, trying to second guess his actions, trying to prevent violence by offering submissiveness.

'All that action this morning,' Elliott murmured, 'it's made me feel randy. I think we'll go upstairs.'

160

It was what she had dreaded most. The celibacy of the last few months had been her sole refuge.

It was rape, though she did not fight. He threw her onto the bed, peeling off her clothes, snapping whatever would not yield readily to his hands. Then he was on her, like a pig snuffling for truffles. She thought she would lose consciousness as he thrust his way into her. This was worse than rape. Elliott enjoyed her, her revulsion was not lost on him, and he enjoyed this too. If she had fought his triumph would have been complete.

This sets the seal on my comeback, Elliott thought, as he lay back and gouged Susan's face with his hand. Playfully, but with a suggestion of pain. I have regained total control over my wife. He fell asleep and marked it with a deep snoring.

Susan watched him as she carefully sat up. His black head was buried in the pillow with a hint of a smile on his face. Like this he looked innocent and boyish. There was still a pink softness in his cheeks that had stayed with him since childhood. When his eye lids were closed the malice in him was not apparent. Susan saw the man that might have been, the man she thought she had married. When the lids were open they revealed eyes which could not hide the thoughts she knew so well. They betrayed the malicious patterns of his brain.

Susan got up, took some clothes into the girls' bedroom and dressed quietly. She was outwardly calm but panic surged close to her surface. This coupling with Elliott would be the last. She tried to stop her nerve fleeing by digging her fingers into her wrists, adding to the marks Elliott had made. If she did not leave him now she never would. She could not kill him or take her own life and leave the girls to him, though such thoughts had flicked through her mind. But she had to get away. For refuge she had the choice of Edwin, Rowena or her father, a trio of scant possibilities, and all within a stone's throw of her hateful husband. Kathryn had left a phone number with Rita and Susan thought of this but Kathryn was somewhere on the motorway. All her ideas crashed down blind alleys but this did not stop her from packing a case for the girls, taking the car and driving to where her daughters were staying.

* * *

Edwin looked through the morning newspaper. He had bathed and changed, and the conversation with Kathryn had calmed him though Griffiths had phoned him to say he was on his way.

As the strike had progressed Edwin saw less of Griffiths. He had tended to keep away from the union offices as much as possible, more so as his own road became violent and personal. His paper told him that the power workers were refusing to help the miners, which came as no surprise. Workers were splitting into separate groups, divided and weakened as they bowed to government pressure or bribes. The book's oldest tricks were still the most effective but he was still amazed by how quickly a way of life was being dismantled. That damned woman had seen the way and had struck whilst his lot dithered. Rapid direct action supported by a backdrop of lies aimed at people's basest instincts was all it took.

The Labour Party Conference was starting next Monday. He had almost forgotten about it. After the events of the last few weeks it seemed irrelevant. Never had he felt more on the outside of things, that whatever he did would be no use. This defeatism was stealthy and pervasive. He saw how miners returned to work, how they bent their heads and talked about having good reasons. There was almost a comfort in saying 'to hell with it' and accepting one's fate but such thoughts left him as soon as he let Griffiths in. There was something about the man, supposedly on his side, that left him cold. He determined to fight on in his own way.

Griffiths tapped his shoulder and went into the front room.

'Haven't seen you for a while,' Griffiths said, 'but you've certainly been busy. Things like this convoy business have got to stop, Edwin.'

He did not answer as Griffiths sat down unasked. He glanced at the paper and shook it.

'It's an important week for us coming up,' Griffiths said, 'with the conference.'

What is the man talking about, Edwin thought. The Labour Party? They had just about washed their hands of the strike. They simpered and made apologies for the picketing and their leader took pains to distance himself. Their opposition to the government was so weak it was shameful. The last word spilt from Edwin's lips.

'What's that?' Griffiths asked.

'Just thinking aloud. You know how things are, there will be more violence before the end. Some of the boys think they have nothing to lose now.'

'And you agree with them?'

'I understand it.'

'I've had a lot of flak already about what happened on the M4. It doesn't help our cause.'

'Blotted my copybook, have I? Come on Mr Griffiths, it's heads you lose, tails you lose, we know that.'

He emphasised the 'Mr' to distance himself from Griffiths, and noticed that his guest was willing to deal in surnames now. Edwin knew he would be going no further in his union career, which was ironic considering the temperament of their president. But this suited him, he had always seen it as a part of his work underground anyway, not a stepping stone for a white collar.

Griffiths looked at him keenly. The man craved a cup of coffee but Edwin had not offered him one.

'What worries me,' Griffiths continued, 'is that if a man like you can get sucked into this type of thing what chance have others got? You've always struck me as a reasoning man.'

'Reason has been tried and tried, but all the Board wants is surrender.'

'But if we went back now the union would be intact, we'd still have a base to fight on.'

Edwin saw no point in the discussion. It would lead to him losing his temper, one facet of him that had been tightly controlled until Elliott had teased it out.

'If you think this lot that governs us has a shred of integrity I suppose what you say might make sense,' Edwin said. 'But I don't. Whatever happens the pits are going to be closed. We might delay it by giving in now but I can see only one end.'

'Yes, but if we can keep them open until the next election things might change.'

'That's straw clutching. Look around you, there's a sack of shit being poured over everything and too many are wallowing in it. A lot of people like what is happening to the miners.'

'Well, we'll have to agree to differ on this,' Griffiths said.

He looked at his watch. Bowles made him feel uncomfortable. He had a class chip on his shoulder which coloured his whole outlook. He was the type of man who made changing the Party so difficult.

'I'm off to the Conference next week,' Griffiths said. 'Can I have your assurance that you won't lead any more actions like we had this morning.'

'Nothing else is planned,' was Edwin's non-committal answer.

'Well at least watch what you say on the phone. There's talk of phone tapping in head office.'

Griffiths left, glad to be gone from the house. Bowles was not playing to their game plan now, he was a liability who would have to be jettisoned.

* * *

'Where are we going, Mam?' Sally asked.

Susan did not know. Her flight had been impetuous, perhaps rash, but very necessary. The girls caught her mood and began to cry.

'I don't want to go back to Daddy,' Sally sobbed. 'He's nasty.'

'Yes, he's nasty to you, Mam,' Sarah added. 'We can hear him shouting, all the time.'

Automatically, Susan thought to defend Elliott, to tell them that he did not mean it, but she stilled her words. His hold on her was cast off and she would never say a word in his favour again. It was hard for her not to join the girls in their tears but she had to maintain her strength. She had made a decision to leave Elliott and somehow she had to keep to it.

She drove past Edwin's house. Its window frames needed painting, the old curtains she had given him years ago still hung limply in the front room and paint flaked from the door. No, here would not do and Edwin was a man, from the same genetic source as Elliott. She had had enough of men. It would have to be Rowena, far from an ideal choice, but the only possible refuge.

'We're going to Granny's,' Susan said, in as strong a voice as she could muster.

They bundled into Rowena's, shattering the tranquillity. The cat scowled and turned tail when it heard the strange sound of children crying and Rowena woke up with a start.

'Whatever's the matter,' she asked, 'has anything happened to Elliott?'

It was some minutes before Susan could calm the girls down. She managed to get them to go into the parlour, to watch the decrepit television, and promised them some of Rowena's treats to follow. Then she sat opposite her mother-in-law and told her the story of her marriage, quickly before it overcame her. Susan was not sure how much the woman took in, or believed, but she let it all out, about Elliott's cheating and latterly, his violence.

'Duw, Duw' was Rowena's constant reaction, though she did not question anything Susan said.

'Can we stay?' Susan asked. 'You have to let us stay, until I think of what to do. We can't go back to him.'

She wished her own mother was still alive, for the first time in a decade she missed her. Rowena might yet prove unhelpful but she did not deny Susan's plea.

'We'll have to see what we can do,' Rowena said. 'I had no idea things were bad but if it's like you say Elliott will be here shortly.'

'Not that quick. He hasn't got the car.'

Feeling a little easier now that she had offered Rowena some of her burden Susan wondered if she should tell her about the fight between the two brothers. She did not do so, thinking that the old woman had enough to absorb already.

'I've just baked a fresh batch of cakes,' Rowena said. 'Take some into the children.'

Anxious faces turned up to Susan as she entered the parlour.

'Don't worry,' she told them, 'nothing will happen here with Gran.'

At least Rowena had not sprung to the the defence of her son, as Susan had expected. It would not be long before Elliott woke up and put two and two together. By coming to his mother she had made public his behaviour, let her see him as he really was.

Rowena sighed in her chair and worked her hands, her knitting discarded. Suddenly she looked tired. Susan saw heavy lines settling around her glasses and thin, silver hair, never set in any particular style. Rowena reached out a hand to Susan.

'Are you telling me true about all this, girl?' she asked.

'Yes, I swear it, on the childrens' lives.'

Rowena mused over this but did not take her eyes from Susan.

'Aye, I reckon it's right enough. You've never been a liar, but by believing you I go against my own.'

Rowena's eyes looked past Susan now, through the window to the top of the mountain that could be seen over her rear wall.

'So, he's following the ways of his father, is he?' Rowena muttered. 'They say that's often the case.'

Susan was puzzled. Was Rowena's mind starting to stray? Stanley Bowles had been a stolid, quiet man, abstemious in his ways, the complete opposite to Elliott. Much more like Edwin.

'What do you mean?' Susan asked. 'Your husband never did

anything like this.'

'No, Stanley didn't, but Elliott's father did.'

Rowena took off her glasses to allow a single tear to escape from her right eye. It was the first sign of emotion Susan had ever seen from her. Did she hear right?

'Do you understand what I'm saying?' Rowena asked, turning to see that the parlour door was tightly shut.

Susan was not sure that she did. Another bombshell bursting around her head was not what she needed. She returned Rowena's wet-eyed stare.

'You don't think it could be possible, do you?' Rowena said.

Susan sank back in her chair and shut her eyes.

'You're not the only woman who has kept secrets,' Rowena said. 'I'll tell you now, before Elliott gets here. I've wanted to tell someone for thirty-five years.'

* * *

Elliott woke up three hours after Susan had left. His arm stretched over to shake her but grabbed at emptiness. He sat up and cleared his head. She she probably gone downstairs to make dinner so he knocked on the floor a few times with a shoe and followed this up with a shout. He stretched, yawned and lay back again, feeling good. He would go out for a drink tonight, he might even take Susan and leave the kids down his mother's.

Susan did not come and Elliott's mood changed. Surely she was not going to go against him again? He got up, put on his bathrobe and went downstairs.

'Where are you?' he shouted.

The house was empty. No wife, no children. He checked the drive and saw that the car had gone. Anger and awareness flooded into his mind. He searched for the number of Susan's school friend, to be told that Susan had been there to pick up the girls. He'd kill the bitch.

* * *

Edwin sat halfway up the hillside. He had not felt like walking further. He settled onto a slab of stone he knew well from his youth. His father had brought him here, before Elliott had been able to walk. It had seemed such a long way then, half a mile from their house. Now he perched with his knees hunched up to his chest,

166

working a hand against the mossed stone. He saw his father's grey face in the stone, and remembered the gentle shyness of the man.

Edwin thought of Kathryn's offer as he watched the occasional car wind its way up the mountain road. The day was fine and crisp and sun caught the roofs of the cars, making each one silver. The top of the valley narrowed into haze and he realised he could no longer pick out landmarks as clearly as he used to. Reading had taken its toll on his eyes. He had probably needed glasses for years. The thought of wearing them made him smile. They were rare at the coalface.

Perhaps Kathryn was right. Was he an endangered species? Animals like that faded away, unable to adapt to changing times, or were artificially preserved in zoos or fenced off reserves. Perhaps his valley had become a reserve, a microcosm of a past no longer needed. Was he too old to change or was it that he did not want to? Kathryn had made him ask questions of himself that he had swept under the carpet for too long. Following the road she suggested did not mean he would become a Ceri Griffiths, yet they all bloody seemed to. Bias, Edwin, that's your curse, boy, bias and pride. He knew himself, at least that was a start, but to eradicate his weaknesses was another matter. Especially as he had a brother who was out to eradicate him.

Brown patches had begun to work their way into the hillside copses. It would be October next week, and the start of another long winter. Edwin made his way back down, thinking he might pick up a book again, to see if their spell had been broken forever.

* * *

Rowena's words were halted when the girls came into the kitchen. They were nervous and wanted to check on their mother. When Susan saw how strung out they were she hated Elliott with a vengeance.

'I'll be in now,' Susan said, 'let me finish talking to Gran.'

Reluctantly, the girls went back to their television.

'Poor dabs,' Rowena said, 'it's awful for children when something like this happens.'

'I couldn't help it,' Susan said, 'I couldn't stop Elliott behaving like he has. He's made me wish I never had children.'

'You don't mean that,' Rowena said, 'though I know how you feel. I felt like it when Elliott came along.'

167

She settled back in the chair and beckoned to the cat, but it stayed away, unsure of the changed atmosphere in the house.

'Things hadn't been right between Stanley and myself since the war,' Rowena began. 'He had wanted to join up. He had this fixation about joining the RAF. Of course, miners could stay home, and I encouraged him. Insisted on it, in fact. He seemed to accept it after bit of sulking, but after the war, when he talked to the lads who had been away he seemed to draw into himself. God, men, they are so daft. Moping about not joining in something which killed millions. He talked to me less and less – and he wasn't exactly chatty to begin with. I suppose you could say I was ripe for straying when Elliott's father came on the scene.'

Rowena saw the question in Susan's face.

'No, I won't say his name. He's long gone now, from the area and from life. He died six years ago, from cancer like Stanley. I heard about it months after. It was something they had in common, smoking like chimneys.

'He was the manager down at the Palace – you remember the old cinema. Debonair, that's what they used to call him. I used to go to the pictures a lot, to get out of Stanley's way, and I took Edwin when he was old enough.'

Rowena stopped and began kneading her hands again. Susan saw she was immersed in the past again, remembering pain.

'He noticed me,' she continued, 'that was the thing. I never felt Stanley was ever interested in me much. We drifted together and married because everybody else did. But this chap made me feel special and I responded to him. Looking back I can see how he really was, a greasy opportunist on the look out for mugs like me, but at the time.... He had a flat above the cinema and we used to meet there. I left Edwin downstairs sometimes and I'm still ashamed of that. It was so cheap. It would have been only a matter of time before the usherettes found out, but I became pregnant almost immediately. I knew it wasn't Stanley's. He never did have much interest in that side of things, and lost it altogether after the war.'

'Did he know about Elliott?'

'Yes. I told him. I couldn't bear the guilt. On a Saturday night when he asked me why I wasn't going down The Palace. He took it so calmly, as if he had expected it. That made it worse for me. I wanted him to rant and rave, and go after that man, but he did-n't. Perhaps he thought he was partly to blame but we never talked about it. We never talked. Elliott's father left the village as soon as I started to show. Got a job at the Odeon in Cardiff then moved on again when Elliott was born. I never heard from him.'

There was a heavy stillness in the room, the air charged with the import of Rowena's confession.

'God, it explains so much,' Susan said. 'Elliott is like his father, isn't he?'

'Yes. The height, hair. That made it harder, too. I saw his father in him more and more as he grew up. And the more Stanley ignored me, the more I thought about it. And I started to blame him, because he never seemed shocked by it. Anything to lessen my guilt. Anger is always good for that but I couldn't keep it up. Stanley never reacted so I just drew into myself. Matched him. When he died and it was obvious Elliott was favouring his father I began to spoil him. I thought I could get him to turn out different, not like the waster the other one was. When he joined the police force and married you I thought I had succeeded.'

Susan's problems were mounting. She had expected Rowena to take Elliott's side and not believe her but this revelation had come out of the blue. Where did it leave her? Where did it leave any of them? Rowena dabbed at her eyes.

'His father hit, too,' she said, 'when I told him I was pregnant. He thought I had tricked him, to get away from Stanley. As if women did that in those days.'

Sarah came into the kitchen, hugging her mother around the neck.

'What are you talking about?' she asked. 'You've been ages.'

Rowena quickly put her glasses back on and fixed a smile on her face.

'Nothing much, lovely,' she answered, 'just the olden days.'

'How old are you now, Gran?'

'Three hundred and ten.'

This was their long standing joke, Rowena adding to her age every time.

'What's Sally doing?' Susan asked.

'Watching cartoons. They're too childish for me.'

A car door slammed in the street, making Susan jump. But she remembered she had the Volvo.

'Right,' Rowena said, 'I'm going to get us all some tea.'

'I'll help,' Susan said. 'Will you ever tell Elliott about this?'

'No, not now. It would make matters worse.'

* * *

Elliott went through possibilities. He dismissed the idea of trips down to the coast or shops. Something told him that this was an attempt to leave him. He could not believe Susan could be this stupid. He phoned her father, keeping his voice steady as he passed the time of day with the old man. It was obvious he knew nothing so this left Edwin and his mother. It had to be Edwin.

He walked down to the village, clenching and unclenching his fists, anger rising like steam within him. A woman acknowledged him as he passed but he did not see her. His mind's eye was clearly focused on Edwin, his interfering, meddling brother. He thumped at Edwin's door before he realised the Volvo was not outside. No answer. He cupped his eyes against the front window to double check. No-one. Just those pathetic bookcases. Fucking books. They summed Edwin up.

His reflection looked back at him from the mirror on Edwin's wall. He stared at its fiery glare. The face was an accuser. It looked at him from somewhere in his past, before he had this permanent gut wrenching temper. He had never been satisfied with anything. Let alone happy. Rugby, all the girls, joining the force, and Susan, had not rid him of the feeling that something better lay around the corner. Something to drive him on to another goal. Once he gained control over anyone, boredom ensued. An idea formed in his mind that if he could punish Edwin he would be free of his demons. They had always been associated with his smug brother.

Susan must be at his mother's. He began the walk to the top of the village, no longer sure of what he might do. Susan was clever. She had gone straight to Rowena knowing that he would not want her drawn into this. But she was only making it worse for herself. He saw a man looking at him strangely and realised he was talking to himself. Loudly.

Using the back entrance to the house he looked into the shed and took one of Edwin's sticks. The one with the stupid badger head. It was an instinctive action. He wanted something of Edwin's in his hand, to sweeten whatever retribution he might mete out. Opening the back door quietly he heard Susan talking to his mother. What lies had she told? Rowena's voice was subdued, perhaps a little shaken, but she trusted him. She was the one person on his side. He would have his family back home very shortly.

Susan saw him first, a dark shape looming out of the kitchen doorway.

'Oh God,' she gasped.

He stepped towards Susan and she tried to shrink back against the wall.

'Elliott,' Rowena cried, 'none of that, now.'

His eyes were filmy and reddened, and he looked at her as if he had difficulty focusing.

'I know she's been telling you a load of nonsense, Mam, but don't you worry. I'll sort it all out and I'll have her gone from here now.'

He grabbed out and pulled Susan to him, slapping her with the back of his hand. It was hard enough for her to taste blood.

Rowena stood up shakily.

'Son,' she said, 'you don't know what you're doing. You're all mixed up. Let her alone now, please Elliott.'

He looked from one woman to another, and saw Sally and Sarah standing in the doorway, too afraid to cry. Four fucking females. He had had a gutsful of the whole lot of them. This was what Edwin had done, turned everyone against him. Even his own mother. He wanted to speak but his brain locked up his mouth. There was a dark fury in him which he could almost taste.

If he lashed out now and kept on lashing out his troubles might be over. He heard his mother pleading with him but her words came from far away. He saw himself playing with her before the blazing fire, poking at it when his father was not around. His father had never been around. It had always been his mother, then Susan.

What was Rowena saying? That he was all mixed up? We'll get your brother here, sort it all out together, she said. What was she talking about, didn't she realise he hated Edwin, hated him so bad he wanted to kill him. Would kill him. The girls were screaming, a cacophony of female noise.

'Shut up,' Elliott shouted, 'shut up. You're doing my head in.'

He sent Susan sprawling against the door. She struck it heavily and sank down to the floor. Rowena tried to place herself between husband and wife, moving awkwardly in her slippers. Elliott held her, pushing his face close to hers. Old, tender memories flooded through him for an instant.

'Mam, what's happening to me?' he groaned. 'What's happening?'

'You're sick, son, very sick. You must stop this now.'

Elliott wanted to. He wanted to go back twenty years. No, that was weakness, useless weakness. Rowena had turned against him. Taken Susan's side. Taken Edwin's side. His brother's face loomed large. The man who had caused all this. He had worked on his family for years, with his crackpot politics and loser ways.

'Where's Edwin?' he shouted. 'I want him.'

He started to shake Rowena.

'I don't know,' she gasped. 'Elliott, you're hurting me.'

Rowena sank to the floor, falling against Susan. Elliott caught hold of Susan's neck and squeezed.

'Give me the car keys. Quickly.'

His clenched fist spoke more eloquently than his garbled words. She gave him the keys.

'Tell Edwin I'll meet him on the railway bridge,' Elliott said. 'He'll know the one.'

He stormed out of the house, scattering furniture in his wake. It was getting dark outside but he drove the Volvo without lights, slamming and screeching his way towards the railway line. He left it with the driver's door open and the keys in the ignition. He had to get out, get some air. It was two hundred yards to the bridge and he ran there, sucking in air desperately like a man drowning. He sat on the first wooden step of the bridge with his lungs searing. A diesel passed and honked at him.

Two brothers had spent good times here but those days were long gone. As defunct as the steam trains that once thrilled young boys. That was another Elliott. Another Edwin. This was the perfect place to finish with the past. As he let himself sink into the blackness of his thoughts Elliott noticed the stick was still in his hand.

★ ★ ★

Edwin ignored the phone for a while. He had allowed himself a much more generous allowance of bath water than usual and this was more inviting that any voice on the telephone. No good news ever came to him that way, only requests for his help, and his day had been long. But it kept on ringing. He let it ring twenty times before succumbing. Someone must want him badly. The fraught voice of Susan assaulted his ear when he picked up the phone. In the background he could hear the girls crying.

'It's Elliott,' Susan said, 'I've left him but he's come here. Now he's coming for you.'

Her voice was breathless, on the edge of hysteria.

'Hold on,' he said, 'talk slower. Where are you, first of all?'

'I'm at your mother's. I didn't know where else to go.'

Edwin sighed and knew there would be no end to this day.

'What's happened?' he asked.

'I couldn't stand it any longer,' Susan said. 'I just had to get out of there. I've taken the car and the girls are with me.'

'Yes, I can hear them. And you say Elliott is coming here?'

'No, not to your house. He wants to meet you at the old railway bridge. Edwin, he's off his head. I thought he was going to kill me, and he pushed Rowena over.'

'Is she hurt?'

'No, just shaken. Don't go to him, he'll hurt you. I'll phone the police.'

'They're his own.'

'Not now they won't be. You haven't seen him. He's out of control. Everything is out of control.'

'I'll go the bridge,' Edwin said, 'see if I can talk to him. Don't worry.'

The last words sounded hopelessly optimistic and he put the phone down quickly, before Susan could say anything else. He might be talked out of it and that would not do.

He unplugged the bath, dressed and was out of the house before the water had drained. Whatever happened at the bridge would be a turning point. Strands of his destiny were converging, but he had no control over them. Elliott's job had no influence over him now, he should have realised that when he heard of Susan's assault. That was a prelude to tonight, which he sensed would see the final splitting apart of two brothers.

He saw Elliott sitting on the steps of the bridge, hunched up with something in his hand. It was hard to make out what in the gloom of dusk. Thirty years fell away and his short-trousered little brother was there, hanging around him and the older boys, begging flattened pennies. Edwin had liked looking after him then, replacing their father. Dad had never seemed interested in his younger son. He knew why his brother had chosen this place.

For a moment he stayed under the cover of trees and tried to collect his senses. Violence must be avoided. He mouthed this to himself like a litany. If he had been a religious man he might have even tried prayer, asking for a miracle of understanding to descend upon them.

Edwin stepped into view and his brother saw him. He stood up quickly and Edwin saw the walking stick in his hand.

'Fuck me,' Elliott shouted, 'I didn't think you'd have the bottle to come.'

He tapped the stick against the rusted railings of the bridge, continuing a habit picked up on picket control.

'So, big brother has come to sort me out.'

Edwin stopped several yards from the bridge. What light was left in the evening fell on Elliott's face. It made his red-rimmed eyes gleam. His careful grooming had collapsed. He was dishevelled, his eyes almost popping.

'This has gone too far,' Edwin said.

'You're right,' Elliott yelled, 'dead fucking right. I've let it go on, let you mess around with my wife's head. You've turned everyone against me, you short-arsed bastard.'

Edwin kept out of the swinging range of the stick, expecting it to descend on him at any moment. Perhaps Susan's idea of phoning the police had been the right one.

'What's the matter?' Elliott said, his voice dropping to a whisper. 'Fraid what I might do to you? And you a hard miner. Remember when we used to hang around here, when we were kids? You were top dog then, always older, always bigger. That's why I've got you here, this is where I want it to end.'

Edwin wanted to remonstrate with him but felt his own anger rising, to combat reason. They were opposites in viewpoint, temperament and lifestyle, yet still bound together by a blood tie. Frustration seethed in him.

'It doesn't have to be like this,' Edwin muttered. 'You're going to cock up your life completely if you carry on.'

'Cock up my fucking life, be buggered. And you should know, shouldn't you, Mr Fucking Success Story.'

Elliott lunged at Edwin, raising the stick above his head. Edwin ducked away from the blow, holding up his hands and still trying to calm him, though he knew he might as well piss into the wind. His brother did not hear him. They had regressed to their teens, when Edwin had struggled to control an Elliott growing stronger without hurting him. But this time he was not throwing lamb

174

chops, he was trying to brain him with a heavy stick. Three times Elliott cut the air with his weapon. Its arc brushed his hair but did not connect. Elliott's rage made him easier to dodge. He stood opposite Edwin like a mad, blinded swordsman flailing at unseen enemies. Edwin saw him as he must have been on the picket lines, uniformed and out of control. He slipped past him and ran up the bridge steps.

'Hah, running, are you, you cowardly bastard. You can't run from me, boy.'

It was no use. Edwin knew he would have to close with him. He hoped to minimise their difference in size by getting above Elliott. If he could overpower him, perhaps knock him out, his dementia might leave him. Elliott charged up the steps and lunged at him. Edwin caught the stick on his left shoulder and was knocked off balance. Elliott was on him, slashing and kicking.

★ ★ ★

He had seen Edwin standing in the trees, thinking he was under cover, the stupid little sod. That his brother had come filled him with a gratification he could scarcely contain. It bubbled out of him, telling him that this was the solution to all his problems. It would be self-defence. Edwin came at him with a stick, his well known walking stick, then he fell from the railway bridge, onto the hard, bone breaking track. Yes, that would be the story and the pain in his head would be over.

He sat calmly as Edwin approached him. Edwin would try to talk to him, to play the 'brother card' but this man had never felt more a stranger. He was a curse on the Bowles family, and was not needed. His grip on the stick tightened and he stood up as Edwin neared him, shutting his ears to his useless talk. Let the fool babble on, and get closer. He was just waiting for the right moment to strike. If he could get Edwin down he'd drag him to the top of the bridge and drop him onto the line. If a train was approaching so much the better.

He swung at Edwin but the little bastard was too quick. More blows missed their mark and Edwin was past him and up the bridge.

★ ★ ★

Edwin was knocked to the ground. He had braced himself for Elliott's charge but could not withstand the force of it. Elliott had a forty pound weight advantage reinforced by his rage. He managed to wrench the stick away from him but his brother fell on top of him, digging at him with his fists. Some blows were blocked, others struck his face. Blood was flowing from somewhere. Elliott tried to butt him with his head but he managed to work his knee between them, and hold him off. He had to get clear or his brother would succeed in his fratricide. He gathered his strength into one push and succeeded in rolling Elliott away from him. Edwin did not hold back now. He swung out with his own fists, connecting solidly with Elliott's head. This knocked him down a few steps, allowing him to break free again. He ran to the top of the bridge, trying to maintain his footing on the uneven planks, staying away from the edges.

There would have been time to flee when Elliott was down but Edwin stayed put. Elliott closed with him again. They locked arms on opposite shoulders and tried to wrestle each other to the ground. This suited Edwin more, his lack of height was not so much of a disadvantage and he was able to make use of the confined space. Even so, Elliott forced him against the railings, where they stayed for several minutes.

'You can't keep this up, you bastard,' Elliott hissed through his clenched teeth. 'You'll have to let go, and then I'll have you.'

Edwin did not answer, he needed all his breath. Their heads were so close they rubbed against each other as they swayed. He would never forget the distorted fury on Elliott's face, all the more fearful for its lack of rationality. His brother's bulging eyes were the last things he saw as the railing gave way and they tumbled to the railway track below. Edwin felt he floated through the air for the few seconds of their fall. Instant vertigo shot through him and he was not sure if he lost consciousness or not when they hit the ground. As his head cleared he realised he still had hold of Elliott's jacket. Elliott had landed under him, on his back.

Elliott was still breathing. In a surprisingly deep and measured way.

'Elliott,' Edwin whispered, not daring to move, 'are you all right?'

His brother did not answer. Edwin saw that they straddled one track of the railway. Elliott was spread-eagled across it, lying with his head at a strange angle. His neck seemed distorted, as if unseen hands had rearranged it. He had broken his back, Edwin was sure of it. The track would have snapped it like a stick, especially with the weight of his own body to help.

Carefully he lifted himself away from his brother, stifling the complaints of his bruised body to stand up on a sleeper. Elliott must not be moved. A man had broken his back down the pit once and he had recovered to walk again because men had known what to do. Help was needed.

Edwin took off his coat and draped it over Elliott. Then he heard something, a slow, grinding noise he knew so well and cried out in frustration. If he did not move Elliott he would be crushed. Like a penny.

For a moment he wondered if he could flag the train down. He could not take the chance that he would be seen in the darkening night. The face of Billy Tucker loomed large. He could see the headlight of the engine as it came around the long bend that skirted the village. Edwin put his arms under Elliott and began to move him as carefully as he could. But he was a deadweight and would not move easily. As the train neared he resorted to tugging him away from the track. Every jerk and jar of his brother was a blow to him but he pulled Elliott clear of the track, seconds before the diesel thundered past. Its whistle screamed at him as the driver belatedly saw them and was followed by the screech of brakes.

Edwin put his ear to Elliott's mouth and felt hot breath. Elliott's face was at rest, it showed no sign of their fight or the bitterness behind it. In the last few minutes Edwin had forgotten it himself. He brushed hair away from Elliott's forehead in an instinctive brotherly action. Then he lay beside him and got his wind back. They were far enough away from street-lights for the sky to gleam blue-black; stars were beginning to prick their way through. It had been ages since he had looked up at the sky. In a corner of his mind Edwin heard voices and the rays of torches probed the railway tracks.

'There they are, by the line,' someone shouted.

'I didn't hit anyone, I'm sure of it,' another voice said.

Uniforms gathered round Edwin. He recognised one of them. Probert, Elliott's sergeant.

The torchlight made Edwin shut his eyes. He wished he could have shut out what had happened as easily.

A hand shook him, alerting him again.

'What's been going here?' Probert asked. 'You are Edwin

177

Bowles, aren't you?'

'Don't touch my brother,' Edwin cried. 'I think his back is broken.'

★ ★ ★

Susan spooned soup into Elliott's mouth. She tried to catch the drops that spilled from it but had not yet perfected the technique. It had been a long time since she had fed her mother this way and she had never been as helpless as Elliott was now. He opened his mouth obediently but tried to chew the soup as if it was solid food. This caused more liquid to escape and a napkin tied around his throat caught the excess. His eyes stared past Susan, towards whatever world his mind now lived in. It was three days before Christmas.

Her world had been on a tilt since Elliott's accident. She called it his accident. He had broken the fifth vertebra of his backbone in the fall from the railway bridge. It made him tetraplegic, with just movement in his head and arms. Not much in the arms. And he was brain damaged.

Elliott's mind had gone. He had crushed his head into the ground and something had died inside. Susan was no longer interested in the medical details. For months now she had received the laywoman's guide to back injuries, brain damage, and the care of victims. She was also a victim, tied to him and to an uncertain future.

Elliott was in a spinal rehabilitation centre near Cardiff. It was a place where broken-backed people were moved to after a spell of hospital assessment, though usually with their minds intact. They could be helped to come to terms with the awful reality of their injury. For tetraplegics it was particularly bleak. To be bed-bound always, having to rely on others for everything, the cycle of food to waste no longer under personal control. The body an arbitrary attachment to a brain which had absolved its control of it. And there was a constant risk of chest infection. Many died within two years, their mind rejecting the effort required to stay alive.

He lay like an overgrown doll. Susan had combed back his hair in the way he had always kept it. He had never looked more handsome. His was a flawless face, but faraway eyes gave it an untypical calm with which she still could not come to terms. Elliott had

178

been a man of extremes but now all his fire was gone. She held his hand, moist and flaccid. As unresponsive as his heart had been in the last year.

She had not yet collected all her thoughts together, but she felt a sad blend of memory and unfulfilment. She could not abandon Elliott now, but she had not withered when she learned of the reality of his condition. The likelihood of his early death took away the antagonism that had so recently been her lot. She did not forget what he had done, but knew the price he had paid. Susan tried to look forward, away from her bleak marriage.

She left Elliott to the care of the nurses, taking a last look at his black head on the pillow from the doorway. For a moment she was in the line of his eyes but they did not see her. In the corridor the male charge nurse approached her.

'He's looking better this morning, Mrs Bowles,' the man said. 'I remember him when he played rugby. He could have gone all the way.'

Susan walked out into winter sunshine. Shafts of pale light pushed through the clouds, arrowing the far contours of the mountains. Her new hatchback waited for her. She had sold the Volvo as soon as possible. That had always been Elliott's car, not theirs.

It had been a strange and fraught time. The shock of the fight, the long investigation of Edwin, the bewilderment of her daughters and her attempts to protect them from the wild chain of events. The rampant village talk had been hard to deal with. But the oppressor Elliott had been removed. Calm was replacing him. Something she realised she had not had for many years. A slow and sure process that was rebuilding her. She could plan her day, do anything she wanted without Elliott's persecution. When the authorities had broached the subject she had made it quite clear that she would never have Elliott home again. Not with his two sets of disability. Within a month she had gone back to Rita's group, and had been warmly welcomed.

Susan's future was not hopeless and she had no money problems. Elliott was insured to the hilt and although there were many details to sort out with the police, she was not worried about practical matters. That the girls had been deprived of a father caused her more concern. She hoped to make it up to them and nurture an image of a kinder Elliott. Susan started the car and played a cassette, from Kathryn, by a woman she had never heard of before. She enjoyed the music, the flow of the guitar and inter-mingled words pleased her, even if she did not understand all of them. For a second she saw Elliott beside her, ripping the tape out of the machine and calling it stupid, weird nonsense, turning on the sport full blast on the radio. She increased speed and felt light and free. And without guilt.

★ ★ ★

When it had looked likely that Elliott would die they wanted to pin a murder charge on Edwin. The media drooled on it for a week. What could be better for them, the policeman and his brother the striking miner, a Cain and Abel scenario enacted in a backward Welsh valley. And no-one had to invent it. National tabloids sniffed around the village as the news broke but ranks closed against them and they found out little. Rowena's secret was never threatened. Between them, Rowena and Susan decided to let Edwin remain ignorant.

'This family has had enough shocks,' Rowena said. 'It may not be right but it's better for Edwin not to be told. You know what he's like for thinking. Something like this would start him off all over again, he'd go back over his whole life, examining his rela-tionship with Elliott. Examining me.'

Susan thought Edwin's guilt might be lessened with him know-ing, but she did not go against Rowena.

The more the police dug the better it was for Edwin. His bat-tered face went in his favour and Susan and Rowena's testimonies were vital. When some newspapers, deprived of a fratricide, tried to make Edwin a crazy Red the village rallied around him. London newsmen learned not to enter The Merlin. The village understood the pain of brother fighting brother, it knew what must be going through Edwin's head. Quiet, loner Edwin. He stood trial in December on charges of causing bodily harm but by then his acquittal was a formality. Self defence was the only pos-sible verdict. In his case justice had lived up to its name and the irony of this was not lost of him. A system that was so flawed and weighted against his own had come up trumps for him. If only he could win for the men like he had won for himself.

In the wake of the fight Griffiths relieved Edwin of his union duties. Discreetly, with much emphasis on the need to ease his mind of additional worries. At that time no-one knew if he was going to prison or not. He had been charged and let out on bail which the union put up. Even the police did not think he would be going anywhere.

His solicitor cautioned Edwin against seeing Elliott but he went anyway, with Susan. She drove him down in her new car on a cold, bright winter's day. He hated hospitals and had rarely been in one. They had a certain air, the smell of disinfectant mixed with space and dread, and often cloying heat. People being well cared for, but by strangers.

When Edwin walked into Elliott's room he thought his brother saw him. From ten feet those black eyes fixed on him and he tensed for outburst, such was his conditioning. His shoulders flexed defensively and he felt old bruises again but Elliott was not staring at him. His eyes were dead, working on some distant automatic pilot. Edwin was sweating, it poured out of him as he approached his brother, who lay so still on his special bed, a contraption linked to multiple wires and levers.

'He can only move his head,' Susan whispered. 'The hands jerk sometimes but there's no control there.'

Already she talked of Elliott as an object.

The waste of it all. Not just Elliott's present state but the last twenty years. Their relationship had dripped away, like water into sand, until it became all sharp angles and distant rivalry and, latterly, hatred. Seeing Elliott lying practically comatose Edwin could almost taste their failure as brothers. Such failures that they had used politics as an excuse, when bigger men might have put it to one side and maintained a fraternal alliance.

He reached out a hand and touched Elliott on the shoulder, gently, as if he was a new born baby. His brother had the same lack of control over his life, but without a future of growth. Edwin had been over the fight countless times in his mind, looking for ways he might have handled it differently. If he had ran away, if the railing had not failed, if he had not gone in the first place. Every time his brain played back images was a torture. A chain of thoughts that stretched back to early childhood. Susan was talking to him.

'It wasn't your fault,' she said. 'You have to believe that, Edwin. The girls have lost their father, more or less, and I don't want their only uncle going mad.'

'But if I hadn't gone to the bridge?'

'He would have found you somewhere else, you know that. He

was unhinged that night, he had been for a long time. When he came to Rowena's something had finally burst in him. When the strike started he changed quickly, things I'd seen in him for years started to take over him.'

'He never got over our father dying.'

Susan almost told him then. It would have been easy to let it spill out but Rowena was right, it would churn troubled waters still further. She knew Edwin would increase his burden of guilt and start to feel an unhealthy amount of pity for Elliott. If Elliott was to die within a few years she wanted Edwin to be as ready for it as possible. Like she was.

They lapsed into silence. Elliott was now Edwin's equal in this. Susan watched each man and wondered at their history. Edwin's eyes strayed from his brother, to the window, and back again. She knew he longed to be back in the valley, the distant contours of which could be glimpsed from the window. Walking the mountains which seemed a part of him. Edwin squeezed his brother's shoulder and gently touched his face with his fingers. Susan sensed the frisson of love in the touch and willed her eyes not to fill.

'Come on, it's time to go,' she said.

As they drove back to the valley Edwin sat still in the new car, lost in thought. The visit had shaken him, he had seen the evidence of his failure as a brother. If he had not reacted so badly when Elliott had joined the police force, not shown his viewpoint so openly, their relationship might not have deteriorated so dramatically. There were so many things he could have done better, but hindsight was useless and galling. Life must stand as it was and he must deal with it. He no longer had a union position and he was sure the Board would find a way to get rid of him after all that had happened. No job and no role, with a third of his working life left.

'You're quiet,' Susan murmured.

'What's new? Sorry, everything is whirling around in my head.'

'I know. It did in mine but I've had years to prepare for this, the years I've been married to Elliott.'

'Aye.'

He realised how easy his life had been. None of the responsibility of his union work amounted to much in the face of what Susan had endured. His responsibility had been only to himself. The Bowles boys were certainly brothers in selfishness.

182

'You're thinking bad of yourself,' Susan said.

She pulled the car over and stopped.

'You've to get through this, if you give up now you'll be as selfish as Elliott.'

She started the car again and played the tape.

'Kathryn sent me this. Have you heard from her?'

'She's sent me a few letters, but I haven't got around to...'

'Do it. You need something outside of here. You need something new in your life, Ed, like I do. What happened to Elliott was terrible but it has given us another chance, don't you see that? He has released us.'

The quiet and once timid Susan, whose husband lay crippled, was giving him a pep talk. As they approached the village he asked Susan to stop and let him out. Short stabs of sun fought smoky clouds, driven over the valley by a keen wind. Good walking weather.

'You will come for Christmas dinner?' Susan asked.

'People will talk.'

'I'm immune to village chatter now. It was those reporters who got to me. What a lousy bunch they were. I want you to come and I've asked Rowena too. Something usually went wrong at Christmas with Elliott. He found excuses to get called into work or he drank too much down the pub and came back late. It sounds strange but this time we will be more of a family, more of a family without him.'

'You've grown, Susan.'

'I've had good teachers. Rita, Kathryn. And you.'

'I changed my mind about Kathryn Peters, before she went back to London Those articles she wrote were good.'

'Yes, she was sincere. You should take her up on her offer.'

'Perhaps I will, when I get things sorted in here.'

He tapped his head with a finger.

'What about Elliott?' Edwin asked.

'On Christmas Day? I'll go and see him early. Take him a few things, go through the motions.'

'And the girls?'

'They've been a few times but I won't take them at Christmas. Rowena will stay with them. She said she'll stay over until New Year, in fact.'

'I've tried to talk to her about Elliott but I haven't got very far.

He was so much her favourite I thought she'd never bother with me again, but she hasn't been like that at all. What she's really thinking I can't tell.'

'She doesn't show much, you don't either. But I suppose Elliott more than made up for it.'

'What a bunch, eh?'

'Come over about one,' Susan said, 'and don't worry about bringing anything.'

'I certainly will worry. I'm going to get the girls something nice. You too.'

Susan watched him cross the railway bridge and make for the hillside. He stopped at the spot where two brothers had plunged through the railings and rubbed his hand against the new guard. In his duffel coat he looked more gnome-like than ever but Susan liked him and was free to do so openly now.

Edwin was right, the family was a 'bunch'. Full of secrets, repression, unrequited hopes and terminal disappointment. Yet they had all learned from Elliott. Even Rowena had been shaken out of her apathy. Susan determined to persuade Edwin to go to Kathryn's college. She would keep a sisterly eye on him from now on.

★ ★ ★

Edwin climbed quickly. Seeing Elliott lying so helpless was an image that time would never dim. The family trait of stifling emotion with diffidence had been blown away. If he was to change, to become a more rounded human being, he would have to keep it this way. And not deny the tears that stalked his eyes now.

Christmas would be a start. For years he had made excuses if people had asked him round, even invented other places for him to go to. It was the time when his aloneness was at its most naked. Yes, he would go to Susan's, try to be a genial uncle and hope such behaviour would come naturally in time.

He kept his head down and leaned slightly into the wind. It tried to push him back down, yet he sucked in the rushing air, until it made him light headed. By the time he gained the top of the ridge his heart pounded against his chest and he felt the sick dizziness which came with over-exertion. But he was used to this elemental buffeting and it was always worth it.

He looked about him, at the sweep of his valley and the distant folds of adjacent valleys. Height here never affected him. This was a different type of climb, familiar and under his control. He sat behind the ruin of a stone wall which deflected the wind over him and remembered sheltering in the same spot at Christmas last year. Since then he had experienced the most confusing, charged and violent times of his life. A war which had encompassed his family, politics and creed of living. Jumbled images flashed through his mind. Elliott as a young boy, the obscured face of his father, the actions of the strike, and the bridge. Always the bridge. He could smell its damp wood and feel the cold railings against his back and see stars revolve in the sky. And his brother lying so still and unseeing.

Guilt had been his lot since then, and a depression that fed on it. Pieces of it were present in him still, perhaps they would always be there, but they were no longer his whole feeling. There was light too, despite the virtual destruction of Elliott and the blasting away of the hopes of his working comrades. It would be easy to believe that his future was all dark. But he would not do it. He clapped his hands together. Sheep which had sidled close to him were startled and offered their blank eyes as they fled. He had been wrong to think the affairs of his workmates could be enough. It was not, and Susan had been right. He had to learn other things.

Edwin stood up and walked along the ridge. It amazed him to think that so few ever came here, even in summer. He was stepping over the backbone of his land. All its tortured history lay under his feet. He wanted to take the solitude of the hillside into his hands, crumple it into a ball, and eat it. Such was his addiction and sense of oneness with the spirit of this place.

He thought of his last talk with Kathryn Peters. It had taken an English woman to revitalise his feeling for Wales. And it *was* Wales, not just 'the valley'. It had always lain close to the surface, chipping away at his consciousness. Sometimes lifting him up, often shrouding him with doubt. His brother had no such doubts. Elliott had always hated Wales and things Welsh. In this way he had hated himself. It had been another self-inflicted cross for him to bear.

Edwin determined to make another attempt to learn the language that should have been his by right. That would be one signpost of change. And he *would* take up Kathryn's offer. That would be another. To broaden his horizons without denying his roots.

He started his descent, skirting farmhouses and boundary walls, fixing the familiar slanting lines of the village. It had been there for a long time, and if the strike was lost it would be there still. A bitter wind had got up but he did not feel it as he walked home. Looking forward to Christmas.

The Author: Roger Granelli is a professional guitarist as well as the author of short stories and two previous novels, *Crystal Spirit*, about Wales and the Spanish Civil war, and *Out of Nowhere*, the story of a jazz guitarist in America. After working in Britain, Europe and America he returned to Wales in the year of the Miners' Strike.

Dark Edge was written with the support of an Arts Council of Wales Writer's Bursary.